C000003126

I'd like to say a special *'Thank You'* to Margot
for all of her thoughts and insights.
Also mention, Gwen, Mag, Kathy, Ronny, and Rosie.

"If, ten years ago, I had had any clue or even an inkling that life was quite so fleeting, then at least three of the four most important people in both our lives would have been there to witness the day of the celebration of our marriage. Although I know that this sunshine is from them and they are all here in spirit. Thank you very much to all the important people who are here celebrating with us.

Emma and I would like to raise a toast to
Sid & Connie, Ron & Margot.
We miss you all very much. Cheers."

Emma and my wedding day. Edinburgh. 8th April 2006. (After 28 years of courtship!)
Emma and my wedding party. The Lodge. 30th April 2006.

"Men, intensively trained and experienced in the ways of war, ought to be regarded as skilled tradesmen, and paid as such. It is no excuse for not so treating them that there is no demand for their special skills outside the armed services."

Patrick Dalzel-Job - Commander in the field of 30AU.
Arctic Snow to Dust of Normandy.

"When I heard they (the Nazi/NASA rocket scientists) were being made national heroes I was disgusted. It was not only showing disrespect to us… (the slave workers who died in their thousands working in the Nordhausen tunnels) but to their own dead.
Thousands, hundreds of thousands of Allied soldiers died to liberate Europe, to defeat Hitler and these people were the mainstays of Hitler's reign of terror and there they were being fated like heroes, it's just… (tears)…(silence)…"

Andrew Herskovits
At fourteen years of age he was a forced slave labourer at Mittlewerke, working on V2/A4 rockets. This is a quote from interview in 'The Hunt for Hitler's Scientists'.
Windfall Films/PBS documentary shown on Channel 5 April 2005.

Prologue

20th July 1969. Eastwood, England.

'Tranquillity base here. The Eagle has landed' the small crackled voice sounded as though it was actually from a tiny American contained within the small wooden box that he was watching intently. Ron Guy wished it were. He sat motionless, bathed in the pale flickering blue light. He could feel the bile rising in his throat, his anger barely under control, while wondering if that Eagle was still holding the Swastika as it landed on the moon.

This was wrong. He knew it with all of his heart and soul and on the very day of the first anniversary of his brother-in-law, Guy (Ghee) Wilthew's suspicious death. Looking down at the young boy, just a toddler, his first grandchild, he considered what kind of world he had helped to create, in his own small way, during World War Two...

December 2005. Runwell, England.

I constantly found myself wondering why I found it so hard to do these visits. The grounds surrounding the mental hospital were actually a beautiful place, tranquil, wide-open green spaces. I loved my Grandad dearly, thought of him more as a father than a grandfather. My real father having disappeared so early in my life.

Maybe it was because I saw so much of myself in him and it scared me. Then of course there was the obvious hard work of trying to deal with a bipolar, a manic depressive, on the constant cycle of almost hysterical highs, followed by the inevitable, black, lows. That and the sudden appearance of the paranoia.

Had I made a mistake sorting out that computer and internet connection for my Grandad? He'd expressed a need to start writing, surely that had to help him start to recover from the loss of his beloved Margot, but how can anyone recover from the loss of fifty-three years of passionate companionship?

It had seemed to work initially, Ron had taken to the computer a few of years ago, like a duck to water, he seemed to understand the inner workings of it better than I did, much to my surprise.

I often took Ron to the local pub; *The Quart Pot*, or others, for lunch, when his mood swings seemed stable enough for him to be allowed leave from the ward. I recall one of the previous conversations with Grandad over lunch as I strolled from the car up towards the ward.

"How's the writing going Grandad? Are you still working on your religion? Why don't you finally tell us all about all your wartime stories in your book?" I was well aware of Ron's incessant scribbling, after he had become too paranoid about his computer to continue using it. I always found myself in awe, incredulous as to Ron's philosophical and religious knowledge, it was just amazing and appeared endless, I often found myself wondering where had it all come from.

"It is not a religion it is my philosophy of 'Isims' and it is going to be a best seller. You don't believe me do you?"

"No I don't." I smiled.

"You just wait and see...Confucius was in his seventies before he wrote his best work... You know how Bill Gates keeps control of the likes of you?" Ron grinned maniacally at me.

"No, Grandad I don't, you're not going to start down that road again are you?" I tried to distract him from that course of conversation and Bill Gates was certainly one of his favourite topics.

"Ahhgg! You've never really listened to me have you?" Ron smiled.

"Yep, every word Grandad" I grinned back at him.

"You know the CIA have been watching my computer again?" The manic grin spread wide.

"Yep, just like Bill watches mine, except he can't cause I use an Apple Mac, so there." I quipped back, not wanting to engage in his obvious paranoid fantasies.

"I was a Red Indian Brave. They're watching me because I used to work with Ian Fleming..." A huge beaming grin spreads slowly across his face. "You don't believe me do you?"

"No, I don't." I was continually surprised and worried at the scale to which

Ron's fantasies were starting to reach and didn't really know how to placate and steer him away from them.

My attention clicked back to the here and now, the electronic nurses voice, "Hello"

"Hi, I'm here to see Ron Guy." The security door buzzes open. I wondered why there's any security at all, no-one ever checked my coming and going, and I could be anyone.

The place is really very difficult to take in, sombre, neglected, but I know the nurses do their very best, always cheerful, trying to make a difference. Despite the fact that Ron had led numerous mutinies among the easily led patients, encouraging them to refuse medication and escape the wards and generally making the nurses work time a lot more difficult than it would be without his presence.

As I turned into Ron's room, I stopped in my tracks. Surely it can't have been that long since the last visit. I know I've been way too busy trying to make a go of a new freelance position in London, but Ron's aged about ten years in the last three weeks.

The tears well up, my throat constricts. "Hi Grandad" my voice squeaks out, doing the best I can to sound cheerful.

It is obvious the dark, black, depression must have set back in straight after the last visit, when Ron stops drinking and eating. His eyes have sunken back into their sockets, dark black rings, and his skull clearly visible under the dehydrated skin. The cycle was repeating. Ron had always been as strong as an ox, even in his eighties he was plenty strong enough to look after himself in almost any situation. But surely no one, however strong, can take that kind of self inflicted abuse, especially when the very person inflicting it was so strong willed as to be impossible to turn once his mind was made up on something, by anything or anyone.

I tried hard to compose my emotions as I sat down next to the bed. Ron tries hard to sit up slowly, but sinks back down to the pillow.

"Hi Gé, thanks for coming." The voice is deep, resonant, but slow and now very, very weak.

I knew instinctively this was going to be the last time I would ever see my

Grandad. I reached out and took Ron's large and still powerful hand, leaned forward and kissed him on the cheek, the familiar smell of him, accentuated by the moment.

"You know the manner of your death... is just as important as the manner... in which you live your life... look after yourself, Gé." His voice trails off, as his eyes slowly roll back into the painfully deep eye sockets. The last breath I heard rasped out of the back of Ron's throat, as his whole body seemed somehow to deflate.

But I didn't really see much of that; my eyes are far too blurred with tears...

Ron Guy passed away in Southend General Hospital a few days later while surrounded by many of his large family.

I wasn't there I felt that I had already said my last goodbye...

•   •   •

April 2006. Eastwood, England.

I had arranged to meet Margot, my aunt (Ron and Margot's fifth child of six) at 'Bluebells' my Grandparents small semi-detached home. It had been standing empty for too long now. Of all the possessions, collected over fifty odd years of family life, Margot wanted her mother's grand piano. Even though my Grandmother's musical abilities were obviously declining as I grew up I could still remember the loud and complex notes as they turned the pedestrians heads as they walked down the Close under the shade of the large trees in the small front garden, peering into the leadlight windows of the lounge to try and see the source of the wonderful music.

If anything could be said to contain someone's spirit the old piano certainly contained my Nan's.

The piano took up a considerable amount of the space in the moderately sized front room. The walls were stained nicotine yellow and dusty, covered in varying white rectangles where the family portraits and paintings had once hung. They had been removed a couple of years ago for safe keeping after local young lowlife had thrown stones at the windows and even a firework through the glass panes they had broken and Ron had made them even more determined to be a nuisance by giving chase up the short Close. *(They were possibly behaving just as Ron had done in his own way as a boy growing up in Dagenham, London.)*

As the men who had come to remove the piano began to dismantle it, I headed up the narrow overly steep stairs where I had played games on the dangerously high shelf as a child, the pedals had been missing for a long time and I knew they were probably going to be in one of the attics. It had been six years since Grandad had slept in the marital bedroom, once Margot had passed away he had preferred a single bed in the spare room downstairs.

It had been at least a few years since I had been the there, the last time was when I'd asked a good friend, Chris to arrange a PC and internet connection for Ron to use for his writing, I thought it might be a help, how wrong I was! As I entered the room the computer and printer were still there on the desk, but now buried, hidden under a mass of paper, there was paper spread over the entire room. It was impossible not to tread on something, mainly roll-up cigarette butts and paper *(I was amazed the whole place had not gone up in flames!)*. As I picked up one pile of scribbled notes one word jumped out from the mass and smacked me right between the eyes, MURDER! Followed by the name, Guy Wilthew, the name of my Nan's father who, I knew, had died when she was about three, of Tuberculosis, it was thought. It was also the name of his son, her brother, my great uncle. I knew my great uncle had been on his motorbike somewhere in Brittany on 20th July 1968 with his girlfriend, Barbara, when they had hit a tractor with no lights on in the dark. Barbara had walked away, untouched, Guy had been in a coma for eight days before dying. I also knew from Nan that Guy Wilthew had been a wireless operator (Musiker - Musician) working with the French communists (Rote Kapelle – Red Orchestra – as the Germans referred to them) during the war against the Nazi's. Other than that no one article stood out, it was just a mass of work all over the bed, the floor and some of the walls.

Grandad's handwriting was a graceful script but this had all been written with many different pens and a multitude of colours, had numerous mistakes crossed through, blobs of ink smeared across the lines, the physical energy almost jumping out, a visible thing, some of the pages were just pure spectrums of colour. Capital letters that slowly increased in size and scale and eventually seemed to shout from the page then transform into mathematical symbols, there were pages and pages of multi-coloured explosions in minute detail, a visual disturbance, a mental disturbance. Felt tip pens of every colour, paints of all types, various drawing implements and piles of paper stuffed and stacked into every space. Maps and charts on the walls, covered in notes and dates, newspapers, magazines and books lying open and scattered about.

My original purpose popped back to mind, attic, pedals...

There were three small attic spaces filled to the top with old boxes, ancient magazines, plenty of 'Westcliff High School for Girls' textbooks and school work, *(and a good collection of their wooden Maxply Tennis racquets too)*, sheet music, paintings, even a huge French Bible nearly too heavy to lift, but most of it was junk. I found the piano pedals fairly quickly, leaning up against the sloping beams of the roof above, as I pulled them out a large tarnished silver tin box was uncovered as more junk slipped down against my ankles.

The front room now had an unfamiliar echo, which seemed to get more pronounced as the piano left in pieces. I felt numb. I was devoid of feelings. I had expected to be a lot more emotional.

I waved goodbye to my aunt and the leaving truck and then headed back into the house and upstairs.

The scene in front of me certainly captured a mind in total turmoil; anyone could be forgiven for using the term 'crazy!' I spent the next hours reading small sections, perusing the maps and trying to make sense of the charts and endless symbols, kinds of mathematical symbols about dates and times and 'magic' numbers. This was the work of months, more likely years.

There were stories of Ron's childhood and his parents. One told a detailed account of his father, Frank, stepping out into a busy street to stop a bolting horse from careering into the shoppers, others told of meeting Margot in France. Some told war stories, the subject that as a child I so much wanted to hear about. But there was also a lot of... unintelligible mess and endless information about welding and pipe fitting but all of it jumping about from one subject to another, like a download of mixed computer files all being opened accidentally in one go, there was also a great deal of personal, private, upsetting information, things that he could not possibly have ever wanted others to know about, it was all mixed up…

Nothing in my grandparent's house had ever been particularly cared for; in fact the whole house and family had existed in a perpetual state of mess! Even the certificate my Nan had received from Dwight D. Eisenhower for helping Allied airmen shot down over occupied France was covered in stains when most would surely have carefully displayed it, proudly and prominently for all to see. *(Which is exactly what my aunt Margot (her fifth child) had now done with it).*

As Nan had told me the story she had been giggling like a child, an infectious laugh that thankfully had frequently been heard even later in her life.

'It was your mother, Gwen (Ron & Margot's first child) who spoiled it as a toddler when she had decided to use a drawer instead of the toilet!' Then she turned back to the sink and the view over the garden and her feeding birds at their tables *(They were wild birds but she had always considered them her friends).*

The dirty oxidizing tin box I had found in the attic contained neatly bundled letters, tied in a red satin ribbon, their love letters exchanged during and shortly after the war.

Underneath were Margot's French Identity papers, stamped with a red Swastika then three folded maps of Europe printed on fine cloth, maybe silk, a green beret with gold Royal Marine badge, a blackened dagger, photos and other notes and letters.

The last things I removed were some oil painted portraits of Ron painted by Margot, one of which was on the very canvas of his kitbag and started during the French liberation, another of Ron as a 'Pirate' holding a gold heart shaped locket in one hand and his dagger in the other and a third was a simple oil painted profile of Grandad as a young Royal Marine Commando.

•   •   •

I sat in my home, a small red brick cottage on a country farm estate, searching through the photographs and papers. I had thought I would have a quick peruse, but I found myself carefully studying every photograph.

Framed in grey cardboard, three group pictures, 413 King's Squad June 1943, B-Troop Littlehampton May 1944 and Sniper Course April 1944, there was Grandad's unmistakable family looks with a sweet young innocent smile from the opposite corners of two of the groups of young men and a few others (see photo's).

Sniper Course! I had always wondered at the knowledge he seemed to possess while helping me 'zero in' my air-rifle sights when I was a young teenager, although I still managed to 'pepper' Bluebells windows with numerous pellet holes, despite what I now know to have been expert tuition!

As I made my way through the memorabilia I felt a growing excitement, my eye wandered to one of the portraits of Ron as a Royal Marine, it drew me in until I stood in front of it, none of the portraits were in particularly good condition, the paint had begun to flake away from the canvas or board and the colours were masked under layers of grime and dust. I flipped over the painting. On the back, RM GUY CHX3904 • 30AU. His number and unit demarcation. I had always known Ron was a Royal Marine Commando, had been part of a Commando Brigade, 42 and 44, possibly 30 had been mentioned, but I'd never heard of 30AU.

I opened up the laptop. Within half an hour I had discovered that 30AU was the abbreviation for 30 Assault Unit. It was a Commando Unit involved in many varied operations from 1942 onwards and the liberation of France and invasion of Germany. A covert special operations unit.

It was a unit dreamt up and commanded by *Ian Fleming*! A wartime Top Secret Intelligence Unit! *Ian Fleming* himself had called them his 'Red Indians'!

The hairs along the back of my neck and arms stood on end, my whole body tingled, as I remembered my lunchtime conversation with Grandad, 'I was a Red Indian Brave, I worked with *Ian Fleming*.' It had been true!

Although I had been a boyhood fan of *James Bond* I had never read any of the novels, but now here it was in front of me on the Wikipedia website. *Ian Fleming* had used it in his first Bond novel '*Casino Royale*' had referred to *Bond* during the war as a Red Indian, four times, twice in the last chapter. It was the literary *James Bond*'s wartime unit.

Could that possibly also mean that Ron was being watched by the CIA? That statement had been made by my Grandfather on many occasions, normally when referring to his computer, but I had always ignored it. Put it down to his mental condition, after all he was under psychiatric care at that time! But if the first part was true, could the second be true also? Could 30AU have been involved in something that was still having repercussions today, over sixty years later?

I continued searching for information online, I found there was also a book about 30AU *'Attain by Surprise' edited by David Nutting* a Royal Air Force Officer that had been attached to the unit as part of Operation 'Crossbow' which targeted V1 and V2 sites after D-Day. After ordering the book from Amazon, I had an agonising two-day wait for the mailman to deliver it.

When it arrived the book opened naturally at the photographs in the centre section and the tears welled up, blurring the vision of Grandad wrapped in a Swastika flag, a wide grin staring back out from the page. A photo that Ron would probably never have seen? Or one that he would not care to have ever seen?

The forward talked about the reunions at Littlehampton in *The Marine* Pub. One quick phone call to the Landlord and I had procured the telephone number of Richard Reed, member of the 30AU veterans association and the address of the 30AU website. I looked back to the pile of photos, flicking through them I found it. Guy, Paddy, Reed – written on the back.

The voice answering the phone sounded strong and direct. "Oh wonderful. Ron Guy, a lovely man, I knew him very well."

"I would love to get as much information as I can, I'm afraid I know very little about his wartime experiences. I've been trying to get on the website, but the link no longer seems to work." I explained.

"The website, I'm sorry to say has gone offline. My grandson, Stuart, who originally built it has been unwell, he has been unable to continue it. I remember Ron very, very well, we were close." Richard's voice hushed in revere.

"I'd really like to meet with you and show you the things I've found. I'd love to know more about his unit, his war and what he did. He would never talk about it. But I guess there could be some very good reasons for that, so I should be prepared for some nasty shocks, maybe?"

"Well, it was a tough time, some bad things happened, we were all very young and of course it was all top secret then and some still is even now, I think. It was a specialist intelligence unit. There were only about a hundred of us in three troops when we landed at Normandy, all hand-picked men, each trained in specific abilities. The Marine wing of which we were part was divided into A troop, B troop and X troop, although these troops were very fluid, we also had many casualties along the way. Mostly we were split into small groups of about eight and sent on specific missions. Nobody knew what the other groups were doing. We had a specific task all information based on 'need-to-know', the aim was to just complete the mission, following our orders. The Marines main job was just to keep the Naval Officers alive actually, they were the ones who really knew what was going on.

I was intending to go down to Littlehampton for September, it is quite a journey for me, so I normally stay overnight. Are you far from Littlehampton?"

September, that's months! For me that seemed an age away, I wanted to meet with Richard right now, today. I had been excited by every word and the insight into my Grandfather's past. Reluctantly, I had to accept the timescale for the reunion but arranged to meet Richard near his home in a couple of week's time and said my goodbyes.

May 2006. Norfolk England.

Cromer in Norfolk was a beautiful part of the country and one that Emma and I were very fond of. Emma, my wife had previously lived in the area with her parents for many years. Dickie had been insistent on meeting first at the local pub. I wondered why? Why did he seem nervous about meeting me? Why was he reluctant to give away his address? Although in this day and age people had to be careful, there were just so many crazy things happening throughout the world. Or was there? I often found myself wondering if it was all just an over-hyped media, was the whole world just following America's media lead into a spiral of fear and violence?

The pub was crowded in the nice warm sunny spring weather. Dickie had said that he would be wearing his Royal Marine Green Beret to identify himself. But as Emma and I walked through the many people outside the pub we could not see it, then the flash of green caught the eye, but it was on the wooden table.

Dickie was wearing well, had an air of happiness and well being that had been missing in Grandad for such a very long time before his death.

"You look so young and healthy!" I could tell Lisa was a strong character, I took an instant liking to this couple and they seemed genuinely pleased to meet us.

"Thank you, well I can tell you I wasn't a good person to be around when I came back from the war, very unpleasant. Thankfully Lisa here was a trained psychiatric nurse knew how to handle me, got me straightened out very quickly didn't you?" They smiled warmly at each other. " I was so lucky to have met her and had a career before the war started, something to come back too, get stuck into, lose myself in."

To me it was a heart-warming sight, the contentedness and ease they had with each other.

"Unfortunately Ron never had any of that, no career to fall back on and a wife that was probably just as traumatised by the war as he was, lost in an unfamiliar country. I think he had a very hard time trying to adjust back into civilian life, maybe never even got over it all. At nineteen he was, as you were, a highly trained heavily armed soldier, running around Europe at the very zenith of human history, feeling like a superman, the world at his feet. At that age men feel indestructible, invincible, I know I did and I certainly wasn't a trained soldier, how could it ever be possible to come back down from that? I know he didn't work for two years after leaving the Marines. It was a bad time for him, very hard. Constant nightmares." I stopped myself from going on. I wanted to try and stay upbeat, not drag on about negative aspects.

"I must admit we were both very nervous about meeting you after the terrible stabbing of our grandson, Stuart, and all of the stories you constantly hear on the news broadcasts, you just can't be too careful."

"You're grandson was attacked?"

"Yes, stabbed twenty-five times for his mobile phone, would you believe it, then left for dead in the street. Amazingly he seems to have made a complete physical recovery after about a year. That was the reason the original 30AU website went offline. After the long process of recovery he had found he just could not bear to be in this country, he left as quickly as he could, Australia, he's back now. Still I see your website has come along nicely." Richard smiled.

"Yes thanks, I was surprised there was not one already when I looked online, I guess I must have just missed Stuart's and as there didn't appear to be anything I started mine immediately. I'm hoping to make it as comprehensive a record of your unit as it is possible to do." I was troubled. Later that afternoon I found myself constantly wondering if that mugging could have been related to the same fear Ron had about being watched, about his belief that Guy Wilthew had been murdered in connection with his wartime actions. It did seem too much of a coincidence. Was it possible it had happened because of his website? (*I wondered what a conspiracy theorist would have made of all this? Certainly when I later looked at the police records it seemed entirely unlikely, but was that the point!?*), maybe I was just getting as paranoid as Ron, maybe I should just forget it and carry on, but at that time the thought would not go away as we spent some time relaxing after lunch.

Dickie's converted bungalow stood facing the wide expanse of grey sea off of the North Norfolk coast in a little dead end street, surrounded by a typically English country garden.

"You know I can feel as if I'm in your Grandfather's presence with you here, back in time, it's strange." Dickie sat heavily in the floral patterned armchair, which stood with its back to the sea in the front of the large living room.

The remark caught me off guard, touched an emotion. I unzipped the portfolio and placed the digitally re-printed portrait '*Beau Bête*' on the sofa. He was here with us. I had scanned the original painting, one of several portraits Margot had completed, and spent a long time re-touching in Photoshop before having some copies re-printed.

"Well would you look at that! Just as I remember him. I remember he always had a very modern haircut, sharp, suited him. He was quite an attraction to the girls we met along the way you know."

"This was painted by my Grandmother, Margot, she was a member of the

Maquis, French resistance, they met during the liberation of Vannes in Brittany, were you with him then?" I enquired.

"No, I don't think I was, although I'm not sure where I would have been. The Maquis were wonderful, saved us many casualties, time and time again. Helping us avoid trouble. How wonderful that it led to a marriage and a huge family by the sound of it.

"Yep I'm the eldest of thirty odd grandchildren and the great grandchildren have started piling up now as well." I smiled.

"Why on earth did he never get in touch with all us Marines again, after all we went through together?" Dickie mused.

"This is a print I have had done to give to *The Marine* pub, I was hoping you would allow me to accompany you to the reunion?" I asked, hopefully.

Dickie looked across at Lisa.

"I'd be happy to pick you up, maybe meet half way, drive you down…" I offered.

"Wonderful, yes I'd be happy to accept." Dickie seemed pleased, Lisa looked concerned.

"I'll look after him Lisa. If I can keep up that is." I watched Lisa's face come round to the idea.

"So, let's have a look at what you have in that smart metal case" said Dickie, evidently as impatient as I was to view the collection of 30AU memorabilia.

"All of this is new to me. I found these in an old tin box stored at my Grandparents house. They lived a fairly eccentric life style, I'm not sure that anything was kept deliberately, or just lost within everything else that cluttered their tiny house. I do remember as a small boy finding some Nazi flags, hidden away under the stairs among the junk that filled every cupboard. Could it have been the flag he has on his shoulders in this photo in the book Attain by Surprise? This picture here?" I- flicked open to the photo section of the book.

"Oh, so he had it did he! We did track down a few of the flags but not all." Dickie set eyes on the F-S fighting knife. "Only one thousand of that type ever made. Pattern One - Type Two, Fairburn and Sykes changed the design slightly from the original Type One, which had a three-inch cross guard. How wonderful, he kept it all these years. What I wouldn't give to be able to pass mine on to my grandson. I got rid of all my wartime things straight away, couldn't bear to have them lying about." Dickie felt the weight of the solid metal dagger. "Sixty years since I held a real one of these."

I wondered if his grandson might have been on his mind at that point.

"Ian Fleming's Red Indians?" Again I felt the pang of guilt. As long as I lived I would never be able to understand why I hadn't listened to Grandad when he'd tried to tell me. Why had I ignored him so utterly?

"Yes, that's right, although none of the 30AU Officers thought very much of Fleming, I have to say. Although of course the whole unit would never have existed if it had not been for his brilliant idea and his fortitude in seeing it come into being while he was in the Admiralty. His bosses, one of whom was Rear Admiral John Godfrey, were dead set against the idea at first, so I'm told. Although I think the idea was actually based on a German unit 'The AbwehrKommando' but I believe he was entirely responsible for the units early successes and spent a great deal of time and energy compiling his infamous 'Black List' of intelligence targets. I think a lot of our missions were thought up and planned by him personally. But Fleming wrote his Bond novels long after the war, he wasn't famous then, simply another Commander. Apparently he used to call us his 'Red Indians,' I'm not sure it was an appropriate analogy." smiled Dickie.

"I guess I should be thankful to Commander Fleming as well, if he hadn't had that brilliant idea, I would never have existed, my Nan and Grandad would never have met! Still I guess you could say that about any one of a million decisions that go on to make a family." My mind drifted back again to that last lunch with Grandad, 'I was a Red Indian Brave.' These words kept repeating in my head, but this phrase had so often been accompanied with seemingly ridiculous comments like 'the CIA or MI5 are watching me.' Maybe all that manic, colour-streaked writing ought not to be thrown away (as some of it had been already). I now realised, if I could muster the fortitude, I should read it all. The problem might be sifting the relevant and true from what could have been warped or effected by medicinal mind altering drugs or time.

Dickie then asked about Ron's death.

"He had mental problems after he lost Margot, bipolar, depression, he was discharged from the Marines out in the Far East, Hong Kong, after the war, schizophrenia, the letter had said." It felt awkward to talk about this.

"I'm sorry to hear that, it was a hard time, many 30AU men had problems, some good men, Officers too, although I'm very surprised to hear you say that, I had Ron down as strong, mentally and physically. I'm very surprised actually. Although the boys who ended up out in the Far East had a tough time from what I hear. Very tough. Thankfully I was HO, Hostilities Only, never ended up out there. I think they all had a very, very hard time out there…" Dickie went quiet, looking into himself.

"My Grandad was heartbroken when my Nan died, we all were she was a wonderful lady. But for Ron it was like a whole large part of himself was missing. I suppose during those six years, all he wanted was to be with my Nan."

"It must have been very difficult. I don't know what I would do without my better half. It is no fun getting old you know," said Dickie, with an instinctive attempt to gently lighten the conversation. "Anyway, back to this case. What else have you got in there?"

I carefully unfolded the fragile cloth maps onto the floor I had discovered they had been marked with some small circles and notations.

"Ah right, these are the silk escape maps we were issued before certain missions, for use if captured, they are an important historical artefact, you really should get these into a museum you know. They were printed onto silk for durability and the fact that they were so light and could be folded down extremely small to be sown into battledress seams, or helmet comforters." Dickie informed me.

"I wanted to ask you about these markings." I pointed out the notes scribbled in ink that had sunken into the fine weave of the silk and faded, making it blend in to the rest of the map markings and not very noticeable. "Here, right dead centre of Germany, just south of the Harz mountains, in Thuringia, Gotha and Ohrdruf, are circled and it looks like SIII marked, also slightly further North, Bleidroche and V2 -near Nordhausen and Blankenburg, it looks like HV and HW. Any idea as to what they might be indicating?"

"I'm not too sure, I was never anywhere near that area, although I do know that some of our teams were down that way and they were very successful. I think Lambie went down that way, yes, he captured a Professor, working on guided bombs I think, Wagner I think his name was." Dickie's face screwed up in concentration as he tried to look at the markings.

"Wagner? Maybe the HW? How about this mark up here near Bremerhaven, Z29 and it looks like, Euro and a place called Buxtehude?" I looked up, eager for any inkling of recognition or information.

"Ah, yes, now that was a ship, or two ships, and Buxtehude was an Airstrip. I wasn't there with that unit but I do know they captured a German Destroyer with some very important people on board so I'm told, important Nazi's I think and loads of technical info about new weapons. They were trying to escape, on their way to South America or the Far East or some place hot, apparently, until 30AU got hold of them anyway! Yes, yes and Tambach, yes I remember, Schloss Castle, that was old 'Sancho' Glanville, his team captured the entire German Naval records, everything, hidden in the vaults of the castle. I think they shipped about five tons of paperwork from there, in the Russian sector, before the Russians turned up. I think there were also a few very important German Admirals hiding out there as well and his team of eight men captured the whole lot." Dickie smiled, eager and happy to be able to fill in some gaps.

"How about some of these men, here, Swann, 'Ganger' Gates, Rush and Higgins? Do you remember them, still in contact with them?" I asked, handing Dickie some of the pictures.

"Well now, I certainly remember faces, all their faces, yes, Rush, I know him very well a very good man, steady, reliable, still involved with us now. Higgins became a professional football player after the war, not sure what happened to him after that. Gates, I don't know. Now Swann, yes, yes he was one for the ladies, never knew what happened to him after the war though and I would guess we never will. I seem to remember he was caught in a compromising position with another Marines wife! Although I don't know if that's true, only what I heard." Dickie smiled lost in his memories for a few seconds.

While poor bored Emma spent some time chatting with Lisa, Dickie showed me the converted attic room upstairs; it had a large open window facing the wide expanse of sea and horizon. It was a room that looked to be entirely dedicated to 30AU; photos of reunions lined the wall, an illustration of the original Beach Hotel in Littlehampton, with a Willys Jeep parked out front, an ornamental representation of a Special Operations Dagger and various other memorabilia.

"Lisa has moved me up here; said she can no longer sleep with my constant snoring!"

Dickie opened some files to show me letters from various councils, 30AU men and relatives. Then something I hadn't really expected for some reason. An old brown, torn and battered photo album, it flicked open straight to a series of photographs. Photos that I had never seen before. Photos that even Ron had probably never seen before his death. All of them contained the men of 30AU and each of one group of pictures had the unmistakable smile of my Grandad, beaming out, a wide youthful smile, and he looked truly happy.

6th September 2006. Littlehampton. England.

We were standing faces skyward looking up at the squeaking pub sign hanging outside The Marine, Littlehampton. In my minds eye I had already replaced Sergeant Paul McGrath, the subject of the pub sign, for the painting I had restored, the painting of Marine Guy, entitled '*Beau Bête*'.

The Marine pub was in a very quiet back street of Littlehampton. It had a blue 'Heritage' plaque on the wall, which spoke of the reunions held over the years at the pub, I found myself wondering again why Ron would have never made contact with any of his old wartime colleagues.

We walked over and moved our bags into the guesthouse. The landlady informed us of an unexpected problem and enquired if we minded sharing a twin room.

"No, no, we don't mind, we're family, well almost." Dickie had answered quickly. Before I had even time to think, but I did not open my mouth after that remark. I felt honoured, humbled. I could not help but wonder if we were even staying in the same room Ron and Dickie had shared nearly sixty years earlier when the men of 30AU were billeted here.

The new landlord, had been working hard to try and turn around the fortunes of the pub. I gave him the portrait and a small photo of Margot and Ron together in France just after they had first met, Margot was wearing Ron's Beret. It seemed right to me that it should hang here in the pub, this was probably the last place of true innocence that Ron ever had, before the war had had a chance to touch him, I guess. Anyway it felt right that a copy of it should hang there.

The landlord seemed genuinely happy to accept the gift and hung it with the other 30AU memorabilia, while I sifted through old dusty cardboard boxes that had been dug out from some place of storage, all of them contained various photo's and documents related to 30AU. The first item to really catch my attention was marked with Lt. Commander Patrick D Job's name, he was said by the Wikipedia website to have possibly been Fleming's very model for his *James Bond* character. The small document was a photocopy of an obviously battered and well worn, 'Special Authorisation' pass.

Dickie informed me that this was the very document that had made General Patton angry enough to christen 30AU 'A bunch of Limey Pirates!'

THE BEARER OF THIS CARD WILL NOT BE INTERFERED WITH IN THE PERFORMANCE OF HIS DUTY BY THE MILITARY POLICE OR ANY OTHER MILITARY ORGANISATION. And the same phrase repeated in French, then signed by Eisenhower.

A lot of these things I borrowed for scanning onto the website.

Over lunch Dickie had had to refuse numerous offers of drinks from the locals once they knew of his connection to the pub. He was embarrassed by the attention. I was pleased, this was the way it should be, these men recognised for the heroes they undoubtedly were.

After lunch we took a very pleasant stroll in the warm sunshine towards the small memorial park at the original seafront location of the Beach Hotel.

"This terrace here was where Royal Marine Colonel Woolley, had his Offices, 30AU headquarters and opposite, there, where those horrible modern flats are now, that was where we used to fall in for inspections and drills." Dickie was still fit, chatting away, enjoying the reminiscences.

We slowly meandered through the small park that had numerous gates, but only one of which was unlocked and on to the small Plaque that remembered the spot.

'10th August 1997, To commemorate the 30 Assault Unit, Royal Marines, Who operated from this site for a period during the World War Two 'WE WILL REMEMBER THEM"

We walked further on towards the sea.

"I think this is still the original wall that used to surround The Beach Hotel." Dickie pointed out the high wall through the bushes behind us as we sat on a bench soaking up the warm sunlight. It was very quiet, relaxing day, kites twisted in the sky above us; dogs chased balls across the wide-open expanse of grass between us and the beach.

"All this grass area here was fenced off with razor wire and barriers, it was full to the brim with vehicles, all kinds of vehicles and we had loads. Apparently our unit had the most vehicles per head of any unit in the Second World War. Our armoury was in one of the outbuildings of the Hotel behind us." Dickie casually pointed behind him.

I could see that Dickie was right back there, in time. Surrounded by the vehicles and men he had been a part of.

"We used to have to do our guard duty all along this seafront and you certainly had to keep your wits about you for the whole time. Red, old Captain Huntingdon-Whiteley, he was a real character, he used to run exercises, trying to sneak up on sentries, or we were supposed to sneak up on him as he kept guard, dead of night, heaven knows how we didn't all end up shot by our own guards! I've tried to ask the local council about a concrete statue of a Jeep or maybe a Humber or Staghound to stand on this grass area. It would seem right to remember how it was then, something the local kids could climb on, be part of their childhood, to help them remember what we went through." Dickie sat back and sighed, enjoying the warmth and the peace.

"Yes, you're right, it should be here, now. Hopefully one day someone might do that." I could already see it in my minds eye, a full size concrete Staghound covered in playing laughing kids, playing at war like I had, like all boys did including my own two, instead of the grim faced Royal Marines in the wartime photos I had just seen at The Marine pub.

That night I could not sleep. Dickie was snoring loudly, although that was not what was keeping me awake. The Landlord of the pub had informed us that he had been at the pub one year exactly and had promised himself to get rid the of stinking, stained, carpet before that year had come to an end. Tomorrow was the 30AU reunion and tonight, now, the carpet was being removed, after last orders.

As we walked in the next afternoon he smiled and handed me another old cardboard box, covered in dust. Amazingly the floor of the pub, underneath the protection of the carpet, looked in remarkably good condition, quite obviously the carpet should have been got rid of a long time ago. He informed me that he had found another box of bits and bobs related to 30AU.

I sat and tried to brush off the dirt and dust. In it were more ancient framed pictures of 30AU memorabilia and a few small folded pieces of brown paper, photocopies. On the first page marked, SECRET and headed 30 Advance Unit, Field Teams, it was a list of Naval Officers and the Royal Marine men that made up each of six special operations teams. A few names caught my attention, Lt. J. Besant. RNVR. I had heard the name, before, many, many years before. It had stuck in my mind as a child because of the way I had heard it had brought to mind the fictional character '*James Bond*', my favourite childhood hero, that and the circumstances under which I had listened to it. Also Turner was a name I had already found in Grandad's scribbles.

The next few pieces of paper made up a list, a target list and top of the list was, Hans von Braun – Son of former Agriculture minister – Rocket engineer in charge at Peenemünde/Nordhausen.

Hans von Braun! Could that be one of the von Braun's the world famous Nazi rocket scientists? That could be the markings on the silk maps, HV? Grandad's maps, I had now also read the name in Ron's memoirs, repeatedly. I had to get to the laptop, get online.

"Ah yes, Fleming's Black list, that was used to make up the 'Black Books' that the 30AU Naval Officers had, lists of Intelligence targets." Dickie seemed very calm as I showed him the pages.

"So is that where the original term 'Black Book' comes from?" I quickly did a web search for von Braun and sifted though the images. Hundreds of links were popping up. Von Braun and his brother had both been Nazi party members, who surrendered to the US army in Bavaria on the 2nd of May 1945.

I looked at the list again, to the entry that referred to the scientist. It was clearly marked, 'Hans von Braun, Peenemünde.'

Why Hans? I guess they did not know their real names at that point or even if it was two men or one, but he was on 30AU target list and possibly placed in the centre of Germany according to Ron's scribbles and these map markings, but the websites and history books all said they surrendered to the US troops in Bavaria.

I found a website that had many photos of that moment of surrender, the historically recorded surrender of the Nazi Rocket scientists.

"It says on these websites that one of the brothers cycled down and bumped into an American GI of the US 44th, who just happened to be an interpreter! Then he supposedly went down and got his officers, only later going to the hotel to get the rest of the scientists, hundreds of them! Who had managed to travel right across the entire length of war torn Germany, together but without any of their families, while four different armies were looking for them! Surely that had to be pretty unlikely? I sat heavily back in the chair, staring intently at the computer screen, letting the realisation wash over me. "This could have been staged!" The thought rattled around inside my head. "Why would they bother to go to such elaborate lengths to hide capturing one of the most famous scientists the world has ever known? Although obviously he wasn't famous then." I said my first thoughts out loud. "These were the very men who started the space race, who put the first American man on the moon and who gave the world the term…'It's not Rocket Science' but if this surrender was staged it would mean that US secret agents were gathered together in Bavaria along with all these Nazi's and scientist's behind the German front lines in front their own US frontline forces, collaborating with SS and other top ranking Nazi's to make sure the 'surrender' was going to be as real as possible. Something the world was going to believe as part of historical fact. For sixty years anyway! That really shows some absolutely incredible foresight on behalf of the US agents, they knew exactly what they wanted well before the end of the war and must have even been in negotiation with top Nazi's long before the invasion. This has serious implications you know, very serious… and effectively it means the entire American space program was built on a lie!.." I glanced up from the laptop screen, I was talking to myself, Dickie had wandered off to talk to other patrons he recognised.

I started to write some bits for the website and scan images for uploading, someone online would know what was true and what not, there were hundreds of conspiracy website people who spent all their time deliberating things such as this.

I quickly learnt that there had been rumours of the von Braun's involvement in war crimes for virtually the whole of their career in the US, but nothing proven. In the sixties a series of court cases had been brought by some French holocaust survivors and although some of these had been successful on various members of the one hundred and twenty eight German scientists the US had taken, which had led to either imprisonment or deportation, none of the cases had managed to stick on either of the von Brauns. There was even an article on one of the conspiracy websites stating that one of the men involved in that 'surrender' was later implicated in the Kennedy assassination conspiracy.

The obvious explanation as why to stage the surrender to US forces was that these men must have been snatched from the Russian sector of Germany.

I already knew that at Yalta near the Black Sea, in February 1945, Churchill, Stalin and Roosevelt had agreed to work together for the downfall of Germany and to split the spoils. Germany had been divided into four parts, British to the West, Russian to the East, American to the South and French to the South East. The agreement stated that anything within these sectors would belong to that country, no matter who captured it. Therefore if von Braun had been captured in the Russian sector he belonged to the Russians according to the Allied Yalta agreement.

But if that was the case, why hide that fact for sixty years? Surely once the Cold War started, the Americans would have enjoyed rubbing that fact in Russia's face?

In my head something still did not quite add up.

●　　　●　　　●

A few of the old Royal Marine Veterans had made it down to the reunion from all over the country, but they were all finding the journey a bit of a challenge. A challenge to be conquered most of them said. I felt honoured to be able to share their stories and show the photo's and items I had collected for the website.

"Oh my goodness, that's Ron Guy! I signed up for the Royal Marines the very same day as Ron." 'Spike' Kelly stood in front of the portrait *'Beau Bête'*. "Always wondered why he never got in touch, why he disappeared? Although I ended up in the Naval wing of 30AU. There were three main sections. Thirty-three, Royal Marines. Thirty-four, Army, although they were just wasted, spent most of their time in Italy, kicking their heels, although they were successful in whatever it was they were up to, but it's still all classified, all secret, it seems to me they were totally wasted. Thirty-six was us, the Navalwing, I have a photo of us all if you'd like to see it sometime. There was also Thirty-five, Royal Air Force, but they only ever sent a few Officers, no more than that, for some specific targets." Spike had a deep rumbling voice and everyone within thirty feet was going to be part of any conversation he had.

"So you were in the Royal Marines with Ron before 30AU?" I had to repeat myself but louder, Spike was starting to go deaf. I wondered if it might be related to wartime explosions. I tried to imagine this bent white haired old man, as he would have been at twenty years old.

"Sorry I'm going a bit deaf, the result of insisting on driving one of the Staghounds when I wasn't supposed to! In Germany we were, nagged the poor driver for days I did. He finally let me have a drive and would you believe it, we were ambushed. I got separated from the Jeep we were supposed to be escorting, explosions and bullets bouncing off the armour plating, my ears rang for days, were never the same again. Eventually found my way back to the frontline, more by luck than judgement!

Oh yes, yes, let me tell you about signing up for 'Hazardous Service'...

Chapter One

1943/1944 Chatham, England.

"Not bloody likely!" Eric 'Curly' Killingback was unimpressed as he was joined in the dark, smoky pub in Chatham, by the four Bootnecks. "What the hell kind of idea is that? You can just get back there and remove my name and right now!"

Ron Guy and three other Royal Marines, had just signed all five of them up for 'Hazardous Service', the request had been posted on the notice board and they had added all five of their names to the fifty or so that were already scribbled in.

"What? Why the hell did you join up if you don't want to get stuck into the Hun?" Guy was taken aback. Joining the Marines had channelled all his aggression in such a positive way. The 'milling' and boxing training he had excelled at. The assault courses and stamina exercises he seemed to find so much easier than the others, he had even found himself top of the target range, he was revelling in being the best. Something that his working class upbringing in East Ham, had meant he had always had to fight for.

The notice had been posted on the board at Chatham Royal Marines Barracks and from the moment Guy had seen it he knew it was just what he wanted. He had already tried to join the Royal Air Force at the onset of war, had actually got in and started training, until they discovered he was only fifteen at the time and had lied about his age. He wanted to fight. Fight anything and anyone, but to be trained, and to fight for his country, that was what he dreamed of, more than anything else. To be chosen for 'Special Operations' would really be something. He could think of nothing else, his mind was made up, that was what he wanted. He was not going to fail.

Guy was now a proud member of 413 King's Squad and felt he truly understood the meaning of 'Esprit de Corps' and certainly knew why they were more commonly referred to as 'Hairy-Arsed Bootnecks', so named after the thick leather Cutlass protection on the neck of the original Royal Marine uniform and... the obvious! His passing out parade had certainly been the proudest moment of his life, so far, seven intensive months of Royal Marine training, he felt good about himself.

The 'Hazardous Service' interview took place unexpectedly a few weeks later, the successful applicants were shipped off to the infamous Achnacarry, Scotland, to complete the rigorous Commando training course and from there to the 'Holding Commando' at Wrexham, where they awaited selection.

The twenty or so Marine Commandos sat impatiently, not really knowing what to expect.

"Guy." He was first to be called, he marched smartly through the door and saluted as the Officer closed the door and resumed his place behind the small desk. The very tall, well over six feet, Royal Marine Captain, held out his hand. "Relax, son. I'm Captain Huntington-Whiteley and this is Captain Hargreaves-Heap. Take a seat." They shook hands and sat as the Officer opened a small file.

"Twenty-eighth of May, twenty-five, that's the same birthday as Commander Fleming, he still hasn't finished celebrating." The Captain smiled to himself.

"Sorry Sir?"

"Nothing, nothing, look, between you and me you're already in, I've looked over your training record and there is no question. Pretty handy with those fists?"

"Well, yes Sir, my grandfather, Sonny Guy, he taught me to Box, he was a bare-knuckle fighter on the London Docks."

"These shooting scores are right up there. I don't suppose you've had any explosives experience?" The Captain asked.

"Well, actually, yes Sir, I used to help my Uncle, he was an industrial demolitions man."

"Really? Well, very good, very good indeed. Any other languages?"

"No Sir." Guy knew something was going to let him down.

"Right, well, get onto that, double quick. We expect at least one other language. I think you're going to be a busy boy Guy. I'm going to get you down for a sniping course, and a couple of explosives courses, and that's in amongst all the usual training we expect from you. You'll be heading straight to Amersham for training, probably with some of the other lads we choose from here. You think you're up to it?"

"Yes Sir, without doubt. Sir." Guy felt himself relax.

"Good boy, good boy, now listen hear, you're now officially a member of Thirty Commando Special Engineering Unit. But it's TOP SECRET, not to be discussed in any way to anyone, or you'll not only find yourself out on your ear, but also in jail and don't forget that! We've had some fantastic success already in Africa, Algiers and Yugoslavia operating in small clandestine groups, but it's pretty intense, dangerous kind of stuff. Basically our job is to move ahead of frontline troops, to get into, as quickly as possible, enemy Head Quarters and installations and gather any and all technical documents or information and equipment, before they can destroy it! To 'Attain by Surprise'. I'm heading off out on operations straight from here so I'm going to walk out with you. That's how you do it Heap old boy, the rest are all yours." He threw a pile of folders at Captain Hargreaves-Heap as they left.

As Guy passed his mates, on the way out, he gave them a nod and a wink, it felt good, and he was pleased with himself.

After Commando training in Achnacarry, Scotland, which Guy had to admit, to anyone who would listen, he had loved, well mostly, Guy found himself on endless training courses and 'Red' also had him running about on a lot of errands from the HQ's and billets.

"Guy, how are you lad? Training going well?" Red looked down at him.

"Excellent Sir, Thank you Sir."

"Good boy, listen hear, I need someone I can trust, can you get this down to Fleming for me?" He leaned down to a battered leather case by the side of his chair and pulled out a plain brown envelope. "Get this down to Commander Fleming at the Admiralty Citadel, NID room thirty, or could be thirty-nine, for his eye's only mind you, no-one else's." He held out the envelope and smiled.

All sorts of questions raced through Guy's mind. Where the hell was the Admiralty Citadel? How was he supposed to know who Commander Fleming was? What did NID stand for? How was he even supposed to get in the place with no pass? Could this be some kind of test?

"Yes Sir. Certainly Sir." He saluted; somehow he thought now was not the best time to be asking silly questions.

It didn't take long to locate the 'Citadel' a huge 'bomb proof' concrete bunker, overlooking Horse Guards Parade ground, in the centre of London. He also now knew that NID stood for Naval Intelligence Division, which was a very well respected body of men. The security surrounding it looked impenetrable. Guy decided on the simplest and most direct approach.

"Wait there!" The Guards seemed unimpressed with his lack of pass and hesitant idea of where he was going and why.

The sound of heels on a hard floor preceded her arrival, a smartly dressed lady, carrying some files.

"Hello Margaret, sorry to have dragged you down here again, this young Marine will not pass his envelope to anyone but Commander Fleming." The Guard smiled his best smile.

"Alright, Ted, I'll deal with it. Who sent you?" She enquired.

"Captain Huntington-Whiteley, Miss, told me for Commander Fleming only."

"Ah 'Red' alright, I'll sign him in, Ted. Come with me, you may have a long wait…"

"Marine Guy, Miss, Ron Guy." He replied.

"I'm *Miss Priestley, follow me then Marine Guy, and keep up or you'll get lost." She smiled and turned heading back into the bunker.

*Miss Margaret Preistley sadly passed away recently and during her lifetime wanted no public recognition of the very important part she played in NID-30AU and as an inspiration to Ian Fleming for 'Miss Petty Pettaval' his original name for the character that became Miss Moneypenny. Miss Preistley a history Don at Leeds University transferred to 30AU from DoNR (Department of Naval Research) in the winter of 1944/5 and played an essential part in the running and administration of 30AU from the Citadel (room 30) and in the compilation of Fleming's 'Black List' of Intelligence targets.

The Citadel, it was like a maze, corridors and rooms in all directions, phones ringing, people rushing about, doors slamming and opening. Room 30 was too small for the three desks, camp bed and cabinets squeezed into it, with no windows, but with the slight hum of air-conditioning, concrete walls covered in maps and photographs and piled high with documents and files of all types. No sooner had she taken her seat and resumed typing when she was interrupted by another 'beep' from the front entrance. Guy found himself sitting on the small camp bed in one corner of the office, on his own, while she marched off and after a short time returned accompanied by a Naval Officer, who she instructed to sit and wait on the bed next to Guy. Both men sat in silence as Miss Priestley continued her typing. They studied the maps of North Africa and Sicily on the walls, which were surrounded by aerial reconnaissance photographs of various installations, until another 'beep' made them all jump. Guy and the Naval Officer smiled slightly to each other as they followed through another part of the maze which eventually led to door number 39, the office door quickly opened and out stepped a very tall 'dapper' looking older man with a smoking cigarette and a drink in a crystal glass tumbler both held in one hand.

He smiled warmly. "Ah, Miss P, lovely to see you."

"Commander Fleming, this is…" she did not have time to finish.

"The names Patrick Dalzel-Job." He stepped boldly forward holding out his hand to the man that towered above him.

"Mr. Job, so pleased to meet you, I've just been reading about your spot of bother in Norway. I don't think we'll find that kind of thing to be any problem." Said Fleming as he ushered Job towards his office.

"Well I had no intention of leaving all those people to die in the inferno I knew their village was going to be in a few hours, no matter what orders I was given." Job sounded defiant.

"I quite understand, come this way." The door slammed shut behind them. Guy caught a quick glance through the door and out of the interior office window, which overlooked the parade ground, it seemed this part of the building was not actually in the Citadel and night was fast approaching.

Many Naval Officers seemed to be coming and going from room thirty-nine

43

as he waited the interminable age to finally deliver his envelope, to which he did not even receive a second glance, let alone a thank you. This now meant that he was stuck in London, late at night, with no-where to go, luckily one of the many secretaries seemed happy to go for a drink as they had both left, which more than made up for it and thankfully 'Red' had Guy as well as Marine Danny Reeves running back and forth up to the Citadel on many occasions so it was a dalliance Guy managed to repeat...

...and so continued his whirlwind of training, Guy had felt well trained after Chatham, when he had finished this lot, he felt like a real 'Man of Steel'.

•   •   •

There had been Explosives, Mine and Demolitions training, both the laying and dismantling of enemy types, detection of booby-traps, setting traps, defusing of Torpedoes and various types of bombs and grenades at HMS Volcano in Cumberland.

Followed by a Street Fighting course in the bombed-out factories and buildings of Battersea, this included the use of approaches by sewers and several other covert ways of getting to, and eliminating, a target.

Intelligence training had involved the recognition of enemy documents, personnel, uniform types and the structure of the Wehrmacht and Kreigsmarines, including the layout and security used in enemy harbours and head quarters.

A Photography course on the best way of recording detailed map, documents, instruments or installations including the interiors of submarines, ships or radar sites.

The driving and control of all types of vehicles, 30AU were the most mobile unit of the war, more vehicles per head than any other unit. Jeeps, trucks, personnel carriers, tanks, Humber scout cars, Staghounds, motorbikes and motorboats, most of these vehicles were stored in a huge grass compound, fenced with razor wire and barriers in front of the Beach Hotel on Littlehampton seafront, where the men of 30AU had been billeted in civilian digs. It caused a few problems, as once they were trained to drive these vehicles the men tended to try and use them on any and all occasions, even for their own personal errands.

Naval Officers and Marines undertook parachute training at Ringway, Manchester.

Glider training on Salisbury Plain, one such flight started off in the normal way, the Marines all lined up with full kit were sat in the Horsa glider as it bumped along the airfield, the four powerful engines of a Halifax bomber pulled the glider easily into the air using a tow wire in the shape of a large 'Y' the top of which attached to each of the gliders wings, once both aircraft were at an altitude of about five hundred feet or so a lever was pulled in the glider, one side released as expected the other jammed. The glider shook wildly from side to side, sending Marines flying into each other, after several pulls on the lever it broke off completely, the pilot struggled with the controls, but it seemed to make no difference. Typically the communication line was connected to the side that had released but eventually the tail man in the Halifax realised what was happening and released the cable from his end and it trailed from the wing for about 20 minutes until the experienced pilot managed to make an almost perfect landing, thankfully without the wire snagging anything solid. Another flight in the same session made an over heavy landing and Plywood and Perspex, splintered and shattered inwards, the runners were shoved up through the floor into the fuselage, there only seemed to be a few minor injuries, so both of the groups were marched into the other glider and towed back into the air within minutes. As the Marines discussed it in the pub, later that evening they were informed that when the same thing had occurred previously it had usually pulled the wing off the glider resulting in the death of everybody on board.*

The Police Procedures Course really stuck in Guy's mind, it had included the training of persons identification from photographs, the handling, disarming and searching of prisoners, criminal psychology, the surveying

*(This incident actually took place on 5th Feb 1945, during training in the interim between France and Germany as the expected and probable method of their entry into Germany)

then breaking and entering of secure buildings and banks and it was also where he'd met the very likeable character, Fusilier John Ramsey (Ramenski) of polish extraction, but with a distinct Glaswegian accent, he was a short man of immense strength and agility who looked as if he'd been punched on the nose a few too many times. The ex-policemen who were part of 30 Assault Unit, as it was now known, had recruited him straight from one Prison or another, apparently he spent most of his time behind bars, but even so was considered by them to be the best 'Peterman' or safe-breaker in Britain so he was the right man to teach them how to break into the banks as well.

Guy accompanied by another couple of Royal Marines and a Naval Lieutenant James Besant, who preferred to be called Jim or Jimmy, had been told to report to Scotland Yard for a safe-breaking course. In the courtyard within the station there must have been about forty safe-boxes of various colours, sizes and makes. Many of which had quite obviously taken a significant amount of explosive to open already. Whether anything remained intact inside them afterwards Guy somehow doubted. Ramsey was always accompanied by a couple of the 30AU, troop thirty-four (Army), ex-policemen at the station and Guy was never quite sure whether they were there to make sure he didn't abscond or because they were explosive experts as well. He quickly came to the conclusion that it was probably both.

"Right lads, now obviously we're only supposed to blow the fucking door off! We want to be able to retrieve anything that might be inside, that's the whole fucking point. We can't fuck about with earpieces, or drills, or cutting equipment, you ain't got the time. The quickest, simplest way of getting what you want as quickly as possible is with this fucking stuff." He held up some plastic explosive. "But it ain't easy, not if you want to fucking read anything afterwards anyway." He smiled broadly.

With that opening speech he preceded to work his way through a few boxes, one of which he used a condom stuffed with a small amount of plastic explosive which he slowly fed into the key mechanism through the key hole before standing back detonating and watching the door gently swing open to reveal the contents to the impressed men. Then it was their turn, firstly in teams of three. The first two boxes failed to open after the ineffectual blasts;

the third box leapt five feet into the air and fell into three pieces with burning paper fluttering about the yard, which they had to quickly extinguish.

"What the fuck did I say at the start?" Ramsey didn't look impressed. "It only took the troop thirty-four guys two fucking go's to get it right." The two troop thirty-four guys both smiled.

After that challenge they quickly got to grips with physics of it and after a couple of days of practice on the seemingly endless supply of police safe boxes of all types and sizes, they had it off perfectly on the majority but some were very much easier to conquer than others.

The police 'Black Museum' was an eye opener for anyone who ever saw it; Guy was stunned that everything in it had been used for one crime or another at some time.

The mountaineering course on the cliffs of North Wales was yet another enjoyment for Guy, apart from one moment when they were being trained to use their gators as hand holds on the rope, for quick abseiling descents. Guy's gator straps caught up and then broke just as he tipped backwards over the edge of the drop, it flipped him over and would certainly have been his death had his ankle not been accidentally looped by the rope as he fell, the rope burns on both hands and the inside of his groin gave him a few sleepless nights. As did the Nettle soup which he had managed not to boil for long enough while on the survival course the following week while trying to survive on a diet of spiders that tasted like peanuts and various other unpalatable items.

Lastly he came to the sniper course, as part of a Special Operations Unit the weapons training was intensive, on every weapon Guy had ever heard of, and plenty he had not. It also meant that each man could choose the weapons he was to use for operations, he felt like a child in a free sweet shop. They could even, if they so desired, use the German weapons which they were also trained to use, although Guy was informed that most, although tempted, did not. Most of the 30AU men had stuck with the Thompson submachine gun, with the seventeen round magazine. Guy decided it would probably be wise to choose the same, although he liked the idea of the one hundred round barrel magazine, despite the added weight. He was also requested to test, alongside the Enfield sniper rifle he already had after the sniper course, the De Lisle

'Special Operations' sniper rifle with sound suppressor. It was a virtually silent weapon, the bolt made more noise than the shot, it did mean that the range was compromised, but Guy now felt that he was quite capable of getting close enough to negate that problem. There were two versions, one with wooden stock and another prototype parachute version with folding stock, he had it modified to include a telescopic sight. He also chose the Browning pistol with thirteen round magazine and a Colt forty-five for close-in fighting and building clearance, which also used the same clips as the De Lisle.

Guy, along with many of the men, even attended the same courses multiple times as new information and equipment became available.

It was now May 1944 and Guy was beginning to wonder if he would ever actually see a Nazi before the war ended, but he really did feel ready for anything. Anything anyone could throw at him.

Even Hitler's 'Master Race'.

Chapter Two

I sat in front of the pile of things I had gathered together from 'Bluebells', which would hopefully reveal more of the story to me. I untied the red ribbon on the first pile of letters, Ron and Margot's love letters. Suddenly a memory popped into my head, a memory of a story that I recalled from my childhood, a tale that my Nan had recounted to me while I was still a young boy and it all flooded back to mind now, in detail.

At the time I had listened intently, knowing that surely all families had experienced these things during the war. Then slowly as I grew up it had slipped back into my mind, just another forgotten childhood memory, until now…

1941, Vannes, France.

The warm sunshine blazed through the tree canopy, the idyllic summers day buzzed and hummed, birds sang, everything seemed at peace in a perfect world. Margot Wilthew lay on her back alone in the meadow, gazing up into the towering branches of the lone lush green tree which was filled with dancing birds, she found herself day dreaming again of that elusive stranger, the hazy shape of a man that she knew was there, but would not come into focus. She felt more relaxed now than she had felt in many a year, she wished with a deep longing that she could just stay here for eternity, an eternity filled with this tranquillity.

Suddenly the sun dimmed, everything faded and became silent, she sat up quickly, between her calves, on the ground, the grass lifted and parted, the rich brown dirt began to rise. Her first thought was a mole, but then an earth covered white finger appeared, followed by a hand slowly pushing its way from the soil. It was bloodied, dirtied, had gaping wounds and bones showing through the mangled flesh. Margot found she could not catch her breath…

She sat bolt upright in her bed, covered in perspiration, gasping for air. Unusually the house seemed full of noise. Her head would not clear. That same recurring nightmare that she just could not shake off. Unintelligible shouts mingling with banging and footsteps filled the house.

It was Sunday morning, early, she recalled going to bed the previous evening, feeling unwell, a temperature. Sunday Morning, everyone else would be at Church, she must be alone in the house. Why was it so noisy? Alone in the house. Alone, apart from the British Royal Air Force Hurricane pilot, asleep in the room above hers.

A sudden near panic gripped her heart. The noise of engines echoed from between the Church and the house in the narrow street in Vannes Brittany, France. Hob nailed boots could be heard on the cobbles, the banging was on the front door.

The Nazi's and they were here for the Airman. She leapt from the bed, nearly falling flat on her face as her wobbly legs caught on the covers. Her first thought; the gun. The small ornate engraved silver handgun, given to her with the unspoken understanding that its one and only use may just be on herself. But she was determined that was not going to be the case, she had to survive, had to fight. The small gun slid into her gown pocket as she hesitated on the stairwell. Should she go to the Airman and try to hide him? Or go to the door and let in the flood of vicious Wehrmacht troopers who would ransack the house of everything? Quickly she came to a decision, she had to try and stop the Germans from entering. She threw herself down the stairs, two steps at a time.

The large solid door of the main entrance had been especially reinforced by local French workmen. It shook in puffs of dust and the scattering tinkle of bits of masonry. The sound of cracking, splintering wood meant that it would certainly not hold very much longer as the Germans patience began to wear thin.

"BIEN, bien, je suis ici, attends, ATTENDS!" She had to try and give herself time to think, she was perspiring heavily, she felt hot, too hot, still probably had a temperature, she was unsteady on her feet, all seven stone of her was visibly shaking as she tried to release the many large heavy rusting bolts and catches.

"Öffnen Sie diese Tür sofort JETZT sofort!, Ouvrez cette porte immédiatement, MAINTENANT, immédiatement!" Deep voiced shouts encouraged her to be as quick as possible.

The banging ceased; as Margot started to try and turn the huge ornate key that was the last lock she could hear the shattering of glass and wood at the garden door.

A single gunshot rang out as a small shaft of daylight burst through the door at her waist height, she jumped and screamed as the wooden splinters pierced her upper thighs, but thankfully the bullet missed her, it zinged off down into the hallway after impacting with the stone work behind her feet.

"HALTEN SIE IHR FEUER AN!" The door erupted inwards as the last lock clanked open. Margot was lifted clean off of her feet and thrown back against the stone pillar behind her, she fell in a crumpled heap as the doorway was filled with huge grey-black shapes storming into the house, heading through in all directions.

She was dazed, barely conscious, her nose full of the musty smell of German soldiers. Her hand instinctively slipped inside her pocket and gripped the tiny gun, she and it felt so very small, insignificant before these huge towering men that paid her no more attention than they would have if she'd been a cat sitting and watching them enter.

Margot had no idea what to do, she so desperately wanted to live, to fight these barbarians, but she quickly made up her mind that although she wanted to live she had no intention of being these soldiers plaything while they raped and tortured her. She had always imagined that if it came to violence she would at least have been able to shoot one or two soldiers first, but the stark realization that filled her now was even that would only give them more opportunity to take her alive and that must not happen. As she looked up into the morning light flooding through the front door her vision was filled with fantastic colour. The stained glass windows of the Cathedral opposite the house. Cathédrale Saint-Pierre-et-Saint-Patern. Brilliant rays of colour all seemed to be aimed directly at her, the sun was rising on the other side of the Church and it was shining or reflecting right through one of the windows.

The windows that she loved so much, that all told such wonderful stories. The windows that had inspired her into the Beaux Art school in Nantes. Tears flooded down her cheeks and blurred the beautiful vision and separated the vivid colours even more as they reached her eyes. She so badly wanted to live, to nurture life, to love.

The sounds of screaming brought her attention back, her mother, she was silhouetted against the colour of the windows, hands clasping at the black metal railings of the Cathedral perimeter, the commotion had obviously emptied the Church, people had begun to push down into the narrow street. Part of the congregation tried desperately to drag Marguerite Wilthew, her mother, back away from the railings that she grasped with grim determination.

Margot slowly closed her eyes; she let herself relax as an insignificant heap on the floor. Her mind was made up, if she was touched she would put the pistol under her chin and fire without hesitation. A strange calm had taken hold. Her body had stopped shivering, she almost felt that the coloured sunlight was warming her through, filling her with strength. She was unsure how long she stayed that way, maybe she had even lost consciousness, but she reacted at the first touch. Margot pulled the gun out as quickly as she was able and felt the cold metal of the barrel on the soft warm skin of her throat.

"NON, NON, que faites-vous?" It was her mother's voice. Her mother was there with her. They embraced crying into each other's hair. Her sister Armelle joined the emotional embrace, as they virtually had to carry her up the stairs. Marguerite was desperately worried about the raging fever that seemed to have such a grip on her frail daughter.

Later that same day as the light began to fade, Margot came round again from that same nightmare. The indistinguishable man always just on the edge of her vision and the corpse hand rising from the ground. She found that her mother was cleaning and bathing the wounds at the top of her thighs, the stinging pain was probably what had brought her round.

"Que s'est il passé, où est l'aviateur ?" Margot began to wonder if it had all been a nightmare, although her stinging legs and badly bruised head and neck were more than enough of a reminder it was not.

"Les Nazis, ils seulement marché éteint, seulement la sortie...., nous ne savons absolument pas où est l'aviateur, il semble simplement avoir disparu, comme volatilisé dans l'air! " Marguerite explained, they had looked everywhere, no trace of him could be found, she was at a loss as to his whereabouts, there seemed to be no escape possible, but nonetheless he was gone and therefore so thankfully were the Germans.

She continued on to tell Margot of the news that had been circulating in the Church as the raid had interrupted the service, the daughter of a local farmer had spotted a single hand sticking out of the ground. Freshly dug earth, the farmers had uncovered twenty or so bodies of the missing local Maquis men, but the man attached to the protruding hand had still been alive, was still alive, just. As unarmed prisoners they had been lined up and gunned down by the Wehrmacht, then buried, probably more than one of them still alive at that point. They did not know if that one man would live out the night.

Margot laid her head back down and gazed up at the ceiling rose. She would never have believed, before the war, that this much suffering was possible, she could not help but feel a pang of guilt as she found herself wondering if that recurring nightmare might just stop now.

Later that night she awoke again, no dreams, she felt better, her mind was filled with one thought. The Airman. No one can just disappear, she walked through the dark silent house up the stairs, the previous mornings search had obviously been thorough, wall panels had been torn off, pieces of furniture broken and shattered. Floorboards and stairs had been removed, not one of the walls had escaped having numerous holes punched into them.

She could hear a faint tap. She walked to the window but could not make out where the noise was coming from. As Margot looked out into the night she slowly realized that the dripping trails heading down the glass were not condensation as she had at first thought, but blood. It looked black now, at night, she reached out to touch it. It was outside. Quickly she opened the window, a blood soaked hand reached down, and the Airman stiffly clambered in through the window. He was pale, cold and soaked in blood from head to foot. Margot clasped a hand to her mouth as she looked at his face. A dagger, his dagger, looked as if it had been pushed through both cheeks, between his jaw, she realized he had been holding it in his teeth, probably all day and the double sided blade had gradually cut back into each side of his mouth. Somehow he had managed to clamber out onto the Mansard rooftops of the adjacent properties and push his way into the creeping ivy that covered some of the exterior walls, where he had hung on, all day and most of the night, unable to move or even remove the dagger from his mouth incase of dropping it or giving himself away.

Marguerite and Armelle her daughter who worked at the local hospital, did the best they could stitching the gaping cheeks, but for the next few days every time he ate or tried yet again to thank them in their own language, the blood began to seep from the sides of his grotesque lopsided grin.*

*(A story that it appears Nan only ever told me, or at least I was the only one still alive. When she recounted it to me it felt true, but I was just a small boy at the time! I have tried to verify it with other members of the family and some had heard about the buried Maquis men and the recurring hand nightmare and also about the ornate engraved silver handgun that she was given, but not the Airman with a dagger through his face.)

Chapter Three

May/June 1944. Littlehampton. England.

"Jesus Christ, what can I do?" Colonel Woolley was becoming red in the face. "We've expressed time and time again the need for absolute secrecy, this is just not acceptable! This Marine is now going to spend a considerable amount of time locked up, and all because of loose talk in the bloody pub! We can't afford to spend the time training you lot, only to go and lock you up for the rest of the bloody War!"

The crammed Dance Hall was silent, they were now all aware that their conversations in the pubs and tea rooms of Littlehampton, must be being monitored, probably by civilians, and if their own people could have heard loose talk, so could the enemy.

The briefing had been called unexpectedly, Guy, Dickie and a few other Marines had just returned from having their photos taken, firstly in units, and then in civilian clothes, with the idea that these photos could then be used for false documents should anyone fall into enemy hands and be trying to escape. It was about midday, they were drinking in The Marine pub, right opposite the civilian digs where they were billeted. It was crowded with American GI's from two US battalions that had moved into the area. A 'friendly' rivalry had built up between 30AU and the newly arrived US troops, as the officers of each tried to show what their men were capable of with various runs and even some abseiling down the side of some large factory buildings. After all their commando and special operations training the men of 30AU were putting the poorly prepared conscripted US GI's to shame. The word went around the pub at speed. 'There's been an arrest, Woolley's on the war path!'

Guy looked about the hall where they had quickly been assembled, it was very unusual for all of 30AU to be together, in fact, he could not remember it before. Everyone, Royal Marines and their Officers, Naval Officers, Royal

Air Force Officers, a couple of American Officers, and even all of the original 30AU members, names that had become renown amongst all the numerous newcomers, McGrath, Brereton, Wyman, Smith, Royale. There had always been one party or another away on some mission or course, but not today.

"The next time you pack your kit bags at your billets, could be the last, let's make sure the rest of our time here goes to plan." Colonel Woolley stomped off the hollow wooden stage as the packed hall slowly emptied to the sounds of shuffling boots and hushed mumbles. No one seemed able to work out who the culprit could have been.

A few days later the whole of 30AU was at attention, with packed canvas kit bags at their sides, on the grass square behind the Beach Hotel and next to Company Head Quarters, which was in 49 South Terrace, the last terraced house of the seafront parade.

A-troop were in the centre, X and B either side, with all the various Officers lined up in front of the Head Office stairs. The staff car drew up, out stepped Commander Fleming. Guy watched as Captain Huntington-Whiteley or 'Red' as all the men now referred to him, stood to attention in front of the three units, Red's uniform looked all over the place, gators too high, shirt un-tucked, webbing tangled, but no-one seemed to care, least of all Commander Fleming who walked straight from the car and greeted him with a warm smile.

"Whiteley, my boy, how the hell are you? Is your family all well? How's that bloody father of yours?"

"Yes Sir, thank you Sir." Red still tried to appear professional despite the fact that Colonel Woolley, standing with the other Officers, had been expecting to greet Commander Fleming and was now going as red in the face as he had been earlier during the dance hall shouting. He stormed over to them both and tried to take charge of the situation by asking Fleming to inspect the men.

Fleming took a cursory look over the unit while he wandered back and forth and then addressed them.

"My Warrior Braves… you've been selected… hand picked… and trained to the best possible standards… with the mix of experience and intense training you have in your ranks…you should be ready for anything…you are…ready… for anything. Believe me it's going to be a busy and intensive few weeks…starting today. If anyone here has any doubts as to their ability to perform the tasks asked of them, now is the time to voice those doubts. But I…do not doubt…a single one of you. I wish you all luck…I only wish…I could be going with you."

Guy felt strangely inspired by the small speech, his skin tingled, he liked the idea of being part of an initiated group of 'Braves'. Cowboys and Indians had been one of his favourite fantasy games as a child and it didn't really feel like all that long ago! Perhaps this was really it, after all the false starts of packing kit, only to be told to unpack it again at the end of the day, could this really be the day they were finally going to go to war.

As they headed off towards the already waiting long column of various vehicles, mainly trucks, armoured cars and Jeeps the drone of Patrick Job's bagpipes started up, mingling with the loud throb of ticking engines and Guy again found it an inspiring, skin tingling, moment.

Although the actual assault turned out still to be many days away as all leave was cancelled to avoid any more loose talk being overheard.

•   •   •

The weather was bad, the Channel seas were rough, the ship swayed incessantly back and forth. Guy felt alright but he watched as many of the men had started to suffer from sea sickness or nerves, he could not tell which. The US troops, sharing the space below decks, seemed to be suffering even worse. Guy had found the American GIs very friendly while they had been waiting to board in the 'mud pit' at Southampton, they all seemed genuinely interested in the British Green Beret teams that they had found in amongst their ranks. Although he had received a reprimand for 'fraternising' with the negro GI's. Guy was informed via his Sergeant from the Colonel himself, that the white US GI's had made a complaint about him in person.

In fact Guy had been enquiring about their 'warrior' ancestry and not really receiving a very warm response from the group of young negro's. He always believed, strongly, that the blacks should be rightfully proud of their tribal and cultural heritage and was continually surprised at the negative way his questions about this were always perceived throughout the whole of his life.

They had now all been stuck aboard ship for two days, for what should have been a three hour crossing at most. There had been a day's delay boarding at Southampton, as the original ship they had been assigned to had been sunk on its outgoing run. After they had eventually boarded this ship, it found itself with no place, or no permission, to land, for two very long days.

The 30AU had been divided into three main groups, Pikeforce (mainly X-troop), Curtforce (a few of A-troop), and Woolforce (by far the largest group and the remainder of all the units, including the field HQ and signals teams). These were so named after the Commanding Officer of each group. But only Guy's group of Woolforce had been delayed by circumstance and had therefore (thankfully) missed their allotted OMAHA beach D-day landings. Although a rumour had started at that time that it was because the US commanders did not want 'limey's' on 'their' beaches.

As they clambered down the cargo nets into the landing craft some of the men became trapped in the ropes, as the seas were still too rough, only with great effort were they released. When they eventually hit the beach one Signals Marine, who landed heavily with the weight of his wireless on his back, jolted and accidentally discharged his weapon, a Sten gun which he had chosen over the Thompson gun that most had, it blew a hole straight through his boot, unfortunately his foot was in it at the time.

As they tried to clear the eventual landing site of UTAH beach St. Marie du Mont, , they were all on foot with no transport, as yet. Guy had never seen anything like it, he looked back at the sea, it was packed with ships of all sizes, some of which were in the process of sinking or even sunk and only just showed masts above the surface, everywhere he looked was filled, the sky was full of planes and barrage balloons, the sea was packed with ships, the beach was virtually hidden beneath men and machines. The deep concussions of Naval bombardments could be heard echoing off the surrounding terrain so that it was not quite possible to tell the direction from which it was coming. The weather was still low and overcast, so most of the aircraft, although audible, were not visible.

Colonel Woolley decided to clear the beach without transport, which was still to be unloaded and would then find itself stuck in the huge columns of vehicles. He tried to make up for some lost time with a fierce speed march, past the bemused GI's, through the hot dusty lanes of the French countryside. Over the next few days the tall thick hedges lining the routes stopped the dust from clearing and so everything became covered in a thick lining of choking dust.

They eventually halted, about an hour before dusk, in a field just outside Sainte Mere Église. Guy began to dig a small dip in which to spend the night, the Marines about him looked on in bewilderment and some amusement. Guy had read and studied as much as was possible of all relevant information during his time training and he had learned that when spending the night outside, in enemy territory, 'digging in' was an essential. He ignored the fact that no one else seemed to be doing likewise. As he tried to relax in his prepared 'hole' he listened to Paddy on the field wireless nearby and learnt that Pikeforce had failed to take their objective of a Radar station at Douvres, the intelligence reports had been completely misled about enemy strength. Curtforce had already achieved their Radar station objectives at Aromanches and were now joining up with Pikeforce to patrol the strong hold at Douvres until a sufficient Commando force was ready to take it.

As Paddy signed off the wireless, the sound of a low flying, fast approaching, aircraft caught the attention of a few of the men, as sounding slightly more intense than the constant aircraft noise had previously been.

"TAKE COVER!" Guy wasn't sure who shouted, he could see standing men diving for cover around the field. Instinctively he pulled his legs up into a foetal position within his dusty scraping and ducked his head down, as a strange whooshing sound followed by a metallic fluttering noise, preceded many small explosions popping off all over the field. It only lasted a couple of minutes, if that. Then the explosions were replaced by the sounds of screaming men. Guy slowly raised his head and looked into a relatively large crater where his legs had been resting only moments before he had pulled them up into as small a ball as he could manage. The next hour became a blur, dead and wounded men appeared to be everywhere, some of them dying slowly, as the Marines with the most medical training tried to stem the flow of hot blood.

The final count was five dead, among them Holmes, Wright, Bentley and Naval Lieutenant Ionides, about twenty were wounded, some terribly, Captain Douglas, Sergeant Smith, Sergeant Ellington, Jones, Long and Tamplin were the only names Guy could recall as he later wrote his first letter home from active service. Guy could not help but reflect that all that intensive training had not helped those men, in any way, and something as simple and basic as 'digging-in' had been missed out. Although if he were honest he knew it would have made very little difference to the body count. Everyone remaining was badly shaken, so this was it, they really were finally in the war. From that moment onwards no one needed to be told to 'dig-in'.

The crater left by the explosion at his feet was considerably deeper than his hole had been and after the few hours of helping to transport the wounded Guy curled up in it and tried to grab a few hours sleep, he had the feeling he was going to need it.

The next morning dawned brightly; it was going to be a hot dusty day. Guy's B-troop now found themselves down to about ten men from the thirty-five or so of the previous day. Orders were quickly issued. Guy was assigned to Nutforce, their job was to make sure the Royal Air Force Intelligence Officer, Flight Lieutenant Nutting remained alive and intact while carrying out part of Operation Crossbow to study the reported 'Ski' sites.

Guy stood nearby and listened in on the two troop Sergeants being briefed. Fleming's intelligence reports for his 'Black List' had been informed of two new and terrifying Nazi weapons, as yet unused by the enemy, they came to be codenamed V1 and V2 and the launch sites they were heading to were in the Neuilly la Foret area and codenamed Crossbows. Some of the transport had now thankfully caught up with the unit during the night and the group gingerly perched themselves on top of the Humber Scout cars for the trip through American lines.

After a brief hold up to gain the US commanders permission to proceed, the three Humber Scout cars travelled the fifteen miles or so behind enemy lines completely unopposed, although the sounds of warfare were all around them. They slowed as they approached the first target. Leaving the vehicles and splitting into two 'recce' groups, Guy found himself with a Sergeant and eight Marines. The rest of the unit went with the other Sergeant Major. The maps prepared with the help of reconnaissance photographs revealed two launch sites, side by side but a few miles apart. Guy's group were to approach the furthest one. Using the thick hedges and ditches they moved slowly and stealthily towards what at first glance appeared to be a normal French farm. Crawling on their belly's for large sections of the approach, Guy as the last man in the group was under orders to signal rearwards to the non-existent men following, if any sniper were watching, it might just delay their trigger finger long enough for the actual patrol to have moved on. Guy finally settled himself away from the rest of his team. He was in a high-sided ditch, slightly raised from the surrounding fields, as he slowly manoeuvred his sniper rifle into position. He was close. Two grey military trucks were parked on a concrete platform. The sight of his first Wehrmacht soldier made Guy's heart race, he followed him with the crosshairs as the grey uniformed man moved around the trucks and then walked over to one side by some young saplings, planted in a straight line next to an angled metallic ramp. Following the line of the ramp, a camouflaged aircraft positioned at the lower end. It was nothing like any airplane Guy had seen before. Obviously unmanned, there was no cockpit. More men came into view, one, four, six, some dressed in the same grey uniform others in boiler suits. They appeared to be preparing the aircraft for flight, a fuel line was attached to the cylinder mounted above and at the rear of the fuselage, but no propeller was visible. Guy tried to see if the rest of his team were in position, but they were all out of sight. His mouth was dry, sweat was dripping into his eyes, his heart rate way too high, he was tense, nervous; he began to wonder if he was going to be able to shoot at these men who stood before him. They looked like normal guys, men just like him and his own team, too young.

Then the image of 'Duke', his troop sergeant, a man he liked and respected from the previous nights bombing, jaw hanging loosely, ripped open by bomb shrapnel, most of his teeth now imbedded elsewhere within his mouth, his trousers torn open, blood pouring from what was left of his testicles, he'd been alive and conscious, at least when the US medics had taken him away. *(He made a very good recovery and even went on to father children).*

He squeezed off the first round he had fired in anger, a head shot. It missed, he'd snatched the trigger. The Germans had obviously heard the sound of the bullet in the air. They froze, looking about. The muffled barrel of the sniper rifle was virtually silent, they had no idea anyone was so close. Then the Bren gun opened up from over to the right, followed by the distinctive thud of Thompson submachine guns. Two of the Wehrmacht men crumpled backwards to the ground, the others scattered, diving for cover. Guy scanned back and forth with the scope, but no target was visible. Then the sound of beating boots, there were more German troops running to take up positions from the far side of a farm building. Too many. Guy felled one. His first kill. He didn't have time to think about it. The rest dived for cover under the ricochet of bullets. But now return fire started thudding into the earth of the bank. It was time to go.

Guy glanced over towards where he thought his men were and they had already started to retreat, running, heads down, along the deep ditch, which they had used to approach. He looked back towards the ramp just in time to see two stick-grenades bouncing across the concrete underneath the aircraft. Some Germans obviously realised they were far too close to them and broke cover, sprinting away and out of sight. Guy had swapped guns, unslung his Thompson and re-slung his rifle, he squeezed off a burst of bullets, unsure if they had hit targets or not. The explosion was massive, an orange and black fireball rose rapidly into the blue sky in the shape of a huge mushroom. But Guy didn't really see very much of it, he was running the other way, trying to catch up with the rest of his team which had already disappeared into the hedgerows.

Thankfully Flight Lieutenant Nutting, who had been with the first team, had had more success. They managed to record a lot of information about the other launch site, including photographs and detailed measurements, all of which were whisked back to NID30 by Hurricane Fighter plane later that evening. This was quickly added to over the next few days in the form of a lot of heavy duty equipment and hardware, some of which was entirely unrecognisable to the men moving it and took a considerable amount of logistics to get it shipped back to Blighty.

The next few days were a mass of activity and over the next few weeks many V1 and even a few V2 sites in early stages of preparation were visited, virtually all of them behind enemy lines and with varying degrees of success. Some new types of torpedo 'pistols' were found on some downed German aircraft. Guy was stunned by the A4/V2 rocket sites, some of them were so big as to defy scale. One concrete structure had been partially destroyed by a 'Tallboy' (Earthquake Bomb) bombing raid but still contained intelligence information of value, mainly about the fuel. Operational procedures were quickly adapted and improved as they gained experience.

Guy began to settle into his new role, that of a trained cold bloodied killer.

But however many times he had to do it, to kill a man or a woman was never easy and there was no easy way to do it.*

(It is never explained why Ron would have been required by his country and 'the-powers-that-be' to kill women. The only explanation I can find was at the National Archives in the 30AU documentation and it was an order to 'Eliminate any witnesses to the Intelligence gathered'. (see Photographs, Documents & Maps))

Beau Bête

Chapter Four

I had found that in amongst the treasured love letters between Ron and Margot there were also other letters, related to the war. Some from Allied airmen or their eternally grateful families, who tried, in many different ways to express just how thankful they were to the people, so far away in foreign lands, that had risked their own lives and those of everyone they knew, to send the members of their families back home, alive...

Dear Marguerite Wilthew,

How can we ever express our gratitude? We will never be able to truly appreciate what you and your kin actually risked to save the lives of our loved ones. To get them home from foreign lands...

6th September 1943. East of Paris, France.

The B17 Flying Fortress 'Lone Wolf' bucked and twisted wildly, the pilot 1st Lt. Alfred Kramer and copilot 2nd Lt. Arthur Swap and crew were on their ninth mission, but this one was proving to be something very different, they wrestled frantically with the smoking controls, two of the planes four engines had stopped and they had started to lose altitude, it was already down to 21,000ft and more importantly they were quickly losing touch with what was left of their Bomber Squadron on their run back to Knettishall (H), near Bury St Edmunds, Norfolk, England.

They had left in the early hours of the morning, three o'clock to be precise but the usual English weather was causing constant problems with the formations and timing of the planned runs over Europe. Bad weather had delayed the formation of the 338 B17's over England. Then the bombing raid on the industrial area of Stuttgart, Germany, had not gone as well as could be wished. The target, a bearings factory and an aircraft components works believed to be essential to the Nazi war machine.

It had been impossible to spot on the cloud covered day and the lead squadron had been forced to circle for over 30 minutes while trying to get a fix on their positions. Over 100 planes didn't get to drop their bombs and the rest just tried to pick out targets of opportunity after turning back for home.

Alfie and Art had begun to worry if they would have enough fuel for the home run and they were not the only ones to have realized the problem. Red fuel warning lights had started to illuminate many cockpits as they headed back towards Paris. Four planes eventually ditched into the channel after running out. The formation had begun to fragment and separate under heavy attack from flak-guns defending the target area and a relentless onslaught from hundreds of enemy fighters, some of which had even been recalled from the Russian front to counter this offensive.

(Although they did not know it at that time, the Germans were throwing everything they had at this bombing raid. Because of the previous attacks on these essential facilities the Germans had guessed what the Allies were aiming to achieve and as a consequence they had run into very fierce defences, they were to lose the entire 563rd Squadron, eleven planes who were running as the 'low' group and four planes from the 'high' group. The total losses for the day were sixty planes and over six hundred men, in one day! It was to have a profound effect on the entire war, the whole of the bombing campaign had to be rethought and re-structured because of the lessons learned from these two weeks in 1943. But it became better able to do the job required of it thereafter).

The crew of 30222 'Lone Wolf' had watched helplessly as four of their formation had spiralled downwards hopelessly out of control. All silently prayed while they looked on for signs of parachutes and bailing men, but the constant barrage and buffeting of the air around the plane and the need to remain vigilant for enemy fighters made it virtually impossible to see the entire descent of any lost aircraft.

After the aborted bombing run, as they turned and headed for home, they had been intercepted by the yellow nosed Hun, like a swarm of hornets the enemy in Messerschmitt 109 and Focke-Wulfe 190 fighter planes had swooped in from above and seemed to know every blind spot and weakness of the huge wallowing American bombers *(who were extremely vulnerable at this stage of their development to frontal attacks)* and with no fighter escort of their own the Nazi's were taking full advantage.

Alfie and Art could feel through their hands on the control columns the added vibrations of the thirteen browning machine guns thudding away throughout the aircraft and hear the hundreds of spent cartridges bouncing around in the fuselage from T/Sgt Eugene Martin the top turret gunner just behind their heads, as the men of the crew desperately fought for their lives.

An FW190 flown by Horst Sternberg, held a sustained burst of cannon fire in a full on frontal attack, the nose of the B17 had started to disintegrate as the bullets ripped through the aluminium and perspex and fire had begun to spread rapidly from the sparking control panels. But amazingly the Bombardier 2nd Lt. Rob Burnett and Navigator 2nd Lt. Richard Bowman had escaped major injury although both were wounded and blood spattered.

S/Sgt. William Vickless, Bill, the right waist gunner found himself for the first time considering when was going to be the right moment to give up the fight and flee, he now knew it was a losing battle. Enemy rounds were thudding into the wings and fuselage; the sounds of screaming wounded men filled the intercom system where just a few minutes before all had been the calm and controlled reporting of enemy fighter movements as they made their attacks.

Art made one last attempt to get the Captains message across above the now constant bell signal and the overly busy intercom system.

"BAIL, BAIL, BAIL. ALL OUT NOW!" He shouted, although within himself he felt more calm and controlled than he had expected to be under the circumstances.

Bill could only just make out the bell above the noise of his gun and the increasing speed of the air flow across the fuselage opening he was firing through, he knew that it was time to go, now, maybe it was too late already. Joe Thomas, the ball turret gunner had scrabbled free of his harnesses and into the fuselage, he was wounded, his eyes stared about wildly, panic. Bill and S/Sgt. Walter Soukup, the other waist gunner screamed at him to bail, but he seemed unable to hear them, frozen. The tail gunner S/Sgt Will Chapman had already bailed, he could see the overwhelming odds they now faced.

The bomber yawed across the sky, twisting sideways through the air, flames from the engines and fuel tanks erupted into the fuselage as scrabbling crewmen tried desperately to reach the exits. Some were too badly wounded to be able to move very quickly, but they all eventually managed to bail.

Arthur Swap had sworn to himself he would be the last man to exit, he would do all he could to keep the plane in check so that the crew could escape. He now realized that any semblance of control was long gone, flames twisted and spiralled down the length of the fuselage towards the cockpit as the plane was now moving backwards and downwards through the air. The fire and smoke billowing from the cockpit as more gaping holes tore themselves into being through the thin aluminium fuselage as Art grabbed at Eugene as he tried to get free of his gun turret straps. They were both thrown heavily into the top of the cockpit cabin, hitting the roof hard as the cockpit fire increased. One second they were engulfed in flames in a tight, dark, confined space, the next they were in a clear blue sky, falling earthwards at an ear splitting speed, which was strangely calming after the turmoil on the inside of the aircraft.

The rushing air extinguished the flames that had begun to shrivel all hair that it had managed to get a hold of. Neither man could remember being aware enough to pull any rip chord.

Art and Bill came round and found themselves on the ground under the silk of their parachutes fairly close to each other. Bill tried desperately to remember some of the lectures the airmen had attended on what to do if shot down, but his mind was entirely filled with pain, a searing pain from every part of his body, he could only remember that even his scalp hurt, it hurt unbelievably, still felt as though it was on fire, before he knelt up and tried to get a grip on his situation.

Art knew they were approximately 120km southeast of Paris, 18km northeast of Troyes, deep in German occupied territory. He crawled free of his parachute and laid on his back, trying to concentrate only on his breathing which felt too shallow, pain and coughing fits followed any breath he tried to take beyond a certain point. He stared skywards, watching the contrails left in the wake of his fellow countrymen, some four miles above him. He could still see the lower swarm of hornets, enemy aircraft still trying to knock others of his countrymen and the rest of his squadron from the sky, he decided just to lay and wait.

He could feel the heat of the mid-morning sun, which had decided to make an appearance too late for them, against his reddened face and it didn't allow him to get much rest before the sounds of chattering birds were accompanied by voices. His brain would not focus enough to let him know the language; he could not understand any words.

"Vite, cherchez le chariot, nous devons le déplacer, aussi rapidement que possible.." The sun was momentarily blocked from view as Arthur tried to focus on the face above him, but he could only see a silhouette.

"Monsieur, pouvez-vous marcher ? Vous avez- les os cassés ? Nous devons vous déplacer, rapidement, je suis désolés. ARE YOU ALRIGHT?"

The next few days for the two men were a blur of pain, heat and thirst. At times they felt as if they had come round in their own coffins as various means of concealment were used to transport them about.

They were initially taken to a tiny village just east of Troyes and hidden with a local farming family who informed them that Joe Thomas had been killed, they had his 'Dogtags' and he had been laid to rest at a local cemetery, his grave adorned with fresh flowers. A lone Me109 obviously with too much fuel and ammunition had made repeated passes at the descending men on parachutes and had used more than one as target practice, Joe's chest and head had been torn apart by the large rounds the aircraft used. The Frenchmen were unable to account for all of the men, certainly some had been captured.

Both Arthur and Bill knew from the lectures they had attended before starting their European bombing sorties, that these people were risking torture and slow death to save their lives. It was not unheard of for the Nazi's to kill entire families or even whole villages if they were found to harbouring Allied airmen.

Both men were only ever concerned for the people helping them, desperately concerned for them, virtually none of the men, women and even children who tried to help, would talk to them. Partly due to the fact that neither spoke one another's language, but mostly because they all knew that the less everyone knew, the less the Germans could gain from them under torture and questioning.

Bill and Arthur knew this to be an essential part of any escape but it certainly did not help their feelings of being lost in total isolation and helplessness. The only thing they could do to help was just to be quiet and try to understand and then do as they were told.

That was until they found themselves in a large wine cellar in Vannes, Morbihan, some days later.

"My name is Marguerite Wilthew, these are my daughters, Armelle and Marguerite." Both men turned and looked at each other, to be spoken to directly and in their own language was so unexpected they were temporarily taken aback.

"Pleased to meet you Ma'am. Copilot Arthur Swap and gunner Sergeant Bill Vickless, at your service. We are so grateful..." She cut him off mid sentence.

"Please, hold your thanks, we have the most difficult part ahead of us yet, you will be held up here for a few days, maybe even weeks, we have about twenty fliers in and around the local area and we are planning on getting you all out together in one go, from one of the small fishing harbours. Please make yourself as comfortable as you are able and do help yourself to any of the wine from that rack there, although I would strongly advise against any drunkenness." She pointed to one of the many large wooden wine racks.

"Please Ma'am, we'll do all we can to make our stay as trouble free for you as we possibly can." Arthur could barely wait to get his hands on a corkscrew.

"If you would like to clean up and redress your wounds and then I invite you to eat with us. Marguerite, our Art teacher, will show you to the bathrooms upstairs and Armelle, who nurses at the local hospital, will help you with your wound dressings, we will dine at three." She turned and left.

A few weeks later, early November, the two American airmen's wounds were completely healed, thankfully the facial burns had been superficial and any remaining scars were minimal. The plans were finalized, the Maquis of Bretagne preferred to move the airmen under the very noses of the Nazi's, in broad daylight and during the busiest times.

The fish market of the large port was a perfect opportunity to load the various airmen into a Lobster catching vessel, which would be leaving port on the evening tide, long after the teeming market had finished.

Arthur and Bill had left themselves unshaven for the last few days, both wore ancient fishermen's clothes, none of which had been washed for some considerable time and all of which stank heavily of fish. Belying the way they felt inside they tried to look as relaxed and confident as possible while carrying their large traditional bags and crates down into the fish market, a few minutes walk, just as the local fishermen had done for centuries before them, down these very cobbled streets and towards the waiting boats.

Margot had insisted on being the one to lead them to the right people, to make sure they made it to the right boat. She and Arthur had developed a close friendship in a short space of time. She walked a short way ahead apparently just another local on her way to the market, wicker basket under her arm. They could just see glimpses of the harbour through the medieval Saint Vincent Ferrier arch at the bottom of the hill on the other side of the market, it was full of stalls trying to display what little they could provide. They marched through, down the sloping cobbled market square, as they neared the arch Margot's confident gait paused for a split second.

The harbour street was full of grey military trucks. Wehrmacht troops, in their great grey coats milled about aimlessly, smoking and chatting to themselves. The Wehrmacht regularly helped themselves to any and all the local produce they cared to take, with a lot of it going directly back to their 'Fatherland' and today they had decided to help themselves at the market.

She had no choice, there was no turning back now, she headed straight at the harbour, through the ancient arch, right at the troops, who all turned to look at the pretty local French girl.

"Hübsche junge Dame, würden Sie sich für eine Zigarette interessieren? Jolie jeune dame, entretiendriez-vous une cigarette?" One Wehrmacht Gefreiter made forwards and held out a packet of cigarettes.

Under normal conditions she would have ignored the advance, but it was unusual for one of the young Germans to speak such fluent French. She paused, leaned forward and took one. As she did so, she glanced back. The two 'French' fishermen behind her were doing exactly as they had been so carefully instructed to do. Not stopping. Arthur even managed a small disapproving glare at the young Nazi troopers as he passed. To Margot's mind it was exactly the look anyone of the real fishermen would have given in similar circumstance. As the German troopers all tried to be the one to light her cigarette the two airmen stomped around the group inadvertently getting in the way of the soldiers who were loading crates onto the trucks and then they disappeared between the trucks heading for the boats. Margot excused herself from the Germans and quickly moved on so that she could give the tiny discreet signal that would indicate the right boat to board.

Both men so longed to say a proper farewell to try and express their gratitude, but both knew it was impossible. They clambered aboard and ducked their heads below decks.

The rest of the escaping men, all dressed as local fishermen, were moved in a carefully choreographed sequence, with perfect timing, from one group of people to the next, so that over the coarse of the entire market day, nineteen men from seven different countries were transferred from their places of hiding in the surrounding countryside and towns into the hold of the Lobster Boat which left for its destination of Lands End, England on the next high tide.*

*(There were other aviators that Family Wilthew helped escape, but only Arthur Swap became very close to Margot. He was later promoted to Colonel and kept a regular correspondence with her from his home in America for the rest of his life, repeatedly offering for her and her family to come and visit, but they never met again).

Chapter Five

23rd June 1944. Normandy, France.

The roads and lanes on the approach to Cherbourg were littered with the bodies of Americans and Germans. The men of 30AU considered the US paratroopers, in contrast to their infantry, excellent well trained soldiers, but most found that they had missed their drop zones and by necessity had been forced to group together and just do the best they could under the circumstances in which they found themselves. Wrecked gliders and dead paratroopers were all too common sights, there were also many groups of German vehicles that had been caught by Allied aircraft and virtually obliterated. Badly burned, mangled and dismembered bodies could lie for anything up to two weeks. The 30AU and most British forces always, when possible, bury their dead immediately, taking careful map references so that they may be retrieved and re-buried, with honour, at a later time. Guy had learned that the US forces had no such orders and left the bodies for whoever was to come along and deal with them after they had moved on. Normally enforced POW's (prisoners of war) groups. It was Guy's first experience of something that he would never be able to completely escape again, the sickly sweet opium of death. A smell that once experienced is never forgotten.

The incessant, thick dust proved to be a real problem for the Allied advance to Cherbourg. Not only did it penetrate everything and seize delicate, life preserving, mechanisms, it also provided the German artillery with very accurate targets. Guy became very frustrated at the cleaning of all five of his weapons, three or even four times a day, on top of cleaning the various troop machineguns, vehicles and all sort of other delicate equipment, to make sure that they were all going to work when called upon. He was stunned that one Marine took a shot clean through the heart as another began to clean his own rifle, it seemed even men trained as intensively as they had been were still vulnerable to the fatigue and mental anguish which always accompanies soldiers under the pressures of war.

All three troops of 30AU had come together at Quettetot, from the various targets and missions that had been their first priorities, they then moved closely behind the US 47th Division front lines, to just north east of Teurtheville-Hague. The main 30AU target, from Fleming's 'Black List', was at Octeville-sur-Mer a Naval Head Quarters in Villa Meurice and the tunnels below it. It stood on a hill overlooking the harbour.

But the Nazi's were putting up quite a fight. The US infantry had been pushed back, repeatedly. To Guy's mind some of the American commanders seemed much too cavalier with the lives of their men, but despite being woefully under trained the GI's were none the less magnificently brave. Those same commanders were refusing to let 30AU ahead of their front lines.

When Colonel Woolley had finally procured permission and was moving 30AU forward to the frontlines, the sounds of huge explosions could be heard reverberating around the low hills. It was the enemy's systematic demolition of the harbour, submarines, ships and equipment. It was unlikely there was going to be any intelligence information remaining by the time the Nazi's had finally capitulated.

The men of 30AU had grown used to taking cover at the sound of all approaching aircraft, the United States Air Force planes seemed to open fire on any and all movement on the ground whether it was Allied or axis troops. Every unit had gone to great pains to paint huge US symbols on all space available. Guy had started to find himself wondering if their first night casualties might just have been by some of these over zealous Allied pilots.

Guy was resting with Powell and a few other Marines when two Messerschmitt 109's broke through the clouds, low, strafing all before them. Guy and Powell watched from cover as the large cannon rounds they used tore apart the canvas of some US field hospital tents, all of which were clearly marked with large red crosses. Jumping to their feet in unison with the outraged men around them, they opened fire at the attackers, which were close enough to be able to see the pilot's faces. Even above the scream of fighter plane engines they could hear the metallic thud of their rounds hitting the body and wings of the aircraft, unfortunately without any obvious effect.

As the noise subsided Guy looked ahead towards Colonel Woolley, who along with the other Marines about him, were just regaining their feet only to be thrown sideways through the air as the Sherman tank they were next to exploded in flames. Two more tanks quickly followed the first. The German artillery was using the rising dust to home in on targets with some accuracy. These tanks had already earned a reputation for trapping their occupants as they regularly erupted into flames. Hence they became known as 'Tommy Cookers'. Only one man escaped this first one, he was on fire as he leapt from the turret and quickly smothered to douse the flames.

"Reeves, look after this, guard it with you're life!" Blood poured down Woolley's face as he staggered to the right, away from the flames while trying to stand. He handed Marine Reeves the intelligence map of Cherbourg, which was quickly stuffed within his battledress (He looked after it for the next fifty years! Until he presented it back to the people of Cherbourg on the fiftieth anniversary). Colonel Woolley and a Marine orderly, the two worst wounded, were easily moved over into the hastily patched up tents of the field hospital.

Their progress forward halted for the time being as Major Evans took control of 30AU. The men spent the time brewing up and made themselves as comfortable as possible.

As dusk began to fall, the crack of a single gunshot rang out above the constant background noise of distant gunfire and explosions. It was followed by a thud, as if a sack of potatoes had hit the dusty earth. From where he was resting Guy rolled to his right from his back onto his front. He looked right and realised he could not remember the Marines name. The man from A troop a few feet away, lay face down in the dust. The bullet hole through the temple seeped a black gel like substance.

An enemy sniper.

Guy crawled quickly forward aware that he was raising dust, he tried to concentrate on his periphery vision as he went, to enable him to pick up the muzzle flash of the next shot. The sound split the air, this time it was followed by a throaty, muffled yelp and another thud. He didn't see the flash, but he thought he had heard the direction. Moving his position to try and get a better look, he discarded the Tommy gun and heavy webbing, folding out the stock of the rifle he brought the scope up to his eye. It was full of dust. He tried to blow it out and then he scanned through the blurred cross hairs towards the farm buildings that were quite some distance away, he could see the obvious vantage point for any sniper. It was the spot he would have chosen, a stone built tower on the side of a small farmhouse. He thought he could just see the outline of his target, set back inside the rough opening of the damaged tower. But the range was too great for his silenced and therefore restricted weapon. Springing to his feet and running, crouched, towards the ditch and hedge that would give him the best cover with which to approach the buildings, another shot rang out. Guy realised that he was involuntarily holding his breath, expecting the impact of a bullet into his body; it didn't come. He hit the bottom of the dry ditch too hard. Slightly winded he coughed out the dust and moved as quickly as possible along the ditch behind the hedge. It was perfect cover from the sniper fire and he easily made a hundred yards or more, the last few yards he crawled slowly out of the ditch, through the hedge. He had a perfect shot. Again he had to blow dust from the scope. Lining the cross hairs, even in the dimming light the outline of a grey helmet, the German sniper didn't appear to have moved. Guy now had an angled shot at his head. He settled himself, tried to ease his breathing and heart rate, he had just started to gently squeeze the trigger when he was suddenly gripped by an unexplained fear. His target had not moved, a muscle. It was a decoy, a corpse. It had started to rain heavy drops making tiny puffs of dust as they landed. He didn't know how or why, but he was filled with an uncontrollable, irresistible, urge to move, he had to move and now. Rolling fast and hard to the left, a shot blasted out and thudded into the ground where he had been. This time, despite the dust trying to fill his eyes, he saw the flash and it was close, in a tree (a position he would never use himself). Guy levelled the rifle took hasty aim at what he believed to be the shape of the target. As the sniper came into focus in the rapidly fading light he yanked at the trigger. At the same moment his scope was filled with a blinding flash. He felt his left arm yanked backwards at the sound of tearing cloth but thankfully no pain. Reloaded, he took second aim, again the scope was filled with muzzle flash, he heard the bullet splitting the air next to his right ear, this time he forced himself to squeeze the trigger slowly, the silenced round left the barrel with barely a puff. Reloaded again in a split second he looked back at the tree in time to see the slowly slipping body drop away. Although he knew he shouldn't and his mind tried hard to stop himself, he could not help but look down at his arm and shoulder where he expected to see torn flesh, but it was only torn cloth. Checking the body through the riflescope he could see no movement whatsoever, but he put another silenced round into it anyway and then stealthily and slowly moved back the way he had come.

No one got much rest that night, at first light the push forward started again, this time 30AU were right at the front of their section of the assault, being supported by self propelled anti-tank guns and a company of US infantry. Marine McGregor was badly wounded by a sniper almost immediately, this time intensive fire poured into the obvious sniper positions while Corporal Connolly sprinted across the field and carried McGregor back on his shoulder, although he was still under fire from multiple snipers. Another Marine, Paddy O'Callagan caught one of the sniper bullets through the thigh tearing open an artery. Guy tried to tourniquet the leg while being covered in hot sticky blood. Medic Squinty Johnson tried came to his aid and was felled with a bullet through the knee. Guy watched Paddy bleed to death in a matter of minutes.

As they again started forward behind the American artillery fire, Sergeant Lofty Whyman took Powell, Brown and Guy over to the right towards a small knoll, to cover the troops flank, as they crested a large hollow in the ground it was filled with people, innocent civilians, about fifty men women and children lined up in front of them at least twenty Wehrmacht troops about to open fire. Lofty and Guy dropped to cover, Powell and Brown had already set the Bren gun that they both operated and opened fire before Guy even had time to bring his gun to the target. The Bren rattled off, people scattering in all directions. Thankfully none of the civilians became mixed with the enemy. The Bren felled at least five; the rest quickly disappeared into the distance.

It took some time to calm the civilians and move them back away from the frontline, which was erupting into a major war zone.

The fighting was intense, street-to-street, and house-to-house, pillboxes were a real problem and had to be dealt with individually. Usually with the attachment of a shaped directional charge, nick named a 'Beehive', which could blow a hole clean through the pill box, both sides, leaving it empty.

The US artillery was very effective and accurate and towards the end of the day the advance quickly made the distance to the outskirts of the massive German Fortress. The self-propelled anti-tank guns opened up on the tunnel entrances. Guy doubted that anyone inside would ever be able to hear again. When the debris and dust had settled Guy and about five other Marines were ordered into the tunnels. As they moved into position what Guy initially took to be smoke came drifting out of the entrance. The Marines held position, unsure as to what to expect. He watched the man closest to the entrance, some fifty or sixty feet further forward than he was, who abruptly stood up and wobbled out into the open and then collapsed onto his side.

"GAS, GAS!"

Guy was unsure who had shouted, but as rapidly as possible moved back the way he had come. Again the large guns opened up on the entrances. This time a sustained barrage directly in line with the tunnels which lasted several minutes. Some of the shells were now travelling a considerable way down inside the tunnels before impact.

Major Evans had also called in artillery fire on the rear entrances of what turned out to be more of an underground fortress than just a series of tunnels and this finally stopped all resistance.

The first group who moved slowly in a dazed shuffle out from the tunnels under white sheet flags seemed unable to grasp any instructions Guy could shout at them, he began to suspect they were deaf, but it turned out they were in fact Georgians who only spoke their native Russian. It seemed the Germans were reluctant to leave as Polish, Roumanians and other Baltic natives left the fortress before the Germans. Eventually Admiral Karl von Schlieben and Kontra-Admiral Hennecke appeared and 30AU Royal Marine Captain Hargreaves-Heap took the formal surrender of about twenty Nazi Officers and some five hundred or more German troops.

The body of the Marine who had succumbed to the gas had been placed on a flat wooden cart that stood near the entrances, all assumed he was dead. It was Powell who noticed something that everyone else had missed that he was still alive, just. They later learned that the efforts to save him had been in vain as he had died a few days later.

The fortress and surrounding town turned out to be heavily booby-trapped and some enemy snipers continued to be a real problem. The Germans had even booby-trapped the bodies of their own men as well as Allied, which if moved would kill anyone within ten feet. It took days. The only bright point for most of the 30AU Marines was the discovery of the Admirals wine cellar.

As suspected virtually all information of any value had been destroyed. The harbour was huge, Guy and a small unit of Marines accompanied Lieutenant Commander Hugill down into the area and was stunned at the expanse of the submarine pens, the fifteen feet thick re-enforced concrete had literally been moved from its foundations by the force of the Germans demolition charges. Fortunately Commander Postlethwaite and Hugill did find examples of some new mine types and an acoustic harbour defence system as well as sixteen torpedoes of various types, but it was not enough to placate Commander Fleming. After Cherbourg 30AU moved into the seaside town of Carteret to rest and refit.

A few days had passed and replacement Marines had started to try and train in the skills with which to stay alive. Royal Marine Captain Curtis awarded F-S fighting knives to resistance fighters who had helped rescue some British Airmen from the sea, this for some reason really upset the Commanders of the US forces who made repeated requests that 30AU should be moved from their sector of operations. Captain Ward relieved Lofty and took command of B-troop after Captain Douglas's wounds from the first night attack had left the Sergeant in temporary control.

Guy was on guard duty outside the large Chateau, which the officers were using as their Head Quarters and he watched as Commander Fleming arrived with his entourage in full naval dress uniform, which stood out starkly against the dirty khaki that the majority were wearing. With a face like thunder he stormed down the gravel path and through the front door, Guy thought for a split second about stopping him for security reasons, but hastily reconsidered under his withering gaze. The many Naval Officers had started to treat the

Chateau as if it were a ship, and were using the balcony above the main entrance as the bridge cum poopdeck and officer's mess area. Their conversations were still clearly audible to anyone who cared to listen and Guy was directly below the balcony at the chateau main entrance and had been quietly listening to their idle banter for the last hour or so.

"This is just not acceptable!" Fleming found the patched up and re-instated Royal Marine Colonel Woolley in mid mouthful. "We've lost a whole bloody troop! And we only had three! What in the hell is going on? It took months to prepare those men, irreplaceable!"

Colonel Woolley had stood up and was going the familiar shade of red as he tried to swallow his food to enable him to retort.

"It's a Bloody War! What do you expect? " He finally managed to get it out. "And irreplaceable! That's a joke, some of them can barely remember their guns! We've had them shooting each other, blowing themselves up in clearly marked mine fields or even with their own bloody explosives!" Woolley's booming voice echoed around the surrounding countryside.

"I EXPECT, I expect us to use our training to avoid that war, at this rate we're not going to learn anything of value because the whole bloody lot of you will be dead!" Fleming tried to calm his voice take a less confrontational approach.

"Look when you've studied the reports it will become clearer." Woolley's calmed his voice in response.

"I've read the bloody reports and it's already perfectly clear. We are NOT a frontline force and you of all people should know that! If the target is too well defended. MISS IT OUT! God knows there is enough of them to be choosey." Fleming grabbed a seat.

Colonel Woolley re-took his seat, he knew instantly he was listening to the obvious. He'd got carried away, hadn't thought it through properly. He was in the wrong.

"You're right, my apologies." He was certainly big enough to admit his mistakes.

"Quite obviously 30AU is now too big to operate as one unit, we have to be selective, not get bogged down in fighting, our mission is far too important.

We have to get this right or we'll never get deployed in Germany. Everyone is looking at us and that deployment is entirely dependant on our successes here! I thought that those small raiding parties down in the Med was not how it would work here, but maybe it is, small raiding parties, a few men in and out quick, without stirring up the hornet's nest. Just as Glanville said before D-Day, old 'Sancho' got it just right down in the Med and he was right all along, I was wrong, he knew it worked from 30 Commando's operations, we've learned the same bloody lessons twice!" Fleming's voice got quieter and quieter. Guy strained listening intently for some considerable time, as Commander Fleming informed the officers of the latest intelligence reports on V1's or what the English press were now calling 'Doodle-bugs' or 'Buzz-bombs' that had started to rain on London. He found himself thinking about his family and if Foxlands Cescent would still be standing when he returned. He stayed well past his allotted Guard duty time listening the all the intricate problems the 30AU officers were having linking up with all the different intelligence sections and elements of 'T' Force and various US complaints about them and how Commander Fleming was proposing to smooth these troublesome obstacles with help of USN Lambie as an American liaison officer, but eventually he had heard enough and he wandered off back to the new replacements, wondering if his salvation may ironically turn out to be his intensive training for 'Hazardous Service'. He also made a mental note not to forget his guns or do anything stupid, he didn't want to end up like one of these stinking bloated, yellowish, green corpses that were lying around everywhere.

•   •   •

The next place of liberation was Granville and the harbour. Guy now found himself in the position of actually being requested by the many and various Naval officers of the unit. He had begun to earn himself the reputation of being 'handy in a scrape' as well as a trained and proficient sniper and as such found himself rushing about from pillar to post in all sections sometimes in A-troop although mostly in B-troop units and every section that requested his presence and that had any important targets to pursue. X-troop tended to find themselves held back slightly in case a parachute infiltration was required but once the Allies had really taken control they found themselves right at the front of the push into Paris.

A section of A-troop also had a serious set back when one of the new replacement Marines managed to accidentally set light to the Mess tent which quickly spread to other areas and destroyed a lot of valuable and essential operational materials.

Commander Job was far too self motivated and restless to spend much of his time waiting at Carteret, while the three units re-organised and received their 'dressing downs' from the Royal Marine Officers and Commander Fleming.

Job was constantly heading out accompanied by two Jeeps, which he deftly directed with the use of a fencing sword he had liberated from somewhere, always followed as closely as possible by an armoured escort vehicle which was used to lay down heavier covering fire should the quicker Jeeps need to back track quickly. They visited many and various targets that may or may not have been on Fleming's 'Black List' but which probably Commander Job had discovered with the help of his very proficient interrogator and interpreter, a young Royal Marine Captain Wheeler of the FIU (Forward Interrogation Unit).

They frequently found themselves in some surprising situations and visited a very long list of Radar stations in various stages of disrepair. Guy marvelled at Commander Job's bravery or recklessness, he still could not quite decide which it was.

On one such occasion Job decided he was going to use his diving equipment and recently accomplished training to try and retrieve documents out of the safe box on a partially sunken German ship near the city of Caen at Blainville on the canal.

The Marine sniper tried to survey the surrounding harbour through the scope on his Enfield Rifle from his position of cover as Job and Wheeler paddled out towards the partially submerged ship. After they reached the ship shells began to erupt in the water around them but the sniper was unable to locate a target with which to return some accurate fire, he fired off a few rounds at possible positions to try and encourage anyone that may be there to stop whatever it was they were doing and keep their heads down, but the shelling continued unabated. Observing through the rifle scope, Job was apparently unconcerned about the situation and proceeded with his self imposed mission despite the explosions on and around the ship and after some considerable time, many hours, they loaded much of the documents they had recovered onto one of the ships own small rafts and paddled back to dockside with the large haul between them. Both seemingly almost oblivious to the shells that continued to fall randomly about the place.

Chapter Six

The love letters were so much easier to read than I had imagined they were going to be, the French was beautifully written. The innocence between the two would be lovers that were separated by the entire globe at the time of writing was something that modern day people have lost, probably forever. I found myself transported back in time, swallowed up in the detail, the fear and the excitement of that eventful period in history...

July/August 1944. Near Rennes, France.

Guy watched as Commander Job stomped across the cabbage field towards the signalling Frenchmen. He wondered if the meeting had been pre-arranged, it seemed that all their movements lately were being entirely dictated by information supplied by these 'casual' meetings. The 30AU team had been informed by the local FFI that the German Garrison that had been occupying Vannes had moved out and fled to St. Malo, which thus far had been by-passed by the liberation, although most of the German units had received orders to fall back to Brest. The Germans at Vannes had used the opportunity that had appeared when General Patton had split his armoured column in two, one part headed towards Paris the other at Brest and as they were not leaving any holding forces behind them the area was filled with moving soldiers of both sides who frequently ran into each other. As Job returned from his meeting he informed the team that he was cancelling the planned operation on St.Malo because new information had just come to light and they were going to move back in the direction they had come from and make camp until the expected dispatches had arrived. Lt. Besant and a small force continued on to take up vigil on some St. Malo targets should they become accessible.

The rest of B-troop eventually settled themselves into an orchard on the outskirts of Vannes and Captain Lessing accompanied by Guy and Marine

Perry and Gates were hedge hopping the surrounding fields to make sure there were going to be no unexpected surprises. As they hopped over a large hedge and onto a small lane an American Jeep slid to a halt in front of them. In it sat a portly looking, many starred US General who called them over.

"What the Hell are you Limey's doing in my sector?" He seemed very unimpressed by their presence and 30AU were the only British unit operating throughout the huge US sector.

Captain Lessing went to produce his 'Special Authorisation' pass signed by Eisenhower himself but the General didn't seem interested in even glancing at it.

"I should have bloody guessed, 30AU, you God damned bunch of Limey Pirates and Gangsters making a nuisance of yourselves all over the place and in my Bloody Sector!" He was still shouting and cursing even as he indicated to his driver to get back on his way.

The four Marines smiled at each other in some amusement and continued on their way.

In the morning Sergeant 'Lofty' Whyman returned on his motorbike with the awaited dispatches. He informed the lads that as he had been expecting their team to have gone right towards St. Malo at the main crossroads, which had been churned up by Patton's tanks as they had split into two sections, he had done the same and soon after had run into a fallen tree across the road. As he'd tried to pull it out of the way a Spandau had opened up on him, an ambush, he had somersaulted into the large ditch lining the road and been stuck there for the whole night, but at first light he had retrieved his bike and papers and headed back this way and luckily stumbled straight into them. (He'd probably homed in on Commander Job's bagpipe playing, which he liked to use to put the fear of God into any enemy that maybe within earshot.) Obviously that had been the warning Commander Job had received from the FFI that had turned the main unit back on its heels, an ambush in waiting. Lofty had been lucky to escape.

As Guy, Perry, Swann and Gates had finished their morning patrol and come back to the orchard they had followed the approach of four French women. Guy had noticed one of them in particular, petite, black hair, striking eyes.

He watched as the older woman struck up a conversation with a Naval Petty Officer and was soon joined by Commander Job and then he strolled over and offered a cigarette to the three girls who now sat together enjoying the sunshine. They spent the next few hours trying to make themselves understood to each other and relaxing.

Guy had the distinct impression that this meeting had certainly been pre-arranged as he watched Commander Job chatting to the mother, who obviously had no idea at that time that in less than three years she would lose one of her precious daughters to one of these 'Hairy-arsed Bootnecks'.

•   •   •

Her blood felt as if it had gone cold, Madame Marguerite Wilthew felt her head swim and the very ground beneath her feet lurch, an overwhelming fear gripped her heart as she looked down at the Swastika stamped envelope that had just arrived through the door at Rue de Chanoines, Vannes, France.

It was 1940 the Nazi's had just overrun the small and ineffectual defences in the invasion of northern France. It would later come out that they had infiltrated areas of the French political system to ease the process.

The letter required that as English citizens Marguerite Wilthew and her two daughters, Armelle and Margot were to pack one case each and report to the towns train station immediately.

Somehow she just knew that whatever happened they must not get on that train!

Thankfully Marguerite was made of stern stuff, she had refused to obey the instructions contained within the letter and waving every official looking piece of paper she could find (people already all knew the Germans loved seeing official documents!), she marched purposefully down to see the new Nazi Kommandant of the town, to point out that the information he had was incorrect.

She stormed into the newly requisitioned offices, briefly found her way blocked by his minions and then tried as forcefully as she was able to make her argument.

The language barrier was initially a problem until they both realised they could most easily converse in English. Which didn't really help the main point of her argument! That she was NOT English, but the widow of an Englishman which was, in her opinion a different thing entirely, she also had to try and explain why her daughter Margot had chosen English as her dual nationality when she had come of age, twenty-one, it was her right to do so under the Law of her country, France. There had been a long drawn out pause, the man before her regarding her up and down thoughtfully. Slowly the Oberführer's face had softened, then suddenly burst into song!

> *God save your gracious King,*
> *Long live your noble King,*
> *Send him victorious,*
> *Happy and glorious,*
> *Long to reign over you,*
> *God save the King…'*

As ludicrous as it sounds and believe it or not but Marguerite would have to suffer that indignity every morning for the next four years! She was ordered to report to this office every morning from that moment onwards, for four long years!

So purely by circumstance she found herself with a perfect opportunity in which to gain important information about the occupying forces, their strengths and weaknesses, their movements and their future intentions, she even managed to get glimpses of harbour plans, installations and maps. She quickly became adept at memorizing and understanding markings and notations then reproducing them later on their own maps. All of which she passed on to the men of the FFI who she knew would put it to good use.

She always tried hard to hate this German, to see him purely and solely as the face of the enemy, a man who had the power of life and death over her and her family. But over a short time she realized the occupation could never be successful when quite obviously even this leader of men didn't want to be here, she quickly found herself even considering the possibility that he could actually have been a loving and devoted family man and he had most likely been forced away from his children and his 'Fatherland' by his Führer's quest for domination and the longer he stayed the more he wanted to go home. Thankfully he had been an older German and appeared to be far less extreme and brainwashed than some of the more eager young Nazi's that he commanded.

Marguerite shook her daydream off, now, at last, she could put all those thoughts and memories behind her, they had been freed, freed by the liberating Allies and she now found herself with the opportunity to do what she could to help them, to pass on all the information and contacts she had.

She called out again to Armelle and Margot encouraging them to get ready to go out as quickly as possible for an important rendezvous that she wanted them all to attend and that Monique had just arrived.

It was a beautiful clear blue August morning it felt somehow more light, colourful and fresh as the vast majority of the locals were rejoicing at the lifting of the sheer weight of the last four years of oppression. The streets of Vannes, Bretagne, France were still full of these jubilant people. The Cathedral and many church bells had been ringing out in celebration all morning.

They had all witnessed four long years of humiliating Nazi occupation, the local towns people who had tried to continue to smile and laugh in face of adversity had lately begun to find it impossible to hide the constant over bearing fear slowly subduing the life and heart from the previously close knit community, turning friend and family against one another, in a spiral of distrust and animosity that was firmly encouraged and supported by the occupying Nazi's.

But it was not a time to rejoice for all the people of France, for some it had been easier to capitulate from the start of the occupation, for the sake of a life, for family, for friends, the repercussions of resistance were horrific, the risks were just too great to take, no-one could really blame them.

There were also those that had found themselves able to use their local knowledge and positions to empower themselves, the small minded officious people who were prepared to give the Nazi's what they wanted for their own personal gain, these people now found themselves in a state of sheer panic, like rats leaving a sinking vessel, but most of them failed to escape, found themselves snatched up by the very people they had betrayed and made to pay for their treachery or greed. They had probably thought the Nazis were there for the long term, or maybe they thought they had been careful enough for their movements and actions to have gone undetected or just maybe they hadn't thought about it at all! But very few actually managed to get away with it.

Then of course there was also the reverse of that scenario.

The Wilthew's heard from a trusted source some considerable time later of the terrible situation that had befallen one of the local women. Margot, who was brought up by the nuns of her family didn't actually know her, although she did recall her pretty face and sweet smile as it had been. She might have nodded to her on occasion as they passed in the street, very subtly, but even though she knew of her patriotic actions she would certainly not openly converse with her. Margot had witnessed for herself the woman being turned away with an abusive phrase from a market stall although at that time she had not really known why. The locals apparently had repeatedly seen German troops and even officers leaving her poorly maintained apartment, near the market, at all times of the day and night.

Once she had heard the news Margot found it difficult to dispel the thoughts from her mind, her minds image of the story as it had been relayed to her.

The poor woman with her previously beautiful hair forcibly cut short and her scalp bleeding, then pushed, pulled and manhandled around the streets in her torn clothes and partially exposed underwear, while the ever increasing crowd shouted abuse, threw things and even spat at her. The peoples anger seemed to feed on itself, a baying mob, once ignited it was a growing force that seemed to thirst for blood, they wanted to make someone suffer as all felt they had. Margot wondered if the enthusiasm of some was fired by their lack of action previously, unfortunately this meant that they were not in possession of all the facts. One of the priests had apparently made a gallant effort to stop the proceedings but to no avail. Margot was surprised that his efforts could have failed and gone unheeded, she knew he had been strong for the people while the Nazi's tried to quell the spirit of the population by force and terror.

Eventually men dragged her off into a side street and yet more gunshots echoed around the narrow lanes of the ancient French town.

Margot knew the woman had almost certainly saved many lives of the areas Maquis with some of the information she had supplied to them. She was actually spying for them! Had been willing to put up her body for use by the enemy while her own community shunned her all for the ultimate ideal of liberation. She should, without doubt, have had a dignified death, if any.

But now the liberation had finally come, Margot was dressing, preparing to leave the house as her mother had quickly instructed.

Monique grumbled as they walked out into the stark light and sharp shadows of a summer's day in a narrow street. She wanted to go alone with Margot, not the whole of her family.

"Vous savez plein bien, Maman ne me permettrait jamais de souhaiter la bienvenue à des troupes unchaperoned, il est juste non fait." Margot explained that her mother had expressly asked them to wait for her, she had some important business or other that she had to attend to and she wanted them there with her.

Margot and Monique goaded each other about various Maquis men that they had both got to know during clandestine operations in the local area as they proceeded up the cobbled street. Marguerite and Armelle were quickly on their heels.

"Maintenant des filles, je ne vais avoir aucun de vous." she said directly to Monique," jétant vos étrangers ronds de bras, ils peuvent être des libérateurs, mais se rappellent qu'ils sont des étrangers tous les mêmes, et ils sont tous les hommes!" Marguerite warned all three girls to act with decorum when expressing their gratitude to the liberating soldiers.

She was very aware of their appearances and their position within the higher echelons of the local society. Marguerite had married at nineteen to a talented Aristocratic English artist in Le Faouët, Guy Wilthew. He had fallen in love, not only with the beautiful ever changing light and scenery of Bretagne but also with Marguerite, the young teenage daughter of the religious painter, Louis Marie Le Leuxhe, whose vacant studio he had rented from his widow, which was opposite the large covered market of the village square. Guy had returned from England every year, without fail, in order to court Marguerite until she was old enough to be given away in marriage and then he decided to stay and to take on the house.

Tragically he had died when his three children were still very young. Margot, his third child, was only about three years old. The death certificate said tuberculosis, but Spanish Flu was also sweeping Europe at that time and it could have been a combination of both.

Marguerite gathered the girls to order at the top of the street, "Nous allons marcher hors de la ville pour un peu. Au verger de Monsieur." and gave them their destination, then led the way to an orchard on the edge of town.

As they entered the large orchard through the rickety wooden gate, fixed precariously onto the dry stonewall, they could already hear the muffled sounds from the camp.

Smoke was drifting through the trees and they caught the smell of cooking food and that musty smell of damp canvas and drying cloth. It was quickly becoming a hot day, the sun was beginning to dry the dew-covered grass and the trees branches were weighed down with loads of bright red apples. As they moved through the short and dense apple trees, that were kept short for ease of harvest, they happened upon three soldiers, scrumping, a large canvas bag stood between them nearly spilling over with their haul.

The three Royal Marines froze in mid action.

Marguerite thought she could say with confidence that the owners and the local people would all be perfectly happy for them to carry on.

The three Marines grinned at the four women and then continued their labours. Monique headed straight for them as Marguerite grabbed at her hand and pulled her back.

"Bonjour." All four women smiled and nodded as they passed.

Monique only had one thing on her mind, cigarettes, and she was hoping to find the American troops who were apparently handing out chocolate and cigarettes to anyone who asked, especially pretty girls!

As the four women finally approached the small military camp just on the edge of the orchard, they could tell that they were now expected. Four more Marines were arriving back to camp just before them.

One of these men in particular caught Margot's attention, sun bleached hair sticking out in spikes from under an unusual woollen helmet comforter when everyone else was wearing either green berets with gold Royal Marine badges or dark blue naval caps and he was even wearing a scarf, in August! In Margot's eyes it added a great deal to his attraction, made him stand out starkly from everyone else around. He had very tanned skin, over thick British army issue trousers, black army boots and a heavily creased shirt, unbuttoned with sleeves rolled high.

Margot who was still very shy, despite her years, dipped her head and tried to avert her eyes but at present he was still preoccupied with off loading the heavy weaponry slung across his shoulders.

Margot had been studying for two years at 'Beaux Arts' a renowned school of art in Nantes when the Germans had invaded her country, as such she had seen and drawn many models whilst learning various drawing and painting techniques and this face and body instantly attracted her artistic eye.

She watched the men settle and very quickly tea was brewing over a small campfire.

Marguerite had pressing information that she needed to pass on to the men in charge, she instructed the girls to stay put while warning them not to be taken in by these young soldiers.

"Beau Bête, celle est toute qu'il est, n'est pas dupée." She headed purposefully toward a young Naval Petty Officer up ahead and was quickly joined by Naval Commander Job.

The first gesture of friendship was an open pack of cigarettes held out to Monique. With a large smile she politely accepted.

As Guy turned toward Margot and offered them to her she asked "American or English?"

"American" he answered, "English are not easy to get, the Yanks have got loads of them and we're in their sector." He smiled while looking straight into her eyes.

She managed to return his steady gaze but she could not control the smile that oddly felt as though it were getting bigger and bigger across her face with no limits. The only words Margot managed to understand, were 'American' and that the 'English were not easy'.

In fact her question had actually been directed at him, not the cigarettes and they had both misunderstood, she thought he had meant he was American. She was slightly upset and disappointed that he was not English and that he thought the English were not easy to deal with. For a short while her usual gay nature was somewhat dulled, but it didn't stop her and Monique whiling away the next hours misunderstanding most of what was being said and Armelle, her sister, taking some photographs on one of her missing brothers precious cameras.

Margot felt her heart give an involuntary flutter when she soon realised their previous misunderstanding and also learnt that this Englishman's name was Guy, the same name as her long departed English father and her missing brother (she later discovered it was his surname and obviously, in France, Guy is pronounced 'Ghee').

"You have... more?" She pointed. Margot had noticed a young Marine Corporal who had started to sketch Monique with a rough home-made stick of charcoal on the side of the large bag that had been used to collect the apples.

"Yes, of course." Corporal Swann said as he looked up, talking through the bouncing cigarette that was stuck to his lips. He snapped it in half and handed her the longer piece.

"You pose?" She asked, laughing as she turned to Ron.

A barrage of jokes, jibes and whistles that Margot had no hope of understanding were directed at Guy from the Marines gathered around.

"Here." She pointed to the sketch of Monique that was being made rather difficult by the lumps and bumps of the apples.

"Hold on, we can use mine." Guy strolled over to his kit and up ended the large bag scattering his things over the grass then using his dagger cut the top of the double stitched seam and with much more of a struggle than he expected, or hoped for, he tore open the canvas with a loud rip, then stretched it between additional knives and his dagger to the felled tree trunk some of them had been sitting on and the ground.

He danced about a bit stupidly and took up his pose with a mock chin high proud look to the sky, a cigarette still hanging from his mouth and a grin and a wink at everyone still standing around. He didn't need to make too much effort at totally ignoring any and all of the remarks that flowed freely from the other Marines of his unit.

He knew they were only jealous!

Chapter Seven

August 1944. Brest Peninsular, France.

The harbour was quiet; it seemed to have been completely untouched by the intensive high level bombing of the area, which had decimated the surrounding French fishing town. The FFI, including Marguerite and Margot, who had helped the small 30AU team form some plans for this operation had constantly been reminded by the German officers Marguerite had had to report to everyday that the US bombers had certainly killed far more French people in these port towns than the Germans ever had. But Guy now knew that they still continued to help the downed Allied airmen escape Nazi capture, as the FFI were well aware of the appalling casualties being inflicted upon the young men of the American bomber squadrons as they tried to locate their targets under almost impossible circumstances and the experienced battle hardened pilots of the Luftwaffe tried with all their might to stop them.

(The French people of the port towns actually had a local joke [Nan once told me, but I can't remember quite how it went. It wouldn't have translated well anyway!] About being able to completely ignore both the German aircraft and the British aircraft, but if anyone spotted a single US plane the whole town would head underground.)

The light was beginning to break, the sky was clear, the sea calm, a slight sea mist gave Guy the impression the day would be a beautiful one, if he got through this morning.

Margot Wilthew, his French Maquis guide had led him through the dark lanes and quiet streets after curfew with the aid of a hand drawn map supplied by her mother, to the attic room of a three-storey house overlooking the harbour and then left in haste. Guy used the scope on his sniper rifle to watch the few German guards who wandered fairly aimlessly about the dockside. He had located the 'Schnellboots' or 'S-Boots' that were called 'Torpedo Fast

Attack Boats' or 'E-Boats' by the Allies. They were 30AU's main targets or more specifically the main target was the Torpedo's they were carrying, thought by Fleming's NID30 intelligence reports, to be of an advanced new type, jet propelled and guided. The three Special Operations Jeeps equipped with Twin Vickers Machine guns, both in the rear and at the front, behind bullet proof plexi-glass armour, were waiting out of sight. They had been slowly manoeuvred from the rear entrance into a small wooden dockyard shed, which looked as though it was about to collapse. The shed leaned alarmingly to one side and had old fishing nets hung just about all over it and from the rafters inside. Three Royal Marine Commandos occupied each Jeep, one driver and one Marine on each gun. They were all on edge; they had been waiting for the signal, itching to go. Captain Lessing, a South African Boer, in the lead Jeep looked at his watch, again.

In a small wooded area on the edge of the coast, next to the town, Lieutenant Commander Job waited with the 'Torpedo Extraction Team' of the unit, all of whom were smoking restlessly, the other three Jeeps and the flatbed US truck they had prepared were crowded with Royal Marines, some sitting astride the cradle fitted to carry the soon to be captured Torpedo. Two naval Torpedo specialists were squeezed into the truck cab with the Marine driver and one Petty Officer.

The Marine sniper glanced at his watch, rotated so that the face was visible on the inside of the left wrist. It was time.

The strolling Guard was between the dark hulls of two boats and briefly silhouetted against the morning light reflecting from the water as the shot squeezed off, virtually silently, from the specially equipped sniper rifle. He twisted and fell over the high harbour side with barely any audible splash. The second had just bent slightly forward to light his cigarette; the brief glow of flame illuminated his face as Guy fired. The Guard's body just seemed to deflate down into the ground almost into a cross-legged squat.

The gulls screamed in alarm as the first Jeep, with Captain Lessing, smashed through the rickety wooden shed doors. The sudden noise made Guy jump slightly as he fired his third shot, which missed the target, a quick flick of the right wrist had the rifle reloaded, the Guard had dropped to one knee at the sudden noise and started to fire his Mauser at the fast approaching Jeeps, Guy knew things were going to really liven up now. The Mauser was not fired for long; the Wehrmacht helmet didn't offer enough side protection.

There was another huge bang and rumble, the third Jeep had snagged one of the many fishing nets on the shed, which had collapsed in a billowing cloud of dust and the remnants of one of the walls was now being dragged along the dockside behind the bobbing cork floats of the ancient fishing net, which was still attached to the Jeeps rear machinegun and the Marine behind it, who was flailing about desperately trying to release himself.

Guy could not help but smile although he only watched him for a few seconds; Kriegsmarines were starting to appear on the E-boats decks, the first few were quickly felled, silently. Now the five still operational Jeeps twin Vickers guns started to make there presence felt. Any Germans attempting to resist now would be keeping their heads very low. It was time for Guy to move.

The sound of more engines could be heard approaching, Commander Job with the other three Jeeps and the truck screeched down over the cobbles and joined the first three vehicles. Marines leapt from their places and started to board the E-boats, tossing in grenades before them. Others moved out into the surrounding palates and canvas covered boxes of equipment. Bursts of machinegun fire could be heard echoing throughout the harbour. The naval Officers quickly located the Torpedo's they had come for, confirming that they were the new design type. Fortuitously there were some on the dockside, which the Germans had not yet loaded aboard the E-boats, which really speeded things up. The fire fight seemed to be over even before Guy had reached it, he immediately leapt onto the deck of the E-boat nearest the truck and started to remove the Nazi flag that hung towards the stern.

"Guy, for fuck sake, we're not here to collect bloody flags, help get this job done!" Corporal Swann was unimpressed. Despite the reprimand Guy still stowed the flag.

(It was also from one of these E-Boat bases at St. Nazaire that Guy, during a search of the technical rooms, 'liberated' a technical drawing set with the name 'GEBR. Wichmann MBH' engraved into it. This he sent to his brother

Ted, who became an engineering draughtsman and used them for his entire career).

The Royal Marines positioned around the harbour and on the boat decks felt as if it had taken an age to get the Torpedo loaded, but in actual fact it had taken less than fifteen minutes.

"JEEPS, JEEPS NOW!" Captain Lessing's shout seemed overly loud, but he was keen to make sure none of his men had strayed out of earshot or more likely still had ringing ears from the grenades going off in the confined spaces below E-boat decks. He tried to count the men back into the vehicles, although he knew they all tried to keep the same places so that missing men would be more easily realised.

The sun had started to colour the horizon orange as the vehicles headed out of the town on the prearranged roads, always different roads to the ones they had approached on, in case they had been observed on the way in and an ambush awaited them on the return trip.

"T three OTTER, calling STAG, T three OTTER, calling STAG, over".

"STAG here T three OTTER- SHEEP C, SHEEP C, over"

After finding the predetermined radio frequency, Paddy reports, "PIKE captured repeat PIKE captured, without loss, over".

"PIKE captured, well done, over out" crackled back the confirmation reply.

The Marines started to relax as they headed back towards Allied lines. Guy had been right, the day was already becoming warm as he tried to make himself comfortable in the bouncing Jeep, he happened to be looking back towards the large truck, which was following the six fast moving Jeeps, as it bounced up onto a level crossing. All the Jeeps had bounced in a similar way as they had crossed the rail tracks, with the Marines in the back of each all holding on in anyway they could.

He guessed that it had been the additional weight of the fifteen CWT. truck and captured Torpedo, which had set it off, or possibly it was one of the new German mines that counted the previous vehicles to a preset trigger number before detonation.

The truck unexpectedly launched into the air, lifted by an orange fireball and then engulfed in black smoke before it had even come back to earth. The two Naval Officers who had been sitting on the flatbed next to the Torpedo were launched high into the air through the fireball, they both landed, still together, in the field running alongside the rail lines. As the truck landed it seemed to explode again, from within, ripping itself apart. The preceding shockwave knocked Guy backwards, painfully bruising his side against the Jeeps bulkhead.

"DEFENSIVE POSITIONS!" Lessing screamed the Marines attention back to the job in hand, it could be an ambush. They were all quickly scattering to make sure this was not going to get any worse than it already was, but no enemy fire was forthcoming.

Captain Lessing jogged back to the burning truck, Guy, Corporal Swann and 'Ganger' Gates had got to the truck cab as quickly as they could, unbelievably the Petty Officer, who had been travelling with the Royal Marine driver in the cab, was still alive and they had dragged him out to safety. He seemed relatively untouched, but was a shivering wreck, unable to communicate coherently. The driver and the two Naval men were quite obviously dead. As Guy approached the field where the two men had been thrown he realised it was a minefield, clearly signed. They would have to be left; there was no option. They were quickly back underway, six Jeeps, heading at speed towards the American lines. All the Marines were now tense and could not help feeling a slight sense of relief when they saw the US column heading their way.

As the 30AU approached, the vehicles of the column slid into defensive positions, soldiers scattering, the 30AU Jeeps stopped in amongst the US troops. Guns were brought to bear. The Royal Marines instinctively raised their own arms at the Americans; it was a dangerous situation, one that should not have been allowed to develop. (It was also a situation that was frequently repeated, especially in Germany when the Nazi's did actually start to dress up as the Allies and infiltrate certain operations). The advancing US troops had obviously thought that they were the leading edge of the assault, that there was nothing between them and the enemy.

Guy was scared, only days previously, trigger happy GI's had shot the Frenchman that Lieutenant Commander Job and Captain Wheeler had been questioning, they had been standing in a front garden, in front of the Frenchman's family, quite innocently and with no danger or any apparent ill feeling, when a truck of passing GI's had opened fire for no obvious reason. The Frenchman had died in the Captain Wheeler's arms, while surrounded by his hysterical family. He knew it would only take one trigger happy GI to set this off into a bloodbath.

"What the hell are you Jerries doing dressed like that?" The US Officer was staring at them in disbelief.

Guy had to admit to himself, his team did look like a suspicious bunch now he came to think about it. Various uniform types and colours, Green Berets, Naval Caps, conflicting arm flashes and a very varied assortment of weaponry held up by unshaven dishevelled bunch of hooligans. All jammed together in US Jeeps. The English soldiers these GI's would have seen up to that point would probably have been mainly army, without transport, trudging along in columns, armed with Enfields and certainly all in the same drab uniforms.

"We're 30 Commando, Combined Ops. If you'd care to take a look at my orders I'm quite sure you'll find it all in order." Job felt just as uneasy.

"Hey, Buddy…" the GI did not get a chance to finish his sentence.

Guy let his Tommy gun swing on his shoulder, his heart pounding, he jumped out of the Jeep and walked straight up to the GI who lowered his gun unsure as to what to expect. Grabbing his shirt with both hands and lifting him backwards. "When you address our Officers you call them SIR, understood?"

Job looked as shocked as everybody else to the reaction, he hadn't expected it, no-one had, Guy knew it was a reaction that any one of the 30AU Marines would have repeated, he just happened to be opposite the man who required to be taught some manners and the correct way of doing things.

Somehow it seemed to defuse the tension and the whole situation eased. The Americans now suddenly seemed convinced that this reaction could only have come from a 'Crazy Limey' and raised guns were quickly replaced by warm smiles.

Chapter Eight

August 1944. Vannes, France.

The cool damp air of the cellar was quite a relief from the last few days of blazing sunshine and the constant clouds of dust that accompanied Allied soldiers as they moved about during the liberation of Northern France in the summertime of 1944.

Ron felt his body and lungs relax as Margot led him by the hand, down into the cellar of the large terraced house that he had taken the opportunity to call on while 30AU were temporarily held up between targets.

'Ganger' Gates and Marine Guy had taken a risk, slipping away from Corporal Swann, by the ancient city wall ramparts and the prison arch, as the three had entered Vannes, Brittany. They had been sent to look for provisions while on a shore leave Rota, but Guy knew that Swann had designs on Margot and had also been using his position to try and keep Guy busy with duties for the last few days, so that he might keep Margot and Ron as far apart as possible.

Margot had given Guy the address, a terraced house in Rue des Chanoines, Vannes, when they had moved into position for the E-boat raid a few days ago and now he had a deep longing to see that smile again before 30AU moved out of the area, probably for good.

As Margot had opened the door, that very smile spread wide across her face, but she knew she could not be seen taking soldiers into the front door of the house. As luck would have it her mother had gone out for a short while and Armelle, her sister, and Margot were alone in the house. Margot wanted to grab the opportunity to try and be alone with this man that attracted her so much. She quickly tried to give them directions to the back door of the house in her broken English. The two Marines walked back uphill along the narrow cobbled street and then ducked down into one of the tiny alleyways between the closely set terraced houses, after a few twists and turns they walked through the open, vine covered gate and into a beautiful garden resplendent in its summer bloom. The birds feeding at the numerous tables seemed completely undisturbed by the two large soldiers entering their domain, the constant hum of bees filled the quiet, still air which was somehow completely detached from the air of the busy, noisy market town in the background. A town that was still very much in the throes of enjoying the new found freedom that the liberation had brought. Margot insisted on taking some photographs on one of her brother Guy's cameras and Armelle enjoyed dictating the poses.

"Ganger, give us a couple of hours mate? I'm not going to go anywhere outside that gate until you get back." Guy looked at his military superior but also, thankfully, his friend.

"Sure, don't do anything I wouldn't." His grin spread into a huge smile as he left, closing the gate quietly behind him.

Armelle disappeared with the camera into the large empty house. Margot and Ron stood facing each other and slowly held hands as they looked into each other's clear bluish grey eyes. Birds, butterflies and bees continued their labour, oblivious to the two completely motionless people, who stood for an age, both wondering how they were going to communicate, both knowing they were already communicating everything they needed to know.

The new looking wooden stairs creaked as the two people headed down into the darkness. Slowly Ron's eyes adjusted to the darkness of the cellar after the dazzling sunshine of the garden. Racks of dusty wine bottles lined the cellar walls, reaching right up into the arched ceiling recesses. As they approached the rear of the cellar, Ron could see one of the large wooden wine racks had been pulled away from the wall. Broken glass crunched underfoot where the remnants of a few bottles littered the floor and many booted footprints had mixed dust and wine together, leaving red footprints heading in all directions. Behind the rack an ominous dark hole had been knocked though the wall. The loosened bricks had been piled to one side or lay strewn about as if it had all been done in a great hurry.

Margot did not let go of Ron's hand as they clambered through the hole and into an even darker brick built tunnel. Guy guessed they were now under the narrow cobbled street between the terraced house and the large church, St. Peters Cathedral. Other smaller brick built tunnels led off at angles from this larger one and the gurgle of water which cascaded through troughs over which they had to carefully step, implied this was part of the sewer system of the town, although the air felt much fresher than that of a sewer.

At the far end another hole had been forced through a beautifully ornate stonewall, a pale patch of bluish lighter coloured stone stood out starkly from the darkness of the bricks surrounding the hole. This one looked to have been made in far less of a hurry, the removed stones had been stacked carefully, awaiting their return into position at some future date. Wonderfully carved stone steps curved past the other side of the wall. Guy climbed through, then turned to help Margot; he looked up the stairwell, which abruptly ended in a solid stonewall a few steps up. They followed the stairwell downward, deeper into the ground.

They passed through an arched doorway with an open solid oak door, studded with short metal spikes and on into a huge Vault, obviously part of the Cathedral above them. It was built from massive ornate carved stones, which arched high into the air and relative darkness above them. Tiny shafts of daylight, some that were brightly coloured, almost spectrums, pierced down from numerous directions, they crisscrossed the space, illuminating the swirling dust, which had still not settled from the recent activities. Guy guessed the rays were being coloured by the massive stained glass windows of the Cathedral above them and the light was piercing some small vents on the main floor. As people strolled in the Cathedral the rays of light flickered and sparkled, turning on and off in a timed, coloured display.

Ron slowly turned full circle as he gazed around the huge space with wide eyes, it was an armoury, an armoury and a treasure trove. Huge bejewelled crucifixes and candelabras caught the sparkling spectrum of light as it reflected around the room, wonderfully ornate gilt frames of mirrors and oil paintings, some as high as the Vault itself adorned the walls, many more were stacked, draped in dust sheets. Margot pulled back some of the sheets sending billowing clouds of dust to dance in the bright coloured beams of daylight. She was talking quickly, Ron could hardly understand a word, his French was still poor, but he knew she was in love, in love with these works of art, with the very church itself, she was animated, excited, happy, happy to be revealing the art of her family, probably the art of the whole area. Magnificent works, paintings that should have been constantly on display, but which had been secreted away in the darkness and dust to preserve them from the clutches of the Nazi's.

"Ceux-ci sont Alphonse Le Luexhe et son frère Luis Le Luexhe, ermmm… my grandfather, religious painters…et son beau-fils, mon père...Guy Wilthew…these are my mother… Marguerite Wilthew…" Margot looked as happy as she had been in a long time.

Beautifully made varnished wooden racks were still lined with rifles and ancient weapons, some of them Guy recognized from his training. Many of them looked to be from the First World War, although there was also plenty of Nazi equipment, wooden crates clearly stamped with Swastika's were stacked in various corners and there were also very obvious spaces, areas of disturbed dust, where weapons and ammunition had been recently and hastily removed. Guy had no doubt that it had all been put to good use, was still being put to good use by the Maquis during the liberation.

Ron took Margot's hand as she continued to uncover paintings that she probably had not laid eyes on in four long years. He swung her round into his arms, her face was still smiling, tears of joy mingled with the dust of the years, she continued to speak quickly in French until the first kiss. To which she gave herself, utterly.

After a few seconds the tears of joy gave way to a flood of emotion, emotion that she had somehow kept in check for all those years while she had had to remain strong. Strong for the family, for her mother, her sister, for her missing brother, strong for the damaged and wounded airmen that had come into their lives so briefly, to be passed on as soon as they were able, strong for the constant battle against an overwhelming tyranny, strong against the seemingly endless murder and torture of innocent, good, people.

Ron felt her whole tiny body racked with sobbing convulsions as she buried her face into his chest. At last she felt secure, secure in these powerful arms that enveloped her and held her tight. She could feel the strength flow from him, the power of a true fighter. She let her emotion leave her, felt herself to be renewed by his strength. She never wanted to leave those arms.

"Marguerite!" Marguerite Wilthew had appeared in the open doorway of the Vault, Armelle stood just behind her. "Vous Bête, l'avez laissée allez cet instant!"

Margot jumped back away from Ron and then paused, her wide shocked eyes looked back and forth between Ron and her mother. She then stepped forward and took Ron's hand again, holding it firmly.

"Vous BÊTE! I have the ear of your Officer, young man, Commander Job was my dinner guest last evening and I fully intend to bring this matter to his attention. I have very important contacts and information, which he will not want to risk with you're ungentlemanly conduct. NOW GET OUT! Do not see my daughter AGAIN!" Marguerite Wilthew's English was perfect, she had just about managed to keep her emotions in check, only slightly raising her voice to emphasise her menace perfectly.

Ron knew better than to even try to protest, he looked down at Margot's large dilated watering eyes. What could he say to try and make her understand? He just didn't have enough French vocabulary to even begin. Margot's grip on his hand held for as long as she could muster the strength. Then he left, looking into Marguerite Wilthew's face as he passed, he tried to convey that his intentions had been entirely honourable with a proud look, which probably just came across to her as that of an arrogant boy.

A boy robbed of his fun.

Chapter Nine

"Hello, Sandy Powell I presume?" I enquired.

"Hi. Good to meet you at last." The hard voice rasped back.

"Hello, Sandy, I am the Grandson of Ron Guy, who served with 30AU… during the war. Have you got time to chat?"

" I know who you are. Oh yes plenty of time, I remember Guy, although I was in A-troop, I think he was in B-troop, but our paths crossed many times. Some of the other lads have already been in touch, they talked about you and your Grandad and the wonderful story of him marrying one of the FFI, the Maquis, a wonderful story. They helped us many, many times. Repeatedly saved our lives, I'm very sure of it." Powell sounded strong, a towering man at one time I was quite sure, but now reduced by age to walking with two sticks. Although without doubt he was still a formidable character. In fact Commander Hugill, one the 30AU Naval officers, in his own book, *'The Hazard Mesh'* written just after the war when everything was still top secret, had renamed Powell as Marine Tower and I could guess why. *(Cdr Hugill went on to head the FIU - Forward Interrogation Unit, in Germany 1945)*

"If you don't mind I'd love to talk over some of your memories about Ian Fleming's 'Red Indians', my Grandad never talked about his wartime and it's only been since his death I have discovered what he was involved in?"

"Of course, of course. I'd love to be of help to you. Although I only ever remember seeing Fleming once, at Minden Barracks Germany, forty-five in his Naval Blues, stood out like a sore thumb he did. Well one such occasion springs immediately to mind. One of our Naval Lieutenants, Hugill his name was…"

•   •   •

August 1944. Brest Peninsular. France.

"Powell, McGrath, Nation and you four, on the double, we're out of here, now, we've got clearance to search these target areas. Let's go." Lieutenant Hugill shouted at the Marines as he came back from the field headquarters at a slow jog along with Lieutenant van Cleef.

Guy had been impressed with Naval Officer Hugill on many occasions, they were worlds apart in education and class and Lieutenant Hugill had been less than impressed with the some of the Marines assigned to him, but Guy had made a concerted effort to try and not disappoint him any further, although after witnessing some of the stupidity himself, it was probably an exercise in futility.

They headed off into the countryside towards St. Pabu. Hugill had been informed there was a heavily defended radar station and initial estimates put the German force anywhere between five hundred and two thousand. As they crossed a bomb-damaged bridge, a few kilometres short of the main target, a large funeral cortege was coming towards them.

Powell listened as Hugill questioned some of the people accompanying the crowd. The four coffins contained the bodies of young men who the Nazi's had suspected of being involved with the Maquis. They had been arrested and held at this stronghold for many days while being tortured and interrogated and eventually their bodies had been dumped outside the perimeter. The wailing women and crying fathers were having an effect on everyone, including the men of the 30AU team. The FFI had been laying a siege to the German stronghold since the liberation had begun and so far the Kommandant had refused to surrender to them twice already. Their estimate of the Germans strength was one thousand five hundred.

Powell had a sneaking and very worrying suspicion that Lieutenant Hugill was going to try and take the surrender of over one thousand Nazi's with just nine men.

Certainly the Germans were not in a very strong position, hated by the local populace, cut off from any kind of relief and with only the expectation of continued bombing raids and artillery fire, maybe now was the time to take that surrender, but it did seem madness to try and accomplish it with just nine men.

They proceeded over the next few kilometres at a very slow rate, doing foot reconnaissance before passing any crests or covered terrain. At St. Pabu itself, the local Mayor, an aged man with lots of white hair, informed them of the exact location and put the estimate of German troops at five hundred. The Maquis made a loud show of wanting to help but Lieutenant Hugill declined all offers, except that of a husband and wife who would lead the second part of the team to a vantage point from which to view the target.

"Right lads, I'm going to go and have a chat with this lot, see if I can't get them to see some sense and pack it in, probably best if you take up positions of cover and I go in alone." Hugill explained his hastily conceived plan.

"Sir, where you go we go." Sergeant McGrath and Marine Powell were the men assigned and responsible for keeping this Naval officer alive and they were not going to be so easily dissuaded.

"Quite right, so be it, lets go." Hugill didn't waste his breath. "We're going to have to make them believe we're part of a much larger force and that they really do have no other options open to them. Van Cleef you take off in our Jeep and find me some Americans and quickly. The rest of you go up to this point here, or wherever our friends here think is the best vantage point from which to support us if we do get into some difficulties."

The Marine sniper looked back and watched as the Jeep he was in pulled away; Hugill tied a white handkerchief to the end of his carbine.

He immediately sprinted off from the Jeep as soon as it reached its destination as directed by the two FFI, then crept into the best position from which to lay down covering fire, should it be required. He scanned the entrenched German defences through the scoped Enfield rifle. He could clearly see some manned anti-aircraft guns and a few machinegun emplacements. The entrance track was a few hundred yards long and as he looked down its length he caught sight of Hugill, McGrath and Powell walking purposefully under the small white flag, towards the main gate. It was certainly an act of extreme bravery considering what they approached. The Marine sniper watched through the crosshairs as the two sentries waved them through and the large gates swung open. He could not help but constantly line the sight of his scope with perfect shots on each of the guards as he studied them.

The sun was at the highest point of the day, the shadows their smallest, thankfully the gates stayed open and the Marine sniper watched as the three men stood awaiting the arrival of someone in authority. After about five minutes four Luftwaffe Officers appeared with a bodyguard of about ten troops. He watched as the highest-ranking German Officer gave the Nazi salute to Lieutenant Hugill and then a conversation began with some slight gesticulations by the men of both parties.

Suddenly after a few minutes of peace and tranquillity, he jumped; machinegun fire erupted from another part of the walled perimeter, which was instantly answered by Marine Freddy Nation manning the Jeeps gun. The Marine sniper rescanned the Officers still in negotiation. Powell jumped forward bringing his large Bren gun to bare on the German Officers who in turn sent off a few of the bodyguard to quell the fire of their own men. Sergeant McGrath ran back to the parapet waving his arms to signal a cease fire and the guns quickly became silent again. This small fright seemed to get everything moving in the right direction again.

The sniper watched all of the Officers move from within the main compound to outside the main gate. Powell and McGrath stayed by the main gate. As he watched, the Kommandant walked passed one of the bodyguards who surreptitiously handed him a grenade as he casually walked on. He lined the crosshairs on the centre of his chest wondering what to do. If he felled him the whole thing might erupt into a firefight and certainly none of his team apart from him would have a chance. He waited and watched ready to fire if it looked like he might try to detonate his grenade. After a few more minutes Lieutenant van Cleef's Jeep re-appeared heading down the entrance track, it pulled up and he gesticulated back behind him. At this the Officers all took seats on the grass and began to exchange cigarettes. Lieutenant Hugill then left with van Cleef in the Jeep. Leaving Powell and McGrath at the main entrance being given some hot drinks, as the sniper continued trying to follow the progress through his scope. Both Powell and McGrath had a few face offs with some very mean looking Afrika Korps troops, but both stood their ground firmly, two men against a possible two thousand!

After about forty minutes maybe an hour, it seemed longer to all, Hugill returned closely followed by an American mechanized unit, mostly tank busters.

The sniper continued to watch the Kommandant who now held the grenade behind his back toying with it. He could only have one thing in mind, but would he try to do it, he continued to hesitate as he watched him fiddling with the grenade, then much to his relief Marine Powell suddenly strode over to him and took the grenade away. The sniper let out a long and deep breath; he hadn't realized he'd even been holding it. He decided now was the time to walk down and re-join his team. As he did so he continued watching and the thought occurred to him he may have been premature as a row instantly took place between the American Commander and the German Kommandant, for a few hesitant moments it looked as if the whole thing was going to turn nasty after all.

Thankfully Lieutenant Hugill managed to regain some control over the abrasive Americans who seemed intent on undoing all the good work of the previous two hours.

At last the Germans began to disarm and line up to be taken prisoner, it turned out there were about three hundred of them.

Powell watched as the prisoners filed past. One man stopped at them and held out a camera.

"English Commando. Congratulations on your victory, I'd like you to have this." The German smiled a broad friendly grin.

Powell glanced at the Marines around him, impressed with his English, none replied as Powell took the camera and slid it into a pocket. Sometime later as they brewed up some tea Powell pulled out the camera and examined it with the idea to take a photo, as he pushed at the release to open the bellows to the lens, he noticed a small wire protruding from one of the joins.

"COVER!" He screamed loud as he threw the camera at the same time the sprung lid flipped open to expose what should have been the lens. It exploded with the force of a grenade. No-one tried to stop Powell as he grabbed his Bren gun and marched off in the direction of the prisoners.

They later found an operational Opel car within the fortress and filled it with anything they could find that looked to be of any use and took it all back to the unit. Mainly toothbrushes and bottles of wine.

"And that is how you succeed my good man, with Bluff and Resolution..." Hugill was pleased with his days work.

When they returned to the rest of the unit they learned that free French had liberated Paris and Pikeforce with most of X-Troop had been right there at the front, apparently Captain Pike was the first to the bar at the Ritz Hotel. They were quickly joined by other parts of the unit to clear Paris of all the intelligence targets and every safe box they could find, over eighty, as well as many other important targets in and around Paris, including French factories that were manufacturing essential parts for the German V, for vengeance, weapons.

They found some important and vital intelligence on where these weapons were being manufactured and who was undertaking the design and overseeing the production of them.

BEAU BÊTE

Chapter Ten

August 1975 Fort William, Scotland.

As a child I spent all of my holidays with my grandparents. School holidays at their modest semi-detached house, in a quiet close, tucked away so near to the fields and woods I loved to play in and family holidays in Scotland. Scotland has always stirred my heart like no other place in the world, even more so as a young boy than it still does now.

The holidays that always began with the endless road journeys into the heart of the highlands of Scotland, mainly remembered for the terrible and constant rows between Margot and Ron. Rows about which was the 'right' road to take, once they had even started to row about whether it should be left or right from the bottom of their own street, taking fifteen minutes to come to a decision. They had fought like cat and dog, or maybe more accurately like cat and cat, for virtually the whole of their lives, but no one could ever accuse their relationship of lacking passion. Passion was evident between them, in every sense.

One such holiday has always stood out in my mind more than any other. The time we stayed in a small croft near to Fort William, which nestled on the lower slopes of the highest mountain on the British Isles, Ben Nevis.

The day we had arrived in the area of Fort William the sky was leaden grey and weighed heavy on the hills. As we crested the road near Spean Bridge in the tattered pale blue Bedford campervan, after many hours driving, my keen, bright, child's eyes locked onto a great green bronze of three massive soldiers which was silhouetted against the early morning horizon.

"Nan, can we stop, can we stop?" I implored my grandparents. (I had instantly recognised the outlines of these soldiers from my toy Airfix collection of Commandos, the squared woollen helmet comforters were unique to them.)

"Ron, we have to stop here." Margot let it be known we were stopping.

"Okay, okay." Ron seemed reluctant.

The sliding door of the Bedford van was torn back against the stoppers as I jumped from the van closely followed by the dog, Husky. I ran out of the car park and up to the base of the statue, which towered above me. The rest of the family slowly forced themselves from the warmth and into the cold dull grey wind of the early day.

I stood looking up into the faces of three magnificent and proud Commandos, who in turn looked to the inspiring, mountainous horizon, all three in their familiar helmet comforters, weapons slung over the shoulders. My Nan had often told me tantalising stories of Grandad as a Royal Marine Commando. But much to my frustration, Grandad would never be drawn on the subject.

The lead Commando was just as I had always imagined Grandad to be, while I played my constant war games amongst school friends.

"Uni-ted we Con-quer." I tried to read out the inscription aloud completely oblivious to the few other members of the public and the loose, grazing sheep who were around the statue. Ron and Margot slowly wandered over to my side. The rest of the family stretched aching limbs and tried to shake the sleep from their heads. As Husky began to worry the sheep.

"Is that you Grandad?" I was over excited at this unexpected find.

"No, no, it's not me." Ron stood back trying to roll a cigarette from his pouch of tobacco, which the stiff cold breeze was making difficult.

"Did you know them?"

He looked up into the hard chiselled bronze faces, making a pretence at trying to discern their features. "No, I don't think so."

"Why is it here, Grandad?"

Margot read out the inscription to him. " In memory of the officers and men of The Commandos, who died in the Second World War. 1939-1945. This country was their training ground."

"So you trained here? Whereabouts did you train Grandad?"

"Well mostly at a place called Achnacarry, just over those hills there, although we did move around all over this area. They even made us run up that mountain with full kit." He pointed to the horizon and the snow peaked mountain of Ben Nevis, whose top was partly obscured by the low grey cloud.

"And your Grandad was always first back." Nan smiled as she reached out to hold my hand, she was feeling the cold wind.

"Can you show me where, please Grandad?"

"Not today, no, but maybe later in the holiday. Let's just finish our journey shall we. Aren't you hungry?" Ron smiled just wanting to get on his way.

A few days later after a constant barrage of requests, Ron had capitulated and taken me to Achnacarry.

Ron and I walked slowly hand in hand through the Oak lined entrance track that led to the Cameron ancestral home. It was a beautiful crisp blue day, the warm sun high in the sky. Husky, Ron and Margot's mongrel dog, raced back and forth chasing scents on the breeze. We had left the rest of the family picnicking and playing around Margot and her easel, while she worked on her oil painting of the wonderful ever-changing light across the Ben Nevis landscape. She loved the highlands of Scotland, probably because they reminded her so much of her homelands in Brittany and Le Faouët.

"That Loch we passed near Fort William on the way here, the one I pointed out as we passed. We practiced amphibious assault landings there while under tracer rounds and live fire from the Officers armed with Bren guns. They had rigged explosive charges at various points and if our landing craft got too close to those they were turned over in the water. I remember one man who was killed there, although I can't remember his name now. We spent many, many days marching these undulating tracks, for endless miles. We had to run up the slopes and we were only allowed to walk when going down the other side."

"Let's do it now Grandad." As I tried to pull him along.

I listened intently to all the stories Ron had to give. I'd tried to get war stories from Grandad many times before but had always failed, until now.

"When we first arrived at the train station, they made us get out of the train on the wrong side for some reason and cross the tracks, then we were marched up to Achnacarry and the Officers led us past three graves just down there, they told us that they were the graves of soldiers who had not obeyed orders correctly while being trained and had died as a result, that had an effect on everyone I can tell you. Over there used to be a loud air-raid siren attached to that wooden bridge, our large huts and tents, which we used as barracks were all lined up over in that field, where those Highland Cattle are. The siren was used for getting us out of our beds and ready for training. When we'd completed our training a few of us ripped the siren off its mountings and threw it in the river, right down there." He pointed to the very spot as we stomped over the wide bridge. "Luckily we weren't caught. Although I did get into trouble for punching an Officer here once…" Grandad was enjoying himself, a rare smile spread wide on his face.

"You punched an Officer, Grandad?" I was incredulous.

The smile dropped. "Ah, yes, well, there was bit more to it than that, but I'll tell you about that when you're bit older." Ron had realised he'd got carried away with his reminiscing.

"You see these huge Oaks?" Ron pointed high into the tree canopy.

"Actually look, the metal rods are still there, they were put through the tree trunks to hold the ropes that stretched across that river, we had to climb and swing across those ropes while Officers exploded charges in the water beneath us, down there. They did the same thing with a small wooden slated rope bridge with no side ropes. We had to run at the bridge as fast as we could and not stop, or slow down, until we hit the ground on the other side, the bridge used to wobble and swing wildly from side to side but if you kept your head up and looked straight ahead and ran as fast as you could the wooden slats were always where your feet needed them to be. But, if you slowed, or looked down, you ended up all the way down there." He pointed down into the rock-strewn river many feet below them and they watched as Husky appeared, splashing out into the water of the river. "Although I don't remember it looking quite as deadly as that when I was last here!" Ron quickly walked on, dragging me along with him and calling for Husky to join them.

My eyes were huge, pupils dilated, I was over stimulated by the stories, wanted to run and leap and be that Commando of my dreams, wanted to explore, hunt and climb, to push myself and train just as Grandad had done.

"See this small rock face here?" Ron pointed to some sheer rocks hidden back behind the large Oaks and Birches. To me at that time it was at least a cliff face or a mountain.

"There were small holes all over it and we were trained to climb it by putting a hand in one of these holes with fingers straight, like this. Then once you're hand is in the hole you make it into a fist and it can't come back out. It holds in solidly until you release your fist."

I decided I needed to try this theory at the very earliest possible opportunity.

"Over here in this field, by those trees, that is where we used to do our hand to hand combat training. Two men, one called Fairburn and the other was called Sykes, they were policemen from Singapore. They had devised a street knife fighting technique and they taught all the Commandos how to do it with specially made daggers that they had designed themselves, called the 'F-S Fighting Knife'. They were hand made by Wilkinson Sword just for the Commandos. Still got mine at home."

"Can I see it when we get home, please? Can you teach me how to do it please Grandad, please?" I looked up with pleading eyes into Grandad's face.

"We'll see, we'll see." His smile took up his whole face.

•   •   •

The next day over the breakfast table a row had erupted. A woman called Barbara had arrived completely out of the blue and uninvited. She was Guy Wilthew's ex-ladyfriend, (Nan's late brother) and Ron hated her and was angry. Ron could not understand how she had managed to find us in the wilds of Scotland when he had expressly forbidden anyone in the family to tell her where we were. I could only make out the jumbled excited sound of arguing, mostly in French. I had met Barbara many times before at my Grandparent's house, 'Bluebells', Fairfield Crescent and I didn't really like her, probably because Grandad seemed to dislike her so much. I had also overheard Ron discussing her with an unknown man just before we had left for Scotland.

I had listened intently, without either of their knowledge, as they talked about Barbara being in a small sports car with an Italian historian boyfriend and one of his colleagues, somewhere in Scotland...

"And they were both killed in the crash?" Grandad seemed surprised.

"Yep, and she walked away, untouched, not a scratch! These are the details of the two men and what they were both working on at the time, I think you'll be interested to read that." I could not see this man. Just hear his deep voice.

"Anything else?" Ron enquired.

"Well Barbara was not her real name, it was Maurice Cruiseau, Guy Wilthew met her during one of the political meetings he'd been attending a few years before he died…"

"No, I'm sorry, I can't find much of anything on 30AU and nothing at all on team thirteen, seems they all but vanished, no records, none of the names you gave to me have led me anywhere. I can't even tell if they came back from Germany, one or two mentions of James Besond, sorry..ermm.. Jim Besant in the archives, but not a lot."

"I wonder why? Thanks mate." I could see the unknown man's hand as he firmly shook Grandad's hand and then left.

I had also learned from my Nan that apparently Barbara had also been with her brother when he had been killed on his motorcycle, when it had hit a tractor at night, with no lights on and driven by a fourteen year old boy.

I remembered back to one of Barbara's last unexpected visits at 'Bluebells'. She always called the grandchildren 'Mon Petit Chou' (my little cabbage? - a term of endearment? Or a reference to the fact she thought she was more knowledgeable than us in some way, that we were her small vegetables?), and insisted that we crawl on all fours on each of her visits to 'test' our intelligence. My Nan had always seemed to enjoy her company, with their shared language and family history. Margot also enjoyed telling all us grandchildren about Barbara's origins from a small Pacific island inhabited solely by cannibals (*I now wonder if that could have been the reason she considered us small vegetables?*). This only added to the general family distrust of this unusual woman who practised Tai Chi naked in the bathroom with the door unlocked! (*Not an image a small boy needs as he is growing up*).

During that visit I had happened upon two large Nazi German flags tucked away in a small space under the stairs and when Nan, Margot, had seen them she'd nearly exploded, for that matter so had Barbara. In fact the whole house had erupted in one of the largest rows I could remember and that was saying something in that household. Things only seemed to settle once Nan had taken the flags into an alley that ran alongside the small semi-detached house, and burnt them. I'd been very upset, the discovery of the captured wartime flags had been a precious moment and along with my other Grandfather *(My Dad's Dad, Fred. A martial arts expert who served with the Royal Berkshires in Burma)* who had a German Luger with live rounds, had started my youthful fascination with all things military. *(I grew out of it)* & *(He sold it)*.

But now, on this holiday morning in the highlands of Scotland, my mind was still really only on one thing. Commandos. Gulping down my breakfast of porridge oats and deciding I could not wait for the age it seemed to take the rest of the family to finish their row and get ready for the day out.

"Nan, I'm going to go and play outside, until everyone is ready to go. Is that okay?" Nan was screaming in French, trying to placate Ron and busy doing the breakfast and looking after everyone, as always.

I grabbed my favourite coat, a camouflaged army coat, which hung by the back door and left quietly. The blue skies of yesterday had disappeared and the early morning was dull grey and overcast with a light drizzle that seemed to make everything even more soaked through than it would if it had actually been raining. But I barely noticed it, I was a Commando with a warm and full stomach and on a mission, a mission that had to succeed. I pulled out the Swiss Army knife that I had nagged and begged for, for so long, and which I'd finally been given on my last birthday, along with stern and strict warnings about what would happen if it were abused. I began to practise the few small knife-fighting movements that I had been shown by Grandad the previous evening in front of the log fire.

I headed up the muddy, stone strewn track that led away from the back of the croft and into the hills.

A large paw print in the mud of the track drew my attention. Our dog, Husky couldn't have made it. It was too small for Husky's paw and the claw marks were way too long and slender. It must have been a Scottish wildcat footprint. Nan had often told me stories about these large ferocious cats that roamed the Highlands of Scotland and I remembered the family pet, Moutmout a domestic/wildcat crossbreed that once fully grown had gone wild in the woods of Eastwood. I would track these prints.

They were easy to follow along the lane for a long way ahead, but became much more difficult to make out when they left the lane and headed between huge boulders that had tumbled from the mountains above, who knows how many years before, into a deep trough in the hills made by the stream which flowed from the mossy ground of the lower slopes that proceeded the main mountain. The prints skirted the edge of a stream and headed into the pines of the forest. Two, red, smallish deer suddenly sprang into view, easily leaping high into the air and over one of the many dry stonewalls that crisscrossed the hills. They disappeared into the thick pines.

Small but loud waterfalls tumbled and cascaded between the boulders making a deep tree lined gorge which swept down into the valley below. The spray from the waterfalls soaked my clothes through thoroughly, but I was oblivious to the discomfort. Looking up at the sky above the nearest waterfall it appeared to me that two small leafless trees were moving up and towards the edge of the wet moss green rocks. A large dark shape continued to come into view always moving upwards, its antlers stark against the low grey cloud. It was a huge silhouetted Stag, standing proud, looking to the horizon. I watched it for an age, mesmerised by its stillness and calm. Eventually and slowly it moved away.

Distracted by the discovery of a large and complete Stag's skeleton and skull I had lost the tracks of the wildcat but had then became exhilarated and thrilled by the climbing of the rocky banks next to tumbling waterfalls, I easily climbed two or three. Maybe I could try out the fist handhold to climb the third or forth rock face stood in the way.

It really did work, I clambered up highest rock face so far, only realising once I was near the top just how high it had actually been. I began to think that maybe I should not have climbed so high, but I knew I could not go backwards now, that would be dangerous, I had to finish the climb.

My breathing was heavy as I pulled myself to standing on the top of the rocks. I turned to look at the wonderful view, right over into the next valley. The sun was beginning to break through the low cloud in a magnificent sunrise above the distant mountains.

A rabbit came into his focus, only a short distance away. It was totally motionless. I was amazed I had not seen it earlier, but its grey fur seemed to blend so perfectly with the green of the grass around it. I too remained as still as I could, trying hard to subdue my heavy breath, with eyes fixed on the rabbit.

Time seemed to wait, expectantly.

I became aware of a tiny movement in the rocks to my left, again only a few feet away. A huge, reddish, tabby cat. It was at least double the size of our pet cat Fluffy. It was a Scottish wildcat, its ears pressed flat, with its eyes riveted on the rabbit. As I watched it, I noticed those sharp yellow eyes flick up to the tree above and to the right. Slowly rotating just my eyes, right, and up to the twisted, gnarled, moss covered leafless tree above. The biggest bird I had ever seen in my life, golden brown plumage, bright golden eyes twinkling in the breaking sunlight. The curve of its black hooked beak and massive talons were the most impressive things I had ever seen. It was magnificent, *(it started my life long fascination with eagles)*. It too had eyes firmly fixed on the motionless rabbit in front of me.

The golden eagle moved first, massive wings, feather fingers spread, uncurled from its body as it dropped downwards from the tree. Legs and talons outstretched. The wildcat darted forward a split second later. The rabbit seemed to run in a complete and tight circle in its panic to escape. The glinting claws of the wildcat were first to strike, the rabbit actually screamed as the claws sank home. I stepped back and stumbled from the wet slippery rock I stood on. Well aware of how close I was to the edge of the drop.

The eagle's talons were now also buried deep into the rabbits flesh as it tried to lift the combined weight of rabbit and wildcat back into the air. The wildcat did not want to release its grip or maybe it could not retract its claws enough to let go and the eagle could certainly not carry the weight of both.

They crashed back to the ground all three animals let out high-pitched screams and hisses. The wildcat released its grip immediately the eagle lashed its beak toward it and at the same moment with a powerful beat of wings the eagle rose majestically into the air carrying away its prize with a victory call that echoed around the valley in the unmistakable way only eagle calls can do.

Silence and calm returned. Silence only broken by my own sobs. I suddenly felt very cold, very wet and very scared. I was wet down to my skin and shivering uncontrollably from both the cold and fear. Looking about through tear filled eyes I realised I was completely lost. I only knew that I could not go back the way I had come. Heading down the easiest slope in front of me. Trying to clear my eyes and stifle my sobs. I did not feel very much like a Commando anymore. A few stumbles later I heard the distant calls of my name from Grandad's large barrel chest. When I came face to face with Ron I burst out crying. Running into his outstretched arms I hugged my face into Ron's warm jumper covered midriff.

"Where on earth have you been? We are all out looking for you." Ron tried hard to control his own emotions.

"I'm …sorry …Grandad, …I …I…got…lost." I managed to sob out in fits.

Quote from Admiralty S.W. Official History of 30AU.

"Considered as a whole, these operations had been successful in the extreme. 30AU operating in the front line or ahead of the general advance, had penetrated the most closely guarded secrets of the German Navy and had seized not only the major part of its key personnel, but also all of its archives. The early promise of the Unit had been abundantly fulfilled and all commitments had been discharged."

Top: **Family Guy**- Ron, Frank(Snr), Dorothy, Frank.
Left: Ron Guy, Royal Marine, CHX3209.
Right: Taken at same time as pictures for use on forged papers if captured.
Bottom: 'Hairyarsed-Bootneck' Guy, third left front.
('Spike' Kelly, first left top, and at least one more went on to 30AU.)

...al Marines, 413th King's Squad (Passed for Duty Saturday, June 5th, 1943)

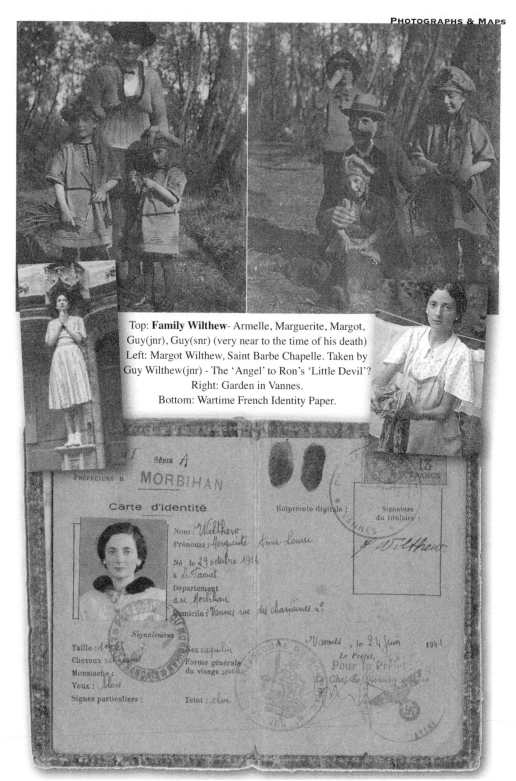

Top: **Family Wilthew**- Armelle, Marguerite, Margot,
Guy(jnr), Guy(snr) (very near to the time of his death)
Left: Margot Wilthew, Saint Barbe Chapelle. Taken by
Guy Wilthew(jnr) - The 'Angel' to Ron's 'Little Devil'?
Right: Garden in Vannes.
Bottom: Wartime French Identity Paper.

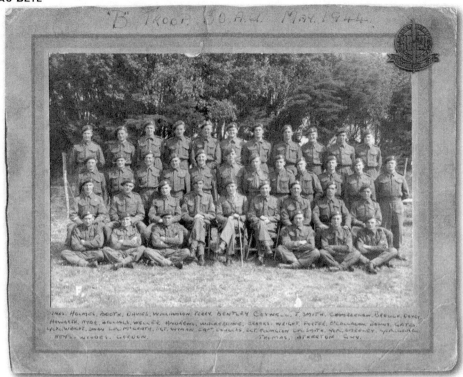

30AU/B Troop - Ron Guy - RM. Bottom right. On first night ashore, D+2 near St. Mere Eglise, three of these men were killed and fourteen wounded by Antipersonnel bombs. (Five killed and twenty wounded in total)

Sniper Course - Ron Guy - RM/30AU. Top left.

The President
OF THE UNITED STATES OF AMERICA
has directed me to express to

MARGUERITE WILTHEW

the gratitude and appreciation of the
American people for gallant service
in assisting the escape of Allied
soldiers from the enemy

DWIGHT D. EISENHOWER
General of the Army
Commanding General United States Forces European Theater

Certificate of gratitude signed by Dwight D. Eisenhower for Margot's assistance in helping
Allied airman evade capture during World War Two.

Left: Vannes France. Armelle, Margot, Guy Wilthew.
Right: Le Faouët St Barbe Fountaine trail, France. Marguerite, Margot, Guy, Armelle Wilthew.

Left: Margot, Guy Wilthew. Right: Vannes France. Guy Wilthew before occupation sits in contemplation under
his childhood portrait painted by his father, Guy Wilthew. Which still hangs there!

Left: Vannes France. Margot in her bedroom on her sister Armelle's Wedding Day.
Right: Vannes France. Margot talented classical piantist. These rooms are unchanged.
Below: On a trip to Lourdes? Many of the Le Luexhe family dedicated their lives to religion. Armelle front seat, Margot behind the wheel.
Bottom: Vannes France. Preist, in apartment that the Cathederal (opposite house), rented from Marguerite Wilthew, with her daughters, Armelle and Margot.

Photos by Guy Wilthew(Jnr)

HEADQUARTERS
EUROPEAN THEATER OF OPERATIONS
P/W and X Detachment
Military Intelligence Service

REPORT FOR THE ADJUTANT GENERAL'S OFFICE

Robert George BENNETT, 2d Lt, O-669984			5 September 1944
(Name)	(Rank)	ASN	(Date)
388 Bomb Group, 563 Bomb Squadron			MIS 1403
(Unit			

		MEMBERS OF CREW		PRESENT OFFICIAL STATUS
PILOT	O-794871	1st Lt Alfred (NMI) KRAMER	RTD	RTD
CO-PILOT	O-675846	2d Lt Arthur M SWAP	RTD	RTD
NAVIGATOR	O-673849	2d Lt Richard Leon BOWMAN	MIA	MIA
BOMBARDIER	O-669984	2d Lt Robert George BENNETT	RTD	RTD
RADIO OPERATOR	36246275	T/Sgt Allan J FRIESS	RTD	RTD
TOP TURRET GUNNER	15105596	T/Sgt Eugene Noel ERWIN	KIA	MIA
BALL TURRET GUNNER	15062895	S/Sgt Joseph Max THOMAS	KIA	KIA
WAIST GUNNER	33285194	S/Sgt William Herman VICKLESS	RTD	RTD
WAIST GUNNER	36221108	S/Sgt Walter Raymond SOUKUP	RTD	RTD
TAIL GUNNER	32170982	S/Sgt William Warren CHAPMAN	MIA	MIA

Date, time and approximate location of plane crash or landing.
6 September 1943 - 1000 hours - The plane crashed 25 miles E of Troyes, France

Nature and extent of damage to plane when source bailed out. Was it on fire, etc?
Exact damage unknown. The nose and cockpit was on fire and pilots instruments destroyed.

At approximately what altitude did source bail out?
20,000 feet

Were any of the crew injured or killed before the plane crashed?
BOWMAN the navigator and Bennett were both injured before jumping.

What members of the crew bailed out? Did their parachutes open?
All the crew jumped and all parachutes believed opened.

Did the plane explode on striking the ground?
No - but it finished burning.

Did source see any other members of the crew dead or alive after reaching the
ground? I saw Kramer, Vickless and Chapman. I heard about all others except Bowman and Swap

Did he receive any information from others as to whether any other members of the crew were dead or alive? If so, give details furnished by his informant and whether the other crew members were identified by name or otherwise.
Bowman and Swap were never seen after jumping. A body believed to be Joe Thomas was found near the plane, dead. All others were known to be safe and they shipped after
Did source examine the wreckage of the plane? reaching Troyes

If the plane crashed in water how far was the plane from land and by what means was source rescued and what life rafts, wreckage, etc., remained on the surface that would have assisted other personnel to keep afloat.

What is source's opinion as to the fate of the other crew members and his reason for his opinion?
I knew that all the member that landed safely were handled by the underground and were sent to various places to hide.

MACR 3129 summary sheet from report for B17F Lone Wolf 42-30222, 8th AF 388th BG 563rd BS.
They lost all eleven aircraft of their Squadron on 6th September 1943 on bombing run to Stuttgart. The 388th Bomber Group was based at Knettishall, Norfolk. England. In the Casualty Questionnaire opposite, Arthur Swap says he was told that Joe was killed after landing, other eye-witness reports and forms filled out by crew members say that it happened in the air and that he was not the only one to be fired at while descending on parachute

AFPPA-12

3127

CASUALTY QUESTIONNAIRE

1. Your name __Swap, Arthur M.__ Rank __Captain__ Serial No. __O-675646__
   Wm. B.   Francis J.
2. Organization __383th__ Op Commander __David__ Rank __Col.__ Sqn CO __Hennagier__ Rank __Lt Col__
   (full name)   (full name)
3. What year __1943__ month __September__ day __6__ did you go down?
4. What was the mission, __Stuttgart Germany__ , target, __ball-bearing plant__ , target
   time, __approx. 10:30 a.m.__ , altitude, __21,000 feet__ route scheduled, _____
   _____ , route flown _____
5. Where were you when you left formation? __about 40 miles Southwest of Strasbourg, Germany.__
6. Did you bail out? __Yes__
7. Did other members of crew bail out? __Yes - all members bailed out.__
8. Tell all you know about when, where, how each person in your aircraft for whom no
   individual questionnaire is attached bailed out. A crew list is attached. Please
   give facts. If you don't know, say: "No Knowledge". __All members of the crew__
   __bailed out before I bailed out.__
9. Where did your aircraft strike the ground? __About 10 miles Northeast of Troyes, France.__
10. What members of your crew were in the aircraft when it struck the ground? (Should
    cross check with 8 above and individual questionnaires) __None__
11. Where were they in aircraft? __xxxx__
12. What was their condition? __xxxx__
13. When, where, and in what condition did you __last__ see any members not already des-
    cribed above? __I met all but four of the crew, two of which were taken prisoner.__
    __I was told by the French people that S/Sgt Joseph Thomas was straffed by an__
    __enemy fighter upon landing, and was killed. Since liberation of German held__
    __prisoners of war I have been in contact with all members of my crew, except the__
    __above mentioned.__

(Any additional information may be written on the back)

that day. Thirteen other airmen were killed nearby.
Map showing planned route to target for 563rd Bomber Squadron mission to bomb Stuttgart.
This crew were on their 9th such mission and it was 388th Bomber Groups 19th mission.
The German fighter pilot was Horst Sternberg (Black 13) FW190 Focke Wulf with 23 victories.

United States
8th Air Force

388th
Bomber Group

563rd
Bomber Squadron
B17F Lone Wolf
42-30222

November 1943. Vannes, France. American Airmen whose B17F Lone Wolf was shot down near Paris after bombing raid on Stuttgart factory, hiding in Rue de Chanoines. Copilot Arthur M Swap & Sgt William H Vickless, transported back to Lands End, England with nineteen other airmen in a French lobster boat.

August 1944. The very day Ron and Margot met, in an orchard near Vannes France.
'Love at first sight' - Cpl.Gates, Monique, Cpl.Swann, Wilthew, Guy. (Photos by Armelle Wilthew)

Right: August 1944. Vannes France. Ron Guy, Margot Wilthew, Cpl. 'Ganger' Gates. Left: On one knee?

Left: May/June 1945. Minden Germany. Flynn, Guy, Cpl.Smedley, Rush, Higgins - B-troop.
Right: May 45 Neumünster Radio HQ Germany. Guy, Cpl.Webber, Reed, Jemmett, McMullon - A-troop.

149

The liberation of Vannes, Morbihan, Bretagne (Brittany), France in the summer of 1944.
Of note:- The SAS wings on the side of Jeep (left) and the three Vickers 'K' rapidfire machine guns on
'La Vengense' (far right). 4th Special Air Service. The Free French of 2e Régiment de Chasseurs Parachutistes.
Taken by Armelle or Margot on one of Guy Wilthew's cameras.

30AU did try to avoid what it considered to be the 'retarding' influence of T-force, although all three were involved most notably in the mission to capture Helmuth Walter, at the north German port town of Keil in May 1945. The Walterwerkes factory were involved in the design and manufacture of the Me163 Komet Rocket plane powered by T-Stoff fuel and also midget submarines and torpedoes amongst much else.

30 [Commando] Assault Unit, Royal Marine Officers, Littlehampton, May 1944.

Lt. G.H.Bailey, Capt. C.R.Lambe, Capt G.Pike, Capt. H.O.Huntington-Whiteley, Capt.R.Douglas, Lt. M.Ryder.

Capt. J.Hargreaves-Heap, Mjr. A.Evans, Col. A.R.Wooley, Capt. K.G.MacGregor, Capt. C.H.Cunningham.

30 [Commando] Assault Unit, B troop, Guildford. January 1945.

Allmark, Howeth, Spurrells, Heys, Hyde, McGregor, Bonny, Wright, Woolcock, Surrey, Cole.

Telford, Rush, Kelly, Manning, Billings, Walkerdine, Pearce, Flynn, Hewitt, Cairns, Lees, Chasty, Gates.

Cpl Muffett, Cpl Godsell, Sgt Kellaway, CSgt Whyman, Capt Lessing, Sgt Harry Smith, Sgt Causley, Cpl Swann, Cpl Poyser.

Taylor, Andrews, L/Cpl Smedley, Cpl Roberts, Jones, Cpl Hutton, LCpl Brough, Williamson, Darwin, Burgoine.

30 [Commando] Assault Unit, A troop, Littlehampton. April 1944.

Freeman, Richmond, Halton, _____?, Owens, Shaw, _____?, _____?, Feeley, _____?, Fischer, Underwood, Byron.

Hedges, Beetlestone, _____?, Townsend, Burgoine, _____?, Bennet, Powell, MacGregor, Gibson, Marshall, Impett, Plaxton, Collis.

Cpl.Connolly, Cpl.Burns, Cpl.Hickling, Sgt Clapson, Cpt. Huntingdon-Whiteley, Sgt.Brereton, Cpl.Auton, Cpl.Watson, Cpl. Goodwin.

Burns, _____Cpl. Booth, _____Brown.

30 [Commando] Assault Unit, X troop, Littlehampton. Spring 1944.

Smudge Smith, Jack Twist, _____?, _____?, _____?, Don Cook, _____?, Welbourne

_____?, McKelvey, _____?, Donald King, Harrison, Sgt. Bob Burchell, Butch Burnett, Ron Simms, _____?, McGrath.

Edwards, Foster, Sgt. Lund, Capt. Pike, Muffet, Taff Edwards, Wilkins.

Harris, Crowe, _____?, Gibbs, Fred Farringdon, Bob Brooks, Bill Powell.

30AU - Navalwing (36), Eckenförde, Germany. December 1945.
This photo was taken in the Christmas of 1945 at the Nazi Torpedo and Submarine testing facility that 30AU had captured. The men of the Navalwing & scientists were there for many months uncovering all the secrets of the German Navy from within the base and also from many of the 'scuttled' vessels in the bay, (including a submarine loaded with 'treasures' apparently. I wonder where they went?).
The main Naval Officer, Patrick Dalzel -Job that Fleming reportedly used as the basis for his most famous character, had already taken the two Marines assigned to him and their Jeep and left for Norway to find his sweetheart that he had met while on other clandestine operations before joining with 30AU - See *'Artic Snow to Dust of Normandy'* - his memoirs.

30.A.U.

___?____?____?____?____?____?____?____?____?____?____?____?____?____?____?____?____?

___?____?____?____?____?____?____?____?____?____?____?____?____?____?____?

____?____?____?   ____?____?____?____?'Spike' Kelly____?____?____?____?____?____?____?____?

___?____?____?____?J Besant____?____?____?____?____?____?____?____?____?

___?____?____?

___?____?____?____?____?____?____?

Nº ADVANCED UNIT   S E C R E T

Copy No. ....30.......

(R.M. WING ADM. INSTR. No.10.)

PROVISIONAL FORMATION OF FIELD TEAMS

1. OBJECT

   To provide 6 field teams for operations which may all be out at the
same time or be employed in relays.

2. DUTIES

(a)   Lieut. Cdr. P. Postlethwaite RNE RNVR
        Captain H.G. Nicholl, R.M.
        3 Scientists
        Lieut .... USN
        1. M.O.A.
        Mne Melton
        No.1. Section "A" Tp.

(b)   Lieut T.J. Glanville RNVR
        Lieut J.W. Rose R.M.
        3 Scientists
        Lieut Dreeker USN
        1. M.O.A.
        Mne Booth
        No.2. Sec "A" Tp.

(c)   Cdr. D.M.C. Curtis DSC RNVR
        T.S.M. J. Brereton(RM Offr.)
        3 Scientists
        Lieut Lunzer RCNVR
        1. M.O.A.
        Mne Higgs
        No. 3 Sec "A" Tp.

(d)   Lieut. Cdr. Harling RNVR
        Lieut. N.M. Brooks R.M.
        3 Scientists
        Lieut Connel RNVR
        1. M.O.A.
        1. W.R.N.
        No.4. Sec "B" Tp.

(e)   Lieut. J. Besant RNVR
        T.S.M. Wynan (RM Offr)
        Captain Wheeler R.M.(F.I.U.)
        3 Scientists
        1. M.O.A.
        Mne Marshall
        No.5. Section "B" Tp.

(f)   Lieut.Cdr. G.G. Turner RNVR
        Captain J.A. Ward R.A.(R.M. Offr.)
        3 Scientists
        Lieut. Cdr. Izzard RNVR
        1. M.O.A.
        1. W.R.N.
        No. 6 Section "B" Tp.

List of six 30AU 'Field Teams' containing some names that were mentioned within my Grandad's scribbles and also the name of J. Besant that had stuck in my mind because when I had heard it as a boy the unknown man had related it to '*James Bond*'. I found the original documents in the National Archives after coming across some poor photocopies at *The Marine* public house, Littlehampton.

Page one from 30AU Target List - Ian Fleming's 'Black List'- headed 'Rockets'.
Top of the list:- Hans von Braun, Engineer at Peenemünde. Hans was probably used in absence of more accurate information at that time, the reference to their father confirms it was relating to the brothers.
Below: The necessity for *'eliminating witnesses'* to successful action and the demolition of the building or ship!? An order for the men of 30AU to be required to 'murder' in the name of their country?

(1)   The customary priorities for secret documents remain in force. These are:

First   – Chefsache, Geheime Kommando Sache.
Second   – Geheim, Nuer Fuer Den Dienstgebrauch.
Third   – Any other documents.

Should any first priority materiel be discovered, an Officer or Senior N.C.O. should be detailed immediately to break off operations and ensure its safe arrival in the Admiralty.

The necessity for avoiding or eliminating witnesses to successful action and for the demolition of any building or ship's cabin which has yielded results and which is likely to be re-occupied by the enemy is emphasized.

(2)   It is important to ensure that every scrap of paper, including ashes, used blotting pads, carbon paper, the contents of waste paper baskets and odd pieces of paper which may be found concealed under furniture, behind maps or mirrors, etc. should be collected and forwarded to the Admiralty. It is also necessary to ensure that all codes, books and cyphers should be kept dry, as water causes the text to disappear.

Care should be taken to see that troops do not meddle or play with any ENIGMA machines which may be captured. It is easy to break the setting of the machine by playing on the keys or altering the plug-ins or junction boxes.

signature of General KEITEL, forbidding the destruction of
documents or equipment after 0800 on May 5th. In the
circumstances, the party under Commander CURTIS showed
exemplary tact, since the total of 30 A.U., "T" force and the
S.A.S. regiment amounted to no more than 500 men while the
strength of the German forces in KIEL was at least 25,000.
Apart from an incident in which a Royal Marine N.C.O. rough
handled a German Officer (the conduct of the Royal Marine was
subsequently held to be justified) the surrender was taken
smoothly and efficiently.

~~49. Although all secret papers had been destroyed, much~~
information was obtained from Officers, Technicians and
Scientists in the area. This was due to the German High
Command having surrendered unconditionally, and to their
having issued orders that all secrets were to be divulged to
the Allies. Otherwise the standstill would have had serious
~~consequences indeed from the intelligence point of view.~~

~~50. A party under Lieut. Commander POSTLETHWAITE seized~~
the T.V.A. at ECKERNFORDE ~~and set up a subsidiary~~ headquarters
~~in the middle of the three testing ranges.~~

55. Soon after the *final* surrender *on May 8th* a party under Commander (E) AYLEN
arrived to conduct the exploitation of the WALTHERWERKE,
where teams from all the intelligence agencies in the
European theatre sent representatives to watch the reconstruction
of the various secret weapons which were being developed on the
basis of the WALTHER systems of propulsion. These included
the U-boats, Types XVII B and XXVI, Torpedoes Types TVII,
TVIII and others in a purely experimental stage, the HATTER
(anti-aircraft rocket bomb) the rocket propelled fighter
plane (Me 262) as well as a number of projects which were
only in the early stages of development.

56. Later representatives arrived from most of the
technical Divisions of the Admiralty especially from D.T.M.(I),
to examine the materiel captured in the KIEL district and to
conduct interrogations of the key personnel. For this
purpose interpreters were provided by F.I.U., officers from
this organization having accompanied 30 A.U. throughout the operation. All the personnel concerned in this work, except for
the U.S. Officers who were billetted with "T" force, were
accommodated and victualled in the 30 A.U. headquarters in
the WALTHERWERKE and the T.V.A.

57. In the meantime Team 5 under Lieut. LAMBIE was
following up the clues it had picked up around HANOVER. On
April 23rd the party started for the HARZ area and proceeded
first to STEINA. Here Prof. WAGNER was captured and from
him a substantial number of documents and much information
relating to the design and production of V-Weapons were
obtained. Altogether twenty six targets in the HARZ district
were investigated, much intelligence material of extreme
value recovered, the more important items being the
following:-

   (a) at BLANKENBURG, HARZ, working drawings of the U-boats
        types XXI and XXIII, together with full information,
        supported by original documents, relating to the
        GLUECKAUF organization and the programme for the
        assembly of U-boat hulls from prefabricated segments.

   (b) in an underground store in the HARZ mountains, specimens,
        in working order, of the latest German radar equipment

/and.......

National Archive Documents pertaining to the 'History of 30AU'. These two pages outline the capture of
Prof. Herbert Wagner designer of the Henschel Hs293 guided glide bomb, already used by the Germans to sink
HMS Egret and transport ship HMT Rohna, killing over 1000 troops. This account pinpoints his capture to
Steina which is NE of Dresden and a very considerable way behind the frontline at that time. There were other
accounts that gave Prof. H. Wagner's location as Blankenburg in the Harz Mountains, both of which were in
the Russian Sector. This fact would explain why the Allies then flew him to Bavaria, alongside one of the von
Braun's to the 'Staged Surrender' for the world's media to record as 'fact' which then enabled them to deny

Southern Germany and Austria. The team, as reformed, consisted of Lieut. Commander GLANVILLE (in command) Lieut. Commander (E) HAYNES, Lieut. BESANT and 5 Royal Marines, transported by a jeep, a Chevrolet armoured car and a 15 cwt. truck. This party started for STUTTGART on April 12th, having first to call at N.T.S. G.2. S.H.A.E.F. in order to obtain clearance from VI Army Group, no reply having been received by Formation H.Q. to repeated enquiries on this account.

32. By April 10th, the strength of the Unit was therefore disposed as follows:-

Team 4	–	with the Guards Armoured Division, destined for the capture of BREMEN.
" 5	–	to cover HANOVER and then to proceed to BREMEN.
" 6	–	to remain with the Canadian Armoured Division; to follow that formation to its eventual destination.
" 7	–	to cover EMDEN with the Polish Armoured Brigade.
" 8	–	to cover Western Holland.
" 10	–	to cover HAMBURG and all points East.
" 55	–	(Lieut. Commander GLANVILLE's team) to cover the evacuation areas in the south.

"X" troop which had been training in the U.K. for an airborne operation against KIEL, which was not now to take place, crossed to the continent on April 9th, and immediately moved up to an advanced H.Q. at OSNABRUCK. It was thought at this time that BREMEN would be the first port to fall and that it would be a convenient place for the Unit to rally and from which the field teams could move forward. In this case "X" troop would relieve "B" troop as the Royal Marine element in teams 4, 5 and 10. When it became apparent that the general advance would pass by BREMEN, this port was left to Team 4, leaving Team 10, with the whole of "X" troop free to press on to HAMBURG and, eventually, to KIEL.

34. A further change in plans was caused by the discovery at HANOVER by Team 5, under Lieut. LAMBIE, of a number of clues leading to the HARZ mountains, which, it was now evident, was a dispersal area for Naval objectives evacuated from the North. In these circumstances Lieut. LAMBIE received a new directive to take his team as quickly as possible to BLANKENBERG (HARZ), despite the fact that this town was in the area of XII Army Group.

35. On April 22, Team 10 (Commander CURTIS) and "X" troop played an important part in the capture of BUXTEHUDE. This was the first purely Naval Intelligence target to be captured in this area. On April 26th, Team 4 (Lieut. Commander JOB), having pressed on ahead of the general advance, were the first troops to enter BREMEN and accepted the surrender of the town from the acting Burgomaster. The team also captured a NARVIK class destroyer which was lying in the harbour. This yielded some interesting documents.

36. On April 29th a new disposition of forces was made. Team 10, with "X" troop and some other Naval Officers joined the S.A.S. Regiment for the crossing of the ELBE and the exploitation of the LUEBECK area. Team 8 was to transfer

/from.....

the Russians their rights according to the Yalta Agreement. (See Maps, P.169). Prof. Wagner went on to a long career in the USA working for their Navy weapons division. These pages are in stark contrast to the 'Historically Recorded' version of events, which according to media film footage and Tom Bower's *The Paperclip Conspiracy* has all of these Nazi scientists happily 'Surrendering' to the Americans rather than being snatched from their family homes by highly trained teams of commandos who were 'Licenced to Kill' witnesses. (See P.157). I think this list of teams is far from complete.

Louis Marie Le Leuxhe with wife and twelve of their fifteen children.
Alphonse second from left. Marguerite Wilthew on fathers lap.

Louis Marie Le Leuxhe. 1847-1896.
French Imperial Court painter, who resigned his
commission in protest at the decadent life style
his employers led. Died while adjusting the clock
on the covered market in Le Faouët.

Alphonse Le Leuxhe. 1880-1914.
Painted by Guy Wilthew.
Louis son, an extremely talented artist himself, was
killed by the Germans in the first few days of World
War One.

Le Faouët covered market square. Painted by Guy Wilthew.

Le Faouët, Le Luexhe family home. (Louis died at the clock in the covered market in 1896. Opposite, left.) Guy Wilthew rented Louis studio in 1898 and fell in love with his daughter, Marguerite, one of fifteen children. Guy and Marguerite took on the house and raised their own three children (Guy, Armelle and Margot) there until Guy's early death of suspected TB or possibly Spanish Flu in 1920. Marguerite Wilthew, wore black and mourned his passing for the rest of her life. When Margot was ten they moved to Vannes to be nearer family friends and a better education.

Guy Wilthew. English aristocrat.
Portrait Artist.
Travelled to Le Faouët and fell in love, not only
with the natural light and landscape but also with
the young daughter of a local artist.

Marguerite Wilthew neé Le Leuxhe.
Painted by Guy Wilthew.
Depicting her deciding between a life dedicated to the
church or whether to accept Guy's proposal of
marriage, as symbolised by the sowing kit. (Unseen).

Marguerite Wilthew.
Unfinished study by Guy Wilthew.
(Unseen by English side of family until visit to
Vannes in April 2007)

Marguerite Wilthew. Unfinished study by Guy Wilthew.
The only painting Margot had of her mother at Bluebells.

Marguerite and Barbe Le Leuxhe by Guy Wilthew. This painting is huge and just stunning!
(Unseen by English side of family until visit to Vannes in April 2007)

**Guy and Marguerite Wilthew,
with their child.**
I think this must be the studio that Guy
originally rented from the widow of Louis-
Marie when he first met the family in Le
Faouët at the turn of the century.
(Unseen by English side of family until
visit to Vannes in April 2007)

Margot Wilthew at Saint Barbe Chapelle
(A truly spiritual place) by Guy Wilthew (Jnr).
The 'Angel' to Ron's 'Little Devil'?

Saint Fiacre Chapelle by Guy Wilthew. (Unseen)
(A painting I find myself transfixed by)

Saint Barbe Fountaine and trail
by Alphonse Le Leuxhe. (Unseen)

Bénitier de l'église Saint Fiacre Chapelle Font
by Guy Wilthew 1914.
The painting that brought to mind the Clogs in
Bluebells Kitchen.
Middle: Barbe Le Leuxhe by Guy Wilthew.

Ron & Margot Guy with their first born, Gwen named after Vannes (Breton: Gwened) my mother.

Mag, Ronny, Margot, Kathy, Margot and Gwen with Rosie on the way. Near Bluebells, with Bluebells.

Ron Guy by Margot Guy.
With Commando dagger in hand. This used to hang in the hall at Bluebells, but only now have I guessed it may have been inspired by General Pattons unofficial name for 30AU 'A bunch of limey Pirates' the nick name he gave them when he first ran into the 'Special Authorisation' orders.

Ron Guy by Margot Guy.
The first sketch of which was started during the liberation of France on the kitbag canvas, although this is not the portrait that was completed on that canvas. Entitled 'Beau Bête' (Beautiful but Stupid Beast) the nick name Madame Wilthew gave Ron Guy upon their first meeting.

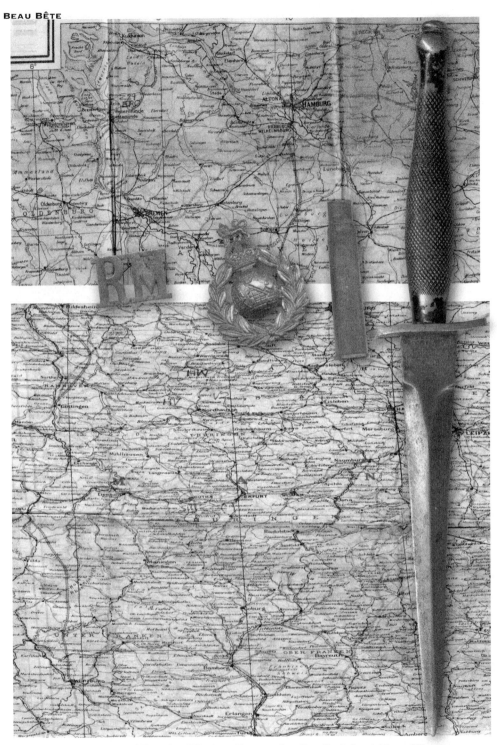

Small sections of Central and Northern Germany from Ron Guy's Special Issue Silk
Escape Maps, found hidden in attic at 'Bluebells' along with Ron & Margot's treasured love letters,
F-S Fighting Knife (pattern1-type2) and these badges and 404 casing.

IN MEMORY OF
MEMBERS OF THE 30 AU
WHO LEFT LITTLEHAMPTON
ON SPECIAL OPERATIONS
DURING WORLD WAR II
AND FAILED TO RETURN

Above: Words by Mr. R. Rush, RM 30AU.
Right: Site of Beach Hotel, 30AU HQ behind.
Below: Plaque on *The Marine* public house.

ARUN DISTRICT COUNCIL
30 ASSAULT UNIT
Secret intelligence-gathering
Royal Marine and Royal Navy
Unit, that took part in the D-Day
landings of 1944 during the second
World War, frequented this Public
House. Former members of
The 30 Assault Unit use
'The Marine' as a base
for their annual
reunion

10th AUGUST 1997
TO COMMEMORATE THE
30 ASSAULT UNIT,
ROYAL MARINES, (30 AURM)
WHO OPERATED FROM THIS SITE
(THE FORMER BEACH HOTEL)
FOR A PERIOD OF TIME
DURING WORLD WAR 2
'WE WILL REMEMBER THEM'

GUY WILTHEW
1870-1920
MARGUERITE WILTHEW
1883-1950
REQUIESCAT IN PACE

GOD BLESS
MARGUERITE ANNE LOUISE GUY
NEÉ WILTHEW
29. 10. 1916 – 30. 5. 2000.
A COURAGEOUS, COMPASSIONATE,
LOVING WIFE, MUM AND NAN.
FOREVER IN OUR HEARTS.
À BIENTÔT OUR BELOVED MARGOT.
ROLAND GEORGE GUY
(RON)
28 MAY 1925 – 5 JANUARY 2006
A LOVING HUSBAND, DAD AND GRANDAD
EVER PROUD OF HIS FAMILY.
PHILOSOPHICAL, BRAVE FIGHTER OF ADVERSITY
ENSEMBLE TOUJOURS.

Le Faouët, France.   Essex, England.   167

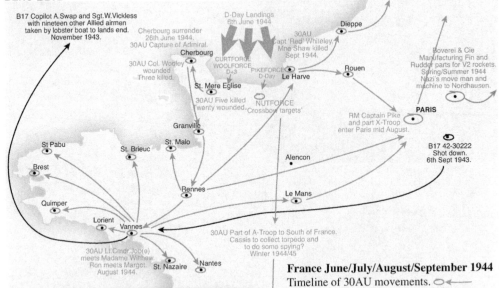

B17 Copilot A.Swap and Sgt.W.Vickless with nineteen other Allied airmen taken by lobster boat to lands end. November 1943.

D-Day Landings 6th June 1944

Dieppe

Cherbourg surrender 26th June 1944. 30AU Capture of Admiral.

30AU Capt 'Red' Whiteley. Mne Shaw killed Sept 1944.

Cherbourg

30AU Col. Wooley wounded Three killed.

CURTFORCE WOOLFORCE D+3

PIKEFORCE D-Day Le Harve

Rouen

Boverei & Cie Manufacturing Fin and Rudder parts for V2 rockets. Spring/Summer 1944 Nazi's move man and machine to Nordhausen.

St. Mere Eglise

30AU Five killed twenty wounded.

NUTFORCE 'Crossbow' targets'

RM Captain Pike and part X-Troop enter Paris mid August.

PARIS

Granville

B17 42-30222 Shot down. 6th Sept 1943.

St Pabu

St. Malo

St. Brieuc

Alencon

Brest

Rennes

Le Mans

Quimper

Lorient

Vannes

30AU Part of A-Troop to South of France. Cassis to collect torpedo and to do some spying? Winter 1944/45

30AU Lt.Cmdr.Job(s) meets Madame Withew. Ron meets Margot. August 1944.

St. Nazaire

Nantes

France June/July/August/September 1944
Timeline of 30AU movements. ○◀─────

Top: 30AU part in Liberation of France.

Left: Royal Marines emblem drawn by Japanese death row prisoner that Ron Guy befriended while on guard duty in Kowloon, Hong Kong. Of note: 'Woolies Looters' addition near base. A reference to the treasures and papers found within the opened enemy safe boxes of Europe and shipped back to...? Or possibly just a reference to the group of six-ish 30AU Royal Marines that were caught stealing a payroll near Paris and returned to their units in disgrace?
(At least one of whom was from Royal Marines 413 King's Squad)

Far Right: Timeline of Allied invasion of Germany, 30AU recorded movements and historical record of Wernher von Braun supposed movements while he rescued five hundred Nazi scientists single handedly?
(He had broken his other arm).

Right: Clark, Angus and Guy. 42 Commando, B-troop. Kowloon, Hong Kong.

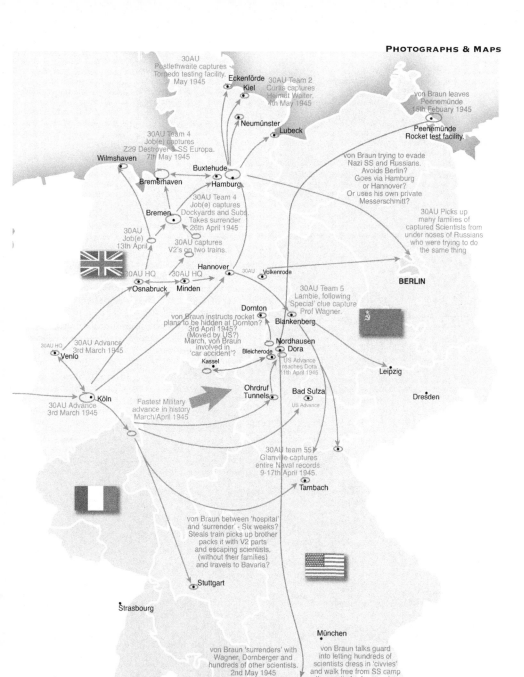

30AU
Postlethwaite captures
Torpedo testing facility,
May 1945

Eckenförde
Kiel

30AU Team 2
Curtis captures
Helmut Walter,
4th May 1945

Neumünster
Lubeck

von Braun leaves
Peenemünde
15th Febuary 1945

Peenemünde
Rocket test facility.

30AU Team 4
Job(e) captures
Z29 Destroyer & SS Europa.
7th May 1945

Wilmshaven

Buxtehude

Bremerhaven
Hamburg

von Braun trying to evade
Nazi SS and Russians.
Avoids Berlin?
Goes via Hamburg
or Hannover?
Or uses his own private
Messerschmitt?

Bremen

30AU Team 4
Job(e) captures
Dockyards and Subs.
Takes surrender
26th April 1945

30AU
Job(e)
13th April

30AU captures
V2's on two trains.

30AU Picks up
many families of
captured Scientists from
under noses of Russians
who were trying to do
the same thing

30AU HQ
Osnabruck

30AU HQ
Minden

Hannover

30AU
Volkenrode

BERLIN

Dornton

von Braun instructs rocket
plans to be hidden at Dornton?
3rd April 1945?
(Moved by US?)
March, von Braun
involved in
'car accident'?

Blankenberg

30AU Team 5
Lambie, following
'Special' clue capture
Prof Wagner.

30AU HQ
Venlo

30AU Advance
3rd March 1945

Bleicherode

Nordhausen
Dora

US Advance
reaches Dora
11th April 1945

Kassel

Leipzig

Köln

30AU Advance
3rd March 1945

Fastest Military
advance in history
March/April 1945

Ohrdruf
Tunnels

Bad Sulza

US Advance

Dresden

30AU team 55
Glanville captures
entire Naval records.
9-17th April 1945.

Tambach

von Braun between 'hospital'
and 'surrender' - Six weeks?
Steals train picks up brother
packs it with V2 parts
and escaping scientists,
(without their families)
and travels to Bavaria?

Stuttgart

Strasbourg

München

von Braun 'surrenders' with
Wagner, Dornberger and
hundreds of other scientists.
2nd May 1945

von Braun talks guard
into letting hundreds of
scientists dress in 'civvies'
and walk free from SS camp
then waits for four weeks
in local hotel?

Oberammergau

Germany March/April/May 1945

○◄— Timeline of 30AU movements in Germany.

○◄— Recorded movements of Wernher von Braun (and his brother?) and the two/five hundred scientists
he took with him across Germany to their eventual 'Surrender' to US troops in Bavaria.

The Yalta Agreement for the downfall of Nazi Germany

British Sector.
Russian Sector.
American Sector.
French Sector.

According to this agreement anything captured or found within these areas
was supposed to belong to the nation indicated regardless of who captured it.

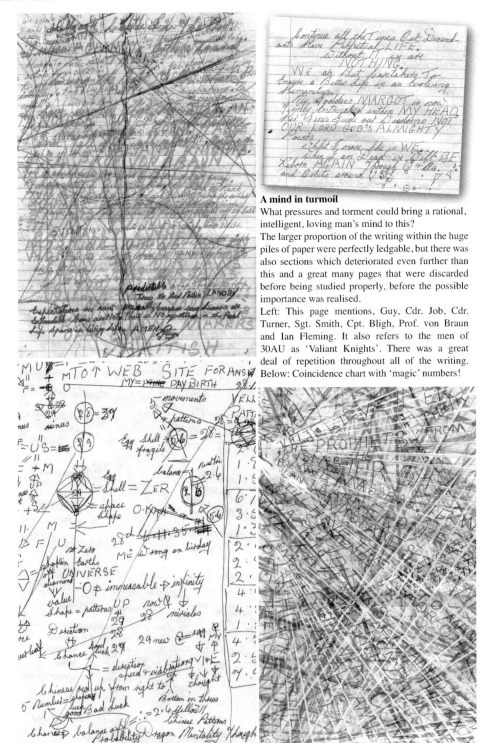

A mind in turmoil

What pressures and torment could bring a rational, intelligent, loving man's mind to this?

The larger proportion of the writing within the huge piles of paper were perfectly ledgable, but there was also sections which deteriorated even further than this and a great many pages that were discarded before being studied properly, before the possible importance was realised.

Left: This page mentions, Guy, Cdr. Job, Cdr. Turner, Sgt. Smith, Cpt. Bligh, Prof. von Braun and Ian Fleming. It also refers to the men of 30AU as 'Valiant Knights'. There was a great deal of repetition throughout all of the writing. Below: Coincidence chart with 'magic' numbers!

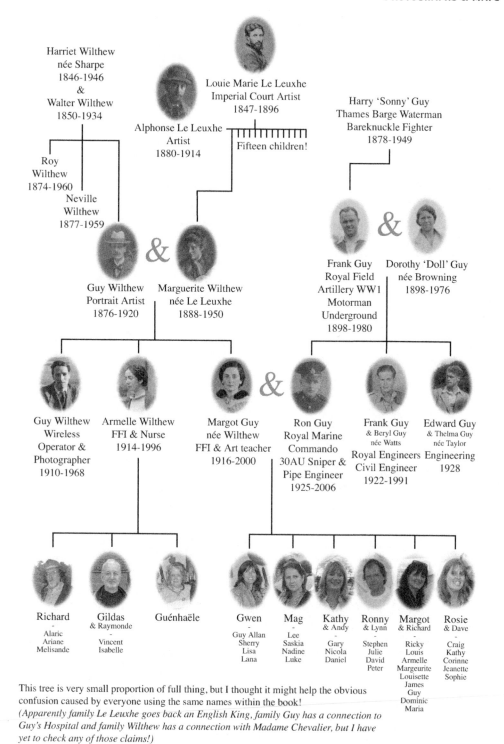

Harriet Wilthew
née Sharpe
1846-1946
&
Walter Wilthew
1850-1934

Louie Marie Le Leuxhe
Imperial Court Artist
1847-1896

Alphonse Le Leuxhe
Artist
1880-1914

Fifteen children!

Harry 'Sonny' Guy
Thames Barge Waterman
Bareknuckle Fighter
1878-1949

Roy
Wilthew
1874-1960

Neville
Wilthew
1877-1959

Frank Guy
Royal Field
Artillery WW1
Motorman
Underground
1898-1980

Dorothy 'Doll' Guy
née Browning
1898-1976

&

Guy Wilthew
Portrait Artist
1876-1920

Marguerite Wilthew
née Le Leuxhe
1888-1950

Guy Wilthew
Wireless
Operator &
Photographer
1910-1968

Armelle Wilthew
FFI & Nurse
1914-1996

Margot Guy
née Wilthew
FFI & Art teacher
1916-2000

&

Ron Guy
Royal Marine
Commando
30AU Sniper &
Pipe Engineer
1925-2006

Frank Guy
& Beryl Guy
née Watts
Royal Engineers
Civil Engineer
1922-1991

Edward Guy
& Thelma Guy
née Taylor
Engineering
1928

Richard
-
Alaric
Ariane
Melisande

Gildas
& Raymonde
-
Vincent
Isabelle

Guénhaële

Gwen
-
Guy Allan
Sherry
Lisa
Lana

Mag
-
Lee
Saskia
Nadine
Luke

Kathy
& Andy
-
Gary
Nicola
Daniel

Ronny
& Lynn
-
Stephen
Julie
David
Peter

Margot
& Richard
-
Ricky
Louis
Armelle
Margeurite
Louisette
James
Guy
Dominic
Maria

Rosie
& Dave
-
Craig
Kathy
Corinne
Jeanette
Sophie

This tree is very small proportion of full thing, but I thought it might help the obvious
confusion caused by everyone using the same names within the book!
*(Apparently family Le Leuxhe goes back an English King, family Guy has a connection to
Guy's Hospital and family Wilthew has a connection with Madame Chevalier, but I have
yet to check any of those claims!)*

Commando Memorial, Spean Bridge.
Near Achnacarry and Fort William, Scotland.
As a small boy on family holiday with Ron &
Margot this statue and countryside made a big
impact on me, that has lasted even to this day.

Beau Bête

Chapter Eleven

September 1944. Le Havre, France.

The Humber Scout car bounced its way through the lanes on the approach to the French port town. Five Marines and Doc, Feeley, and Shaw, perched on top, they all hung on in any way they could. The target was a Bank which the Germans had been using as a Head Quarters and it was in the seaside market square of the town,.

Captain Huntington-Whiteley, Red, had briefed them with the help of a local map and the supplied information from the 51st Highlanders front line, that stated all resistance in the area had ceased.

The Scout car stopped at the prearranged point, the team of nine then proceeded towards the target on foot, along the seafront.

"The Tellermine is the Germans anti-tank mine…" Red began in the middle of the approach to tell them about his research into enemy mines. At that point some German sailors popped up from the beach, hands raised high.

"You two, gets these prisoners back to the pens." Red instructed the first two Marines.

A few minutes later another group approached under a white flag. The next two Marines escorted them back the way they had come, back towards the front line.

The remaining five men rounded the corner of the Square and faced the grand façade of the Bank, a machinegun emplacement nestled in front. Otherwise it all looked quiet. A muzzle flash from the machine gun sent the five Marines running in all directions. Bits of masonry and dust spat out as bullets whizzed off into the air. One Marine dived over a small garden wall straight into a painfully spiked rose bush. Doc and Feeley found themselves further forward in another small garden behind a very low brick wall topped with a privet hedge. The German machine gun threatened to completely demolish the small twelve-inch high wall as Doc and Feeley tried to flatten themselves into the grass behind it.

The Marine couldn't see from his position where Red and Shaw had ended up, but he could hear return fire, which seemed to bring the machinegun noise to an abrupt halt.

After a few minutes he crouched up and peered into the square, a large white flag was being rapidly waved from the tall first floor window of the bank. He could see Doc and Feeley's heads pop up from their place of hiding behind a very low brick wall. Captain Huntington-Whiteley strode purposefully forward, with Shaw at his side, towards the surrendering German troops in the Bank. Then when they were about midway, Doc shouted, they suddenly stopped in their tracks, both fell backwards under a hail of bullets, as grenades exploded, the bangs echoing around the square. The Marine could hear more Wehrmacht troops running into the square but he could not see them from his position. He watched as Doc and Feeley again came under fire, they both jumped up and headed back through a garden arch and up some stairs, Feeley apparently hit, fell out of sight. Doc dived through a door as bullets splintered the wood around him. The Marine could now see the troops closing in on Docs position, about fifteen of them, all firing from close range. Thankfully none of them appeared to have noticed him crouching in the rose bush. Doc reappeared in the doorway; his rifle held high above his head. The Marine breathed a sigh of relief when the Germans did not fire on the surrendering man. He watched as they led him away and a few minutes later one of them picked up a seemingly uninjured Feeley and led him away too. The Marine waited for about forty minutes maybe an hour, replaying the whole incident within his mind. Over and over, what should he have done? What should he do now? Red and Shaw were quite obviously dead. The Germans had not even given them a second glance as they marched their prisoners back across the square. He felt numb, slowly he made his way back down along the seafront, retrieved the Scout car and drove to the Fifty-first Highlanders front line where he found the other four Marines. Later as the 30AU Officers questioned the Marine they did not seem at all impressed he had returned alone.

The Bank turned out to have an underground complex and a force of some two hundred troops when it surrendered to the Highlanders twenty-four hours later. Thankfully Doc and Feeley later returned to 30AU unharmed.

Guy had this story relayed to him by an unnamed Marine in A-troop and the whole of 30AU were extremely upset at this death, Red had been the heart and soul of the unit, they had all literally looked up to him and most had been recruited by him. Guy had genuinely liked the 30AU Captain, Red, he really had been at the very heart of all the men of the unit. At just nineteen the harsh realities of war were beginning to sink in.

After the clearance of Paris, 30AU returned to Littlehampton to re-train and re-equip in preparation for the invasion of Germany, should the Admiralty bosses decide that their operations during OVERLORD warranted continued deployment.

B-troops Captain Lessing was replaced by Captain Ward after the former was hospitalised with alcohol poisoning.

Chapter Twelve

November 2006. Slough, England.

As I pulled up into the small quiet close, I could see one of the UPVC front doors of the numerous terraced houses open in the rear view mirror of the Mini. A very small white haired old man on a walking stick stood adjusting his glasses.

He shouted a salute as I got out of the car stretching limbs after the long journey.

"Hi Mac, how are you?" I extended my hand walking across the sodden freshly cut grass of the verge.

"You know I always wondered what happened to old 'Death and Destruction' Guy" Mac was ready with firm handshake and a large smile.

"Death and Destruction! What was that? A nick name?" I towered over the frail bent old man.

"Yes, yes we all had silly nick names," I noticed the slight frown cross the old man's face as he doubted whether he should have mentioned this fact.

"We were all very young then you know, there was Fighting Joe Jemmett and….Death and Destruction Guy…Storming Sid…and...you know what, I can't even remember now what mine was…how silly is that? Come in, come in, I'm a bit lonely you know, not many visitors." Mac wobbled as his walking stick sank into the soft verge, I couldn't help myself from reaching out and catching his arm, although it probably wasn't needed.

The house is two up two down, small and just starting to show signs of wear and tear.

"Please take it as it comes, have a seat, have a seat, would you like some tea? I'm not too used to visitors now you know." Mac walked through to the kitchen to put the kettle on.

I could feel some kind of connection with this small frail old man, nothing

I could understand, nothing tangible, but something, some element that was there in Grandad and was now in front of me here as well.

"So you were in A-troop in these photos?" pulling out the pictures I had printed off to give Mac.

"Let's have a look, shall we" Mac sits heavily into the low, well-worn armchair covered in blankets by the fire after passing over the tea tray.

"Yes, yes, these were taken in about May or June 1945 at Neumünster Naval Wireless Head Quarters, it was only then that were even allowed to have cameras you know." Mac points and names the characters holding the Nazi flag and in the Jeeps. "Corporal Webber, Jemmett, and... I can't quite remember his name, Reed, maybe. Well would you look at that!" His smile is wide as he studies a photo showing him sitting on Ron's shoulders wearing a vest with Swastika and Eagle on the front, a pipe in the corner of his mouth. "Well I certainly don't remember that." He goes to hand it back.

"No, no, these are for you, they are much more yours than mine and I've got copies of all of them anyway. I've also got these." I unwrapped 'Beau Bête' my Nan's painting of Grandad. He was here in spirit. I also drew out the F-S fighting knife. "You trained to use one of these?" I handed him the heavy Dagger.

"Oh yes, yes, I sold mine to a collector years ago, wow that is heavy, you forget. In the training they made us throw it from one hand to the other as you faced off your opponent, trouble is you always dropped it just when you bloody needed it!" That lovely huge smile spread wide across his face.

"I know, I remember Ron showing me how to do it when I was a kid with a carving knife, I practised for hours!" I wished I could do something more for these men, maybe just by being here I was making a difference.

"I went to the Royal Marines Museum a few years ago and after much hassle and complaining and explanations as to who I was, they finally let me hold one of the old Tommy guns they had on display, I couldn't believe how heavy it was! And I used to run about with a seventeen round magazine in it as if it didn't weigh anything." Mac was enjoying himself.

"I bet you were all pretty damn fit, despite all the fags! Do you know why Ron was moved around all the troops? Did he have discipline problems?" I was continually of the mind that there was more to Ron's story than these men were letting on, and I constantly found myself expecting it to suddenly emerge and bite me.

"No, I don't think so, although he was a hard man, always ready to get stuck into the enemy, he didn't hold back. I do remember talk of a strange turn he had one time, somewhere in northern France I think." Again the slight frown of doubt shows for a split second across his face.

"Strange turn, how do you mean?" I wondered if this might be it.

"I'm not too sure, I really don't know. You know, it could have been because of his skills, we were all trained in different disciplines you know." Mac seemed to deliberately change the subject.

"I do know Ron was trained in mountaineering and a trained sniper, I think he also learned safe breaking and explosives. I guess that all probably explains the name eh…'Death and Destruction', that would seem to cover it! Were you ever in one of the small teams with Ron, maybe in the Harz mountains?" I was unsure of the best way to try and dig for information without asking directly and risking offence.

"No, no, I don't think so, it was very long time ago you know. One time, it was during the period in between France and Germany, actually, when we were all taken back to Blighty to re-train and re-equip. It was October 1944, just after Red's death, Captain Huntingdon-Whiteley, the whole unit took that very hard, it was never quite the same again after he was killed. Bloody Germans were waving their white flag and still shooting, not right, not right… Anyway, they moved us from our Littlehampton billets, which we all loved, while we were away on some secret mission. We did spend some time at The Marine in the meantime, actually we brought some of the Nazi flags we had captured and hung them all over the walls in the pub while we celebrated being back home, well in 'Blighty'. I hated the new digs at Guildford where they moved us to when we got back, we had to get the previous landladies to send on all our stuff and the new Billets charged us twice as much." Mac's face actually showed his disapproval of that decision even now.

"Actually one of the veterans I've spoken to told me why you were all moved from Littlehampton. He'd heard a rumour that it was the Colonel's fault! Supposedly he'd got his landlady's daughter pregnant and he was billeted with the vicar and his wife and that's why you all had to move to Guildford!" I wasn't too sure how Mac might respond to this news, sixty years too late.

"Oh yes, I remember, that was the story that went round, to be honest it didn't surprise me… if it was true… anyway, they issued my team with Arctic Jackets, no explanation and we ended up on a journey all the way down to Cassis, near Marseille, in the south of France. A huge ship was beached on the shore. It had been torpedoed." Mac was smiling again enjoying someone to talk to I hope.

"My step grandfather was on that ship, his name was Ron too, actually they made quite a good double act together, the two Ronnie's, you could never have met two more different people, but they were strangely funny together, always made me laugh when we went out to lunch. Anyway he told me the story, it was the Orford, used for troop transport, he said when it was bombed they ran it aground to save it from sinking, around 1940. He was one of the gunners and because the Orford had been sunk by bombers, when the alarm went off on his next ship the Dempo, somewhere near Naples later in the war, he retrieved his Tin Hat according to 'Orders', got to his gun, which had been deserted by whoever was supposed to be covering it, was scanning about in the sky for the attackers when someone shouted at him. 'RON, we're being torpedoed you bloody idiot get that gun pointed in the right direction!' He still laughs about that today."

"Really, well, well, apparently one of those torpedoes, a T5 or T10 it was, used down in the Med didn't go off and it was some new secret Nazi design and we had to collect it and some other ones from out of some sunken U-Boats, sit on them, in the back of the truck, all the way back to Blighty. One of them had all its metal skin around the front peeled back so you could see the high explosives inside, what a journey that was! Although I don't even think that was the real reason we were down there, something else was going on, not sure what it was, all very hush, hush, secret type stuff. There were lots of us running around down there on various missions. I think they even recovered some torpedoes from a sunken submarine in one of the harbours." Mac's face went blank as he spent the next few seconds trying to recall what that all might have actually been for as he probably had done for years. "Actually I think Ron was down there with us I seem to remember…"

"Really, I haven't found any mention of it in his writing, yet, although that would explain why he is not in the Guildford B-troop photo taken during that winter. Could the trip have been to make contact with the French Communist Resistance group being led from down that way?" I wondered if this could this be a link between 30AU and Guy Wilthew, Nan's brother.

"I guess it could have been, but I don't know. Would you like some more tea?"

"Yes please, no actually, tell you what, how about I make you a cup, you stay there." I got up and headed out into the kitchen.

"Did you ever hear anything about the Nazi rocket scientists or the big tunnels at Ohrdruf, I think from Ron's writings he had nightmares for years about the tunnels at Ohrdruf." I shouted out from the kitchen while filling the kettle.

"Oh yes, I do remember one of their top rocket men came through Buxtehude while we were there" Mac was excited about being able to help directly with a question.

"What was his name, do you remember?" I abandoned the task of filling the kettle.

"Yes, ermm, … Von Braun? Yes, I think so, although I never saw him. I'm not even sure if he was caught by one of our teams or someone else, but he did come through Buxtehude, which was one of the rendezvous for all the small teams that were sent throughout Germany, we all met up again at the German North Sea Command Naval headquarters there. I think he was put on one of the US Dakota's that were flying in and out incessantly from the airfield just north."

I had come back into the living room and was sitting squarely in front of Mac, looking intently into his face.

"What date would that have been, do you remember?" I asked.

"Well now, probably March or April 1945, I guess. From there we all headed up further north again, well, all in different directions." Mac looked at me puzzled as to the sudden intensity of the look.

"I think he might have been caught by a team Ron was in. But in the history books it says he surrendered to the US 44th Army in Bavaria on the 2nd of May." I scribbled some notes.

"Oh, really, oh well, maybe I'm wrong then. None of us really knew much of what was going on. But if we British had got him how did he end up with the US?" His large smile faded in a face of confusion. "Only the Naval officers really knew you know. Now Captain Douglas he was a wonderful Officer, he wrote a book you know 'The History of 30AU' but you know what, when they tried to publish it the government's 'Official Secret's Act' slapped a seventy year ban on it. Now it won't be released until at least two thousand and seventy! He died short while ago. You know, in his obituary the SAS and the SBS claimed him as theirs, but he was 30AU, during the war at least."

"Two thousand and seventy! Bit too long for me, I'd like to know now." I went back to making the tea. My mind spun. Here was Mac, a war hero, one daughter in her fifty's visiting him every three weeks of so, with no grandchildren. Too lonely, it wasn't right, society should recognise these men. I had to quell the emotion rising up inside my chest.

"Do you remember how you found the Americans when you joined with their frontline forces?"

"Oh yes, yes, they were all very friendly, loads of chocolate and very accommodating, when they weren't trying to shoot you anyway. They call it 'friendly-fire' now, but I do not remember it being all that friendly." Again the huge smile crossed his lovely face.

"Of course we all knew that the Americans were our salvation as well, without question. If it hadn't been for their huge sacrifice of young lives none of us would have been there and that is certainly a fact!"

As I left I felt a wave of emotion for this frail old man living on his own, I would certainly be keeping in touch and doing what I could for him.

I also now knew that Fleming had structured the unit in such a clever way that even the men themselves didn't really know how important what they were doing was, or even who and what the targets were or virtually where they even were!

But they did all have snippets of information and tiny clues within each of their stories, things which were confirming Ron's memoirs and if I spent the time visiting and talking to each and every one of them and noting their stories and information a much bigger picture was surely going to emerge.

A picture that none of the men themselves ever even knew they had.

Chapter Thirteen

March/April 1945. Across the Rhine, Germany.

The speed of the advance had been stunning, the US armoured divisions heading into the heart of Germany swamping all opposition before it. Team 13 of ten 30AU men, in two Jeeps, went almost unnoticed as they joined up with the advance a few days before. Jim the teams commander had found with experience that the more organised and well trained the American units were, the more willing they were to accept British Special Forces along side them, they even revelled in it. Sharing their own stories and ample food rations, coffee and any other equipment they had to spare.

Guy was pleased to be operating with Jim again, he had trained along side him for 30AU and had great respect for his abilities. They had spent a hectic few weeks rushing around loads of targets on their way to the Rhine, operational procedures were now just second nature, no-one needed to be told what to do, everyone operated independently as part of a well oiled team. He also appreciated the friendship of the Americans when it was offered. He was mightily impressed by the fighting courage they showed, even under heavy losses, but all of his team had had too much bitter experience of trigger happy GI's and the mistakes that seemed to be too easily made by the Americans during the confusion fighting can bring, for him to feel too warmly towards any of the US troops they met and worked with.

Guy, Blondie, Jock and Mac sat around a small stove in front of their Jeeps. It was early morning, sky, grey and overcast. Heavy dew had settled over everything during the night, making it difficult to warm up. They had spent the cold night in a very rickety wooden shed on the edge of a large farm in rolling picturesque countryside. The farm meant they were now enjoying a well-earned breakfast of bacon and eggs.

Reg and Freddy sauntered up from behind the vehicles. They had spent the last two hours on watch, the hardest two hours of the night, the ones just before dawn. They both looked cold and haggard. The distant concussions of the big guns were a constant now, from one direction or another. Small arms fire could also be heard at various times but they had grown used to the sound and knew instinctively how close it was and if it needed their attention or not. Paddy and Ginger were a short way off, on the wireless, trying to get better signal for the two hourly report that had to be made without fail.

Jim the Navy Lieutenant Commander and Raph of the FIU returned at a brisk pace from a visit to the US officers field HQ. Unusually Jim unfolded a map in front of the team as they scoffed bacon'n'eggs and slurped on over hot, strong tea.

"Right lads this is important and it is probably going to get bit hairy. This hill, Jonastal, is just northeast of us here and well into the Russian Sector, although our intelligence boys say that the Russians are at least one hundred miles from there at this time." He points near the small town of Ohrdruf. Guy pulls out his special issue silk escape maps and decides to take this unusual opportunity to get a good grip on their actual location, should he need to be making a quick get away.

"The US Fourth Armoured is heading to this point here, it is a key military bunker known as SIII. NID30 has ordered us into that bunker, technical information to be retrieved at all costs. They have no clear idea as to what's inside but they certainly want to know. The 89th Infantry recon and 602 anti tank recon troop are coming up this way with the rest of the 89th right behind them. We'll try to come in through that point there and surprise them while they are defending here and here. Get yourselves ready."

Quickly wolfing down the rest of the grub, they gathered up their stuff and re-loaded the Jeeps. The guns and essential equipment were always cleaned and prepared at every opportunity. All was ready to go in a matter of minutes. They were all aware of the sound drifting across the rolling fields. It was the distinctive sound of the US armoured columns on the move, the low rumble of the engines mixed with the unusual high pitched noise of the tracked vehicles.

A bright red sun had started to rise over the low-forested hills and already the sky, which had started off so low and foreboding, had begun to break.

Skirting round the first small village they come to, the sound of small arms fire from behind some large farm buildings, is close enough to send them on a detour to the left to investigate. The Jeeps have to stop quickly as they enter a large courtyard between the warehouses. It is strewn with bodies; everything is eerily still and quiet, no movement, as if time has stopped. The corpses seem evenly spaced across the yard; most are partially dressed in filthy, loose fitting striped prison uniforms. The unblinking eyes are sunken into grotesquely emaciated faces with skeletal grins, they stare blindly back at the shocked Marines who although used to the sight of death have never seen bodies like these before. Pools of blood appear to be still spreading, far too bright and fresh to be flowing from these wasted dead, skeletal forms; it is the only colour in the monochrome scene. The sound of retching from the rear of the second Jeep threatens the contents of all their stomachs.

Again the crack of small arms fire.

"Move, move, move!" Jim's shout brings them all back to the here and now. The vehicles accelerate around the edge of the square. In front of them is a compound, apparently a prison compound surrounded by a huge wire fence, high wooden towers overlook the whole area, but they appear to be unmanned. A large section of the fence has been forced down, inwards. They turn to the right alongside the fence and follow it round to a sentry post. Driving around a German guard laying face down across the entrance road, they enter the compound watched by some US troops next to their vehicles further up by some large wooden barracks. Rag covered skeletons, still alive, do their best to remain standing next to them.

There is no acknowledgement between the two sets of stunned soldiers, before them is a mind numbing sight, more bodies or more accurately skin covered skeletons lie everywhere. Two grey trucks are parked to one side of the entrance, both are piled high with corpses, the rear of the first truck faces them, about twenty skin covered skulls, all facing upwards but with necks bent back so that their eyes and gaping mouths still look towards the paling 30AU men. There are completely naked figures, piled high alongside the wooden huts, which stand next to a large pit, dug deep into the ground. In it are the still smoking, blackened remains of at least a hundred people. A rough wooden, makeshift, gallows creaks under the weight of three hanging naked men, the thin wire around their necks cannot be seen from this distance making them appear to be floating. None of them have ever seen anything like this before; more breakfasts find their way back into the daylight as the ten men wander aimlessly from one nightmare to the next.

The silence is broken by the sound of gunfire, large guns, probably tanks close by. Almost in slow motion and without one word the 30AU team remount the Jeeps and leave.

As their Jeep sped through the deserted road between crops of potatoes they had to swerve to avoid three rag-covered figures that suddenly appeared from the hedges desperately trying to wave them down, to make them stop. Three Englishmen, servicemen, POW's that had managed to slip away from one of the numerous 'death marches'. They had survived on eating cabbage and potatoes, straight from the ground, from the earth that was wet enough to yield to their thin, emaciated limbs. It was impossible to tell how old they were, they could hardly stand, barely able to hold the weight of their own bodies. Guy had his doubts they would live out the day, he grabbed one of the numerous tins of peaches they had recently liberated for themselves, opened it and handed it the nearest man. It was painful even to watch them try and swallow the juice and fruit. They informed the men there was help just a few miles or so back down the road and heading this way, an American column. The three collapsed onto the verge to wait.

One of them was a Londoner from Romford, just down the road from Guy's own home in Dagenham. As they left, Guy tried to give the man his address, "Eight, Foxlands Crescent, Dagenham, just call-in."

He never heard from him.

•   •   •

Two, three, four heavy mortar teams, widely spread, came into view through the trees. There was a line of Sherman tanks firing repeated volleys into the hills beyond the ridge; sporadic heavy machinegun fire was audible from various directions. Return artillery fire sent clumps of mud and stones showering over the two 30AU Jeeps as they cut across the field at an angle from the American armoured forces on their right.

The lead vehicle visibly shook as the twin Vickers machinegun, manned by Reg in the front, opens up in the direction of the barrier that can be seen through the trees. The Jeeps bounce alarmingly over a single railway track. Both vehicles, in a choreographed dance, slide and twist, as the over revving engines pull them up the slope beyond the track and onto the level ground alongside the double wire perimeter fence. Blondie, Jock and Freddy take defensive positions around the team.

Mac and Paddy pulled out the two pairs of large bolt cutters strapped to the wings of the Jeeps, they had seen plenty of action from D-Day to this, they made short work of the two wire-link perimeter fences.

"Right, you two, Ginger and Guy, with me." Jim shouts his orders as both vehicles suddenly lurch to the left then back to the right, the very ground beneath their feet vibrates and moves, the deep rumbling noise coming from the hill must have been similar to an earthquake, everything including the gunfire around them echoing off the hills, seems to pause for a few seconds and then resume. The Marines are used to the close concussion of huge explosions but this was different, deeper, longer, more immense than anything they had felt before. They too, pause, looking at each other.

"C'mon, GO, GO, GO." Jim is the first to wake from the pause. Jim, Ginger and Guy grab and sling the bags they need and are quickly through the fences. They hear the covering fire from the men behind them as they sprint up towards the hill looking for some form of entrance. Strangely all three men stumble together as an odd dizzy sensation suddenly washes over them, blurring their vision and leaving them face down in the mud, but they are quickly recovered and moving back up the slope. More of the hill base comes into view, as they get higher. There is an obvious tunnel entrance right in front of them. Skeletal figures in filthy striped pyjamas, barely able to stand, helping each other stumble forward are leaving the smoking tunnel. They're moving as fast as they can.

"Nie , Nie don't iść w , daleko , Daleko!" the escapees are screaming as the three men approach them, but the 30AU men are unable to understand a word.

Although Guy had already come across enough Polish POW's to understand their sentiment perfectly.

From behind the escaping men, machine gun fire erupts from the tunnel entrance. An SS guard sprays bullets at them, Jim, Guy and Ginger hit the ground again, rolling away from centre of the group and returning fire. The guard crumples backwards and out of sight. The escaping figures now appear to be nothing more than bloody, dirty rags in one big pile on the ground, as the three men regain their feet and move on towards the tunnel.

Guy kicks away the dropped gun lying next to the SS guard who desperately grasps at his bleeding belly, while staring about wildly.

The tunnel immediately widens after the entrance, all three of them are stunned. The entrance looked so small and unfinished but the tunnel, the tunnel is amazing. It is much larger and more brightly lit than they expected, despite the smoke, which is running along the high arched ceiling, the finish of the work is incredible. Guy is reminded of his uncle's fascination with the German architectural school of Bauhaus and this looks like some ultra modern kind of Bauhaus design. It is empty, arching off to the right as it plunges deep into the hill, at least two maybe three hundred yards. The beat of their heavy boots echoes as they run on, more rag covered skeletons are heading towards them, appearing to be unbelievably at odds with the clinical surroundings that they are trying to leave as quickly as they can. Their skeletal grins again implore at the men passing them.

"Nie , Nie , Zostawiać , ZOSTAWIAĆ TERAZ"

The three men come to a standstill, mouths agape, unable to take in the whole picture, unintelligible screams and shouts echo about, assaulting the ears. Opening out in front of them is what appears to be a huge circular, central hub, from around its circumference a myriad of tunnels heading off in all directions. A few figures in white coats and various military uniform types are running about in all directions, without paying any attention to the newcomers. None of the three men have seen anything like it before, stunning, ultra-modern, they feel like they have landed on another planet.

To the left is a large open plan railway station, two platforms, one empty, the other has huge black modern streamlined locomotive adorned with powerful angular graphics, it arches away deep into the tunnels. It appears to have one of these engines at both ends and bristles with antiaircraft guns partially hidden by the studded armour plating. A few people are still trying to board, running through the blasts of steam billowing around the engines at either end as the train slowly begins to accelerate away from the platform.

The three men drift to the metal and glass railing at the floor edge and looking down they can see many more prisoners, moving about in panic, they were trapped two floors below. Most had laid themselves down and appeared to be resigned to their fate. The stronger ones were screaming and shouting at them, but none of the 30AU men recognised a word. Smoke billowed up the central, open atrium, from the floor directly below them, the orange lick of flame could be seen reflecting off the polished concrete and glass all around. Two massive brushed metal, strong room doors stood closed on the second floor, the floor directly below the three men, the bright reflection of a trolley full of gold metal in front of the huge doors added to the orange ripple of the flames growing brighter by the second.

On their right, on the same floor, all three looked up at the yellow flickering gold, Gothic Eagle and Swastika dominating the space before it.

The glass of the balustrade explodes at their legs snapping their attention back. The pop of gunfire from an SS Officer; his black pristine uniform perfectly complimenting his environment. He empties his pistol clip at them from across the atrium. A simultaneous burst of gunfire from all three men sends him sharply back through the door from which he had appeared. A deep, powerful rumble, shaking everything around them, threatens to throw all three to the floor as they move quickly towards the entrance directly below the Gothic Eagle. Large open plan spacious modern offices still occupied by a few wild-eyed people who completely ignore their presence, exits and entrances and corridors head out in all directions.

"Split. Find the strong boxes and be damn quick about it." Jim shouts above the din and vibration.

The door splinters and shatters from the force of the hefty kick, three Marines burst through as the papers re-settle, to Guy's relief the modern wood panelled office room is empty as he recalls the 'eliminate any witnesses' order impressed so indelibly into them during their training. At last, a medium size green safe box stands in the corner.

"Let's get this done and get out, I don't want to be here." Jim looks into the eyes of the two men with him, all three are wide-eyed, pale and scared.

Gradually they had become aware of an increasing mechanical whine, it reminded Guy of the whining gears of the Jeep when travelling at speed, but this noise and vibration was infinitely larger, faster and more powerful. The deep rumbling had become a constant, with occasional violent vibrations, strong enough to shake pictures from the walls.

Ginger moves back into the adjacent office, kneeling by the door he covers the way they had entered. Acting quickly, Guy prepares the plastic explosives from the bags. They were pre-shaped, but had been slightly flattened from transport. He positions the explosives at the key points on the safe box, the directional charges were designed to cut the reinforced bars that ran across the inside of the doors. Jim hands him a detonator from his bag. They run the fuse wire across the office and back out into the room with Ginger. A small thud, which is barely audible above the constant rumble, indicates a successful detonation. The safe door bounces back and forth, billowing the smoke about as they re-enter. Familiar purple folders with gold Swastika and 'Geheime Kommando Sache' phrase they had been trained to recognise, stamped across the front, some of which were quite badly singed and slightly smoking, but all are stuffed quickly into some large fold out canvas carriers they have for the purpose. The folders could contain virtually any kind of information but if it was marked in certain way they had to take it and let their own scientists travelling with them decide if it was current or obsolete.

The atrium rumbles and shakes, it is filling up with acrid blue smoke, screams and shouts are now only barely audible above the din of the fire and the high pitched mechanical whizz, which just seems to go on increasing in speed and power, their ears are starting to sing in a vibration of sheer pain.

Every fibre of their being just wants to carry them away from this place, but the terrified screams from the Polish POW's on the bottom floor draw them back to the balustrade.

"We have to get down there." Ginger shouts it, but he's looking for the other two to take him in the direction they entered. The thickening smoke and intense flames now prevent them from seeing the poor people trapped down below, through watering eyes they stare in amazement at the two enormous metal doors on the floor below. Blue-ish electrical sparks are erupting from the doors and connecting to random metal objects in the area around them, they dart and dance around the trolley, then ping to the balustrade and various girder structures. It looks to be an impossible sight or some kind of optical illusion as the massive strong room doors bend and buckle inwards as the sparks coming from them dance about.

The blast seems somehow to be silent. All three are already running as the shockwave hits them.

In a bizarre mind numbing twist Guy found himself lost, on his own, still running but in the wrong direction, back towards the railing. He can't understand the surreal vision he is part of. It appears that all the fire and smoke are acting in reverse, being sucked back down into the atrium to the floors below. More of the balustrade glass explodes into tiny sparkling shards and is sucked away, downwards. He slides and stumbles in his haste to turn and get away, in the right direction. The very air about him tries to hinder his progress, pulling him backwards. He can see Jim on his own, a fair way ahead of him sprinting up the tunnel they entered through, but no sign of Ginger. Ahead of Jim at the tunnel entrance a couple of their team are cautiously moving forward towards them.

"ENGLISH, ENGLISH! Go back, out, out, NOW, NOW." both Jim and Guy shout loudly their voices sounding very small and insignificant to themselves.

They feel as if they are being pushed along the tunnel as it begins to fill with the whoosh of rushing air. Neither of the running men wants to look behind, they can sense and hear the roar behind them, the faces of the wide eyed men in front of them start to turn a pale shade of orange before they too turn and run.

Guy is thrown through the air out of the tunnel entrance, he hits the ground hard, winded, rolling down the slope, ending on his back looking up into a sight like nothing he has ever seen before. It is an explosion of searing hot fire, but a fire that looks like and is behaving like, a liquid, it seems somehow contained, snaking out of the hillside. It reaches out skywards but slowing, neither rising or falling before it starts to collapse back on itself, accelerating back into the tunnel from where it had emerged. It is gone, quicker than it had come.

Guy pushes himself up from the grass. He feels himself to be heavier and more exhausted than he has felt since Commando training at Achnacarry, although that seems like a distant memory right now.

"Wasser, bitte." Guy finds himself outside next to the German SS guard they had shot as they arrived. He's still holding his belly although now he looks quite calm, but very, very pale.

"Wasser, bitte." Guy stands and looks down into his dying, slightly pink, watery, light blue eyes. In his twentieth year and with no conscious thought whatsoever he makes the decision that will haunt him for the rest of his days, he turns and walks away, he must find Ginger.

He doesn't know it at that moment but those pale blue eyes have burnt an indelible image into the back of his soul.*

*(One awful moment that Guy never told anyone about and no-one ever knew how much it affected him until reading his memoirs after his death, a decision that filled his nightmares and one that he never, ever forgave himself for).

Chapter Fourteen

November 2006. London, England.

"Hello, thanks for getting in touch, I appreciate you taking to time the speak with me, I hope we can help each other." I tried to reassure this stranger we were both on the same side.

"My father was a Royal Marine Captain in 30AU." His voice was calm, strong. "He spent his last years in a mental institution, but we've never been able to prove it was directly linked to his time with 30AU. I do know he tried to reveal certain things earlier in his life when he was in better mental health, which led to a vicious falling out with a 30AU Colonel and some of the other top brass in the unit and he was stopped from proceeding further. I know not how, but he never got over it." His voice remained calm and constant.

"You don't have any of his writings or memoirs do you?' It was worth a try.

"Nothing that seems to make much sense. I'm afraid he cut and burned everything he could from that part of his life. I only have little snippets of stories and innuendo. I think he was convinced that some of the 30AU Officers did very well from their time blowing safes all over Europe. Stories of eighty odd safe boxes blown in Paris alone, other stories of various kinds of treasures found within the many Nazi Headquarters they went through, but no information as solid as those things have ever come to us. He was reported as MIA, Missing in Action at one point and his grandfather having only just heard of the death of his first grandson out in the desert, he panicked and sold the family Abbey and estate, apparently they did recover some of the tapestries and heirlooms after the war. When he finally reappeared from his capture he had rope burns around the neck, he'd been tortured, questioned, by …" The voice had begun to show the slightest hint of emotion.

"My grandfather too spent his last days in a mental institution, it was only there that he finally tried to tell me he had worked with Ian Fleming, been one of his 'Indian Braves'. I'd always known he was a Commando but not 30AU. I thought he was delusional at the time. I ignored it. Now I will always regret that for the rest of my life." It was difficult not to let the emotion come flooding back.

"He was a kind and gentle man, my father." The voice had begun to tremble just slightly with more emotion. "I know that once he found he was unable pull the trigger and his batman had to do the job to avoid him getting killed."

"I'm sure we would all have that problem. You realise that they were under orders to 'eliminate' witnesses, presumably that meant not to leave any witnesses alive, witnesses to the intelligence they gathered. I've just come from the National Archives and seen with my own eye's the document that spells out that directive. The original licence to kill! Surely an illegal order even in wartime? My grandfather was a trained sniper, trained to kill in cold blood. These men were young and witnessing the rape and pillage of Europe by all sides. I don't think most people could ever recover from that. Certainly not the ones with an ounce of humanity anyway." I tried to reassure him.

"He once escaped from the ward, in his sixties he was. Led the police on a merry chase around the neighbourhood on an 'Escape and Evasion' finally took a boat from the harbour and led the coastguard on a merry chase as well, for hours." I could hear the pleasure that recounting that story brought to him. "I wish my mother could still have been alive to hear these things, it would have helped her, a lot. You know my father was always firmly convinced that Von Braun and these other bloody scientists were certainly never 'white as white' as the Americans made them out to be and that it was all connected to 30AU somewhere along the line. They were at the sharp end of all that, I'm sure of it."

"It's strange you should mention that name! Yep, they certainly were. I'm trying to get that truth out. I'm just not yet sure what the best way of putting that truth into the public domain is. No one wants to listen. Publishers are not interested, they will not even speak to you! Newspapers want current stories with which to put the fear of god into everybody. No one wants to know about news from sixty years ago it seems. The website that you emailed me from is beginning to generate some attention but hopefully we can get that to increase, a lot… but we'll see… Let's stay in touch see if we can help each other… "

Chapter Fifteen

As I began to study the Allied invasion of Germany it did appear a pattern was emerging, if the US commanders had known of the existence of these top secret Nazi installations, all concentrated in the heart of Germany, it would certainly explain the thrust of their advance, straight at those targets, in the fastest military advance in history, ever. When you looked at the maps they must have known. The websites that referred to the SIII bunker made it sound like some kind of myth, real or not, no one seemed to know. There were even documents and letters I had found, signed by Eisenhower that specifically directed the Allied reporters of the time away from Ohrdruf and Jonastal and on to Nordhausen instead. Were those orders issued to hide what they had found?

Even the Allied bombing of Dresden, when looked at from this new perspective, far from being undertaken to help the Russians invade, was much more likely to have been ordered to STOP the Russians. Despite that the 'official' line was that Stalin had asked for it to happen (I would never again be able to truly believe another 'official' statement or document (I'm sure he must have asked for help, who wouldn't in his position!)). Surely it would have been undertaken to prevent them being able to use German infrastructure, like the rail and road network, to get in and then out of that central key area in the Harz Mountains. Not to defeat the Germans at all but to make sure all that Nazi technology and know-how ended up in the 'right' hands. I had never been one to heed any of these conspiracy websites before, but now... my heart said one thing, my mind another...

Could this really be all true?... Could ALL of the qualified historians the world had to offer since the war, be so far away from the truth? But they were only making educated guesses based on the 'facts' supplied by the Allies and those Allies wanted some 'facts' to remain forever hidden. Now I had come to believe that it was indeed possible...

There it was again, right in the centre of a bright, almost luminescent spiral of green felt tip writing, the words I had been searching for and slowly finding in amongst this jumbled mass of thoughts and descriptions that Grandad had tried to express in the years before his death. I had also come to believe that he had tried to record his memories and thoughts in such away that it would not put our family at risk from an unseen enemy, or an imaginary enemy, I could still not be sure which.

I had now also discovered, when questioning other family members, Margot, Ronny and Gwen. (Ron and Margot's third, fourth and first children), Ron had talked on a few rare occasions over the years, about putting 'top Hun Scientist responsible for V2 rockets, von Braun' under house arrest, he had also written about and mentioned other scientists, Professor Wagner and a Professor Martin, a V2 fuel chemist, both working on V weapons both captured by 30AU. *(I found myself wondering if Prof. Martin could actually be one and the same person as Prof. von Braun within the writings. Magnus von Braun had trained as a chemist and did work at Nordhausen where the V2's were being assembled, could Ron have confused Martin with Magnus? Or was that just his codename to enable secrets to be kept for 76 years?)* Along side mumbled comments about Guy's (Wilthew) probable murder. Either way, there it was, yet again…'Prof. von Braun'!…

April 1945. Thuringia, Germany.

The Jeeps were travelling fast; the roads were amazingly clear and well maintained. The few faces they did see stared in amazement, some even smiled and waved, rushing off into buildings, no doubt to report to family and friends, the sight of rapidly moving Allied vehicles deep in the heart of Germany.

There were four men in the lead Jeep, Reg manning the captured spandau hastily mounted on the passenger side of the vehicle. They had realised even as soon as the first few weeks after D-Day that even the appearance of force was enough to frequently encourage the surrender of the less experienced Wehrmacht troops. He ducked slightly to hide behind the folded windshield, more to keep out of the cold, early morning April wind than to hide from any enemy sniper who might be taking careful aim. Mac and Jock were bouncing uncomfortably in the back, eyes scanning the scene as they sped past other deserted farm buildings. Mac, compelled to use both hands to support the weight of his Bren, found it pretty difficult to maintain the balance he needed to keep watch on the surrounding terrain.

The driver Fred was now so adept at handling his Jeep he actually relished the moments when he had to take any evasive action. These were the times they had all become hooked on. The adrenalin cursing through their veins, each one feeling the heightened sense of awareness crucial to being far in advance of Allied troops. The knowledge that at any moment, around any corner, a situation could arise they would have to deal with in an instant. Taking snap decisions and immediate actions that might mean and generally did mean they could end up virtually anywhere.

There were five in Blondie's trailing Jeep; Raph manned the Twin Vickers K machine gun mounted behind the bulletproof plexiglass. Guy and Paddy crouched in the back, although they were seated next to the rear-mounted twin Vickers they both held their heavy Thompson submachine guns out in front of them. The De Lisle Carbine silenced and scoped sniper rifle, slung across Guy's back, was a constant encumbrance. He shifted position yet again, trying to move it and had to catch himself from nearly tumbling straight from the back of the Jeep as it rounded an unexpected obstacle. Jim the Royal Navy Lieutenant Commander, squatted uncomfortably in the centre, he was the only one who actually knew exactly what the target was. Everything was strictly on a need to know basis, even he probably didn't know the full story of any expected or probable target. It was rare to head out without a back up target of some sort. Should the primary prove too difficult to achieve, there was always another one, but apparently not this time. This thought worried Jim. He was aware this was an A1 high priority target, which meant the NID30 expected success at almost any cost.

The Marines knew the score, although none of them actually expressed what they were all thinking. They were a small team, nine men, no scientists and last minute preparations deep into the Russian sector of Germany following a 'special' clue (quite what that meant Guy, as yet, did not know). Any technical information or personnel captured in this sector, by national agreement should belong to the Russians. Experience told them this situation implied the capture of technical personnel at enemy installations, with mission information supplied by agents working undercover in the field. Guy had caught some glimpses of Jim's 'Black Book' containing target lists made up from NID30 Commander Fleming's 'Black List'. There had been some photos, one of a young, handsome looking man, stamped with a Swastika, the pages listed several names as well, A1 - Hans Von Braun – V2 Missiles, A1 – Professor Herbert Wagner – Hs 293 Guided Bomb, A1 – Professor Martin – V-Chemist/Fuel and others. Guy knew what A1 meant. Heavy casualties to 30AU were acceptable to the Admiralty, if it led to the completion of a successful mission.

The dark hills at the foot of the Harz mountain range loomed large ahead of the speeding Jeeps, the roads were beginning to narrow, winding back and forth up into the hills, the trees suddenly blocking out all view of the surrounding terrain. As they gained altitude on the twisting tracks, the Marines caught broken glimpses of the valley below, small towns, scattered woods and farmland. Jim knelt up from his position, then signalled with two sharp arm movements for the lead vehicle to pull up into the lightly wooded area on the left, both Jeeps slide to a stop on the soft carpet of pine needles. The young Marines were dismounting their charges even before they had come to a halt, each one running, only slightly crouched, heading into the nearby cover to take up defensive positions around the now stationery vehicles, where only the two men manning the machine guns, Reg and Raph, now remained, back to back.

Taking his compass, Jim checks their bearings on the map. Guy gently lays his Tommy gun down on the mossy bank and then nestles into position to survey the area. He lifts the strap of his sniper rifle over his head, opens the lens cover with a soft click and then placing the scope to his eye, he looks into the valley. Scanning the small village they had skirted around as they approached, he satisfies himself there are no military installations in obvious view. The sound of people starting their day drifts up through the crisp dawn air into the hills from the peaceful basin below. Guy watches a convoy of grey military trucks heading out of the village in the opposite direction to their position. Checking the empty road ahead of the trucks, he sees a huge plume of smoke erupting from the mountainside.

His first thought is explosion but he realizes the billowing column is from a steam engine exiting a hillside tunnel obscured from view. The locomotive emerges at speed in their direction. At first it appears to be carrying a large cylindrical storage tank painted in an olive drab grey, but as the engine clears the trees obscuring the tunnel and track, he can see this is not a storage tank. It has a streamlined nose cone and tail fins, clearly visible through the camouflage netting loosely flapping about at its extreme rear end. It was a huge missile at least forty feet long and five feet wide. He realised he had seen this shape before, only a few days before, or was it weeks it was becoming difficult to keep track of time. His team had been heading into Germany, approaching some wooded land when only a few hundred yards ahead from within the trees a huge missile had erupted from the tree tops accelerating straight up into the clouds shaking the very air around them and illuminating the low clouds from within as it quickly disappeared from sight, it was a jaw dropping vision, the power and speed were not comparable to anything they had seen before. When their Jeeps had arrived at what they thought would be some kind of launch site it was deserted apart from a relatively small metal pyramid bolted firmly to the centre of the road, it was still smoking.

Guy could now make out three of them, lying end to end along the train's length. Despite the tightly secured netting still intact on the last two weapons, the outline was unmistakable. Guy signals to Jim, clicking his fingers loudly, then pointing down into the valley at the rapidly moving cargo. Unhooking his field glasses, Jim looks down in the direction Guy's rifle is pointing, quickly scribbling some notes and the time on the map in front of him. The Lieutenant Commander moves over, pointing at the wireless set in the back of second Jeep. Paddy runs out from his cover to send in the report Jim has just scribbled.

"T one three WILDCAT, calling STAG, T one three WILDCAT, calling STAG, over".

"STAG here T one three WILDCAT - SHEEP B, SHEEP B, over"

Paddy quickly dials in the predetermined radio frequency and reports "ADDER with FANGS repeat ADDER with FANGS heading west SUTTON three zero two zero six, west SUTTON three zero two zero six, west, over".

"ADDER with FANGS west SUTTON three zero two zero six, over out" crackles back the confirmation reply.

Jim signals for Guy to follow him as he secures his map and field glasses and moves back away from the track and into the pine woods behind them. Guy re-slings his De Lisle and grabs the Tommy gun as he sprints off in the direction Jim's heading, they move uphill for several minutes at a fast pace, as they crest the tree lined ridge the next valley comes into view through the pines. Jim and Guy both fall forwards onto their belly's looking through the grass and pine trunks at a large house in the clearing just slightly below and to the right of their position. Guy uses the rifle scope that he'd unslung as he neatly fell into position, Jim his field glasses, both survey the property before them.

A long curving gravel drive with one sentry position and wooden barrier at the tree break, leads round to a large country house, two floors with attic rooms. Two large black limousines are lined up outside the main entrance, one looks pristine and perfectly polished the other is dirty and dull. Both have the small red Nazi flags on each front wing, a guard with his Alsatian dog saunters past the vehicles. Guy can't help but line up the cross hairs of his scope perfectly dead centre of the guards chest. Jim continues scanning the property, there is a narrow, apparently empty, viewing platform on the far side of house and a six foot high perimeter fence that appears to encircle the whole clearing, the only opening is at the small sentry post entrance, where one guard in large grey overcoat is concentrating hard on something in his fingertips.

Jim re-hooks his field glasses and pulls out the map, studying it carefully.

Tapping Guy's shoulder, with two quick points at each of the guards, "Twenty minutes".

The sound of his voice seems clipped and muffled by the dense carpet of pine needles and the trees around and behind them. They both check watches,

Guy stays on his belly as Jim skips over him and disappears back down the ridge.

Guy watches the guards chatting at the main entrance for a few minutes before deciding to move around the ridge to see if he might lessen the amount of blind spots caused by the large pines or possibly even get a bit closer as he's worried that this distance is right on the limit of his rifle. As he moves further up he finds a spot where he can see both a clear view of the property and behind him, glimpses of the valley and town down below. The muffled sound of distant explosions filter up through the forest, as Guy re-scans the town. He watches a huge convoy of grey German military vehicles on the winding roads around the town. The sound of distant explosions gradually intensifies; it is a sound he has become so used to hearing it barely registers as he settles himself into the most comfortable position he can find. He carefully studies the guards' movements, while regulating his breathing and heart beat, relaxing, breathing deeply, in through the nose, out through the mouth. He has rotated the watch on his left wrist so that one small glimpse downward is enough to keep a precise check on the minutes ticking by. His mind now completely blank, the guards appear to finish their conversation, the sleeping dog is yanked back to his feet as his master heads off back towards the house. The cross hairs alternate slowly back and forth, from guard to dog to guard and back again, as the minutes tick down they finally come to rest plumb centre on the entrance guards' face, watching his every move; he looks relaxed. Then his head snaps up looking in the direction of the entrance. From where Guy is, all is silent, but the guard has obviously heard an approaching vehicle, obligingly he leans heavily on the counter weight of the solid wooden barrier, it slowly raises up, gaining momentum the higher it gets, as it hits vertical the Marine sniper gently squeezes the trigger. There is the odd sensation of powerful recoil coupled with the almost inaudible puff of the silenced De Lisle rifle, muffled even more by the dense vegetation. The guard spins perfectly on the spot, his great grey coat billowing out around him, as he seems to sink into the ground. The rifle is re-cocked with a swift, practiced, flick and click of the bolt as the sniper scans across for next target, the dog's head has popped up in the direction of the entrance, it slumps to the floor jerking the masters hand on the lead, who starts to pull it along on the ground completely oblivious to the fact that it is now dead. As he turns to look down he too falls heavily, straight on top of his dog. Somehow Guy had managed to remove himself from the killing of these men just by the distance of the shot, it had become easier with time and experience to remove yourself mentally from what you were doing.

Guy doesn't see the two Jeeps hurtling through the entrance, spraying gravel in all directions as they approach the house. He is up and moving quickly down the steep slope to scale the perimeter fence.

The Jeeps slide to a stop next to the Limousines, their wheels leaving deep troughs in the gravel, the Marines sprinting off in all directions. Reg heads back the way they came, down the drive, Paddy and Blondie to the left of the house, Mac and Freddy to the right, Raph and Jim straight at the front door. Jock checks both the Limousines then crouches down between the two large cars watching Reg going back down the driveway and glancing up at the ridge where Guy should be and watching him falling six foot, flat on his face as he catches his boot gator on a barb at the top of the perimeter fence he's scaling, then shaking himself off and sprinting across the open lawn towards the vehicles. Guy slides down by the vehicles in front of the house near Jock.

"Very graceful DD" Jock smiles sarcastically.

Guy smiles, but ignores him while he tries to remove the small Nazi flag from the Limousine front wing.

"Ain't you got enough of them?" Jock has seen Guy's collection of Nazi flags.

The front door frame splits open with the first hefty kick of Jim's boot, they burst through into a spacious, dark, polished wooden hallway, a large staircase heads up and to the right, and double doors are open on both sides. They have both drawn their pistols; Jim swings into the left opening, Raph to the right. Both rooms are empty, perfectly neat and clean. They can hear the clear sound of hard heeled shoes on hard polished wooden floorboards behind them, both spin and drop down on one knee, right arms extended and supported by the left hand, pistols scanning for a target. A large smartly dressed man rounds the door frame further down the hall, his hands full of paperwork, which scatters in all directions as he raises his hands as fast as he can manage.

"Schießen Sie nicht, schießen Sie nicht, don't shoot, don't shoot!" he screams, his face a perfect picture of shock and bewilderment.

"ON THE FLOOR, AUF DEM FUßBODEN, NOW, NOW" Jim bellows as loudly and as forcefully as he can, pistol aimed straight at the man's face, who kneels slowly and then lays face down amongst the scattered papers.

At the sound of the shouting Guy is up and at the front door of the house, now pistol in hand with Rifle and Tommy gun slung across his back. He steps into the hallway and makes quick sideways movement to put himself in the corner, back to the wall, while his eyes adjust and take in the scene in front of him. Raph is heading up the stairs right arm extended, pistol aiming at the furthest point he can see. Jim is standing above a prone man face down on the floor. With a quick glance left and right Guy runs through to the open doors at the back of the hall, the first room is spacious wooden panelled study, there is drawing board and a huge desk both covered in paperwork and plans, Guy instantly recognises detailed drawings and plans of V weapons. A large safe sits open in the corner it too is overflowing with paperwork and rolls of drawings. Glittering bars of precious metals are stacked neatly in the base of it, gold and silver in colour, Guy guesses at Platinum. He can hear Raph's heavy boot steps running back and forth upstairs, kicking open doors. DD spins out of the study and through the last door at the back of hall into the kitchen. A family sits at the breakfast table, mouths agape mid way through their food they find themselves staring down the barrel of a colt 45 held at arms length. No obvious threat, but his heart sinks, were they going to have to 'eliminate' these witnesses to this intelligence gathering?

Guy strolls over to the wooden table at the side of the large kitchen, lifts the cloth covering half a loaf of bread and starts to cut himself a slice while keeping an eye on the frozen family and glancing through the back kitchen windows he looks at Mac and Freddy squatting by some out buildings keeping a sharp watch on the surrounding woodland with quick head movements, eyes scanning back at the house.

"DD, what the bloody hell do you think you are doing?" Jim's face is calm as he enters the kitchen to the sight of Guy, his mouth stuffed full of bread. "Get outside, get Paddy on the wireless, clear those out buildings, stow those bodies, hide the Jeeps and set up watch, NOW!" his face contorts with an element of anger expressed in the last word.

Guy leaves with a barely audible and unrecognisable "Yeth Mir."

On his way out the front door he catches the sight of Raph grabbing the German captives head and yanking it backwards, his fingers, stuffed painfully into his nostrils. He is shouting repeated questions into the man's upturned face.

"Ya, Ya, Missiles, Vengeance Weapons! A-four, von Braun, von Braun,!" the captive answers back loudly, staring up at Raph.

Paddy is already on the wireless as Guy approaches the Jeeps.

"T one three WILDCAT, calling STAG, T one three WILDCAT, calling STAG, over".

"STAG here T one three WILDCAT - SHEEP A, SHEEP A, over."

"WILDCAT has the RABBIT repeat WILDCAT has the RABBIT, over."

"Well done WILDCAT standby, over out."

•   •   •

Guy had spent a surreal, unusual afternoon watching German military vehicles filing along slowly in one direction or another, they were completely surrounded by the enemy, but an enemy that seemed entirely preoccupied with its own demise, moving about in endless columns around the village that was clearly visible from this vantage point on the ridge. It overlooked both the property, now occupied by his team, and the valley and lowland in the direction they had originally approached. Strangely most of the columns appeared to be moving away from the front rather than towards it. Occasionally low flying fighters would suddenly shatter the silence of the surrounding woodland, appearing to be virtually at the height of the pine tops. To Guy's delight he watched two RAF Mosquito's swoop down into the valley and attack one of the columns of trucks, scattering German infantrymen in all directions. It was a sight that always made the hairs on the back of his neck stand to attention, especially when he had previously witnessed them destroying a locomotive travelling at full speed during the liberation of France.

All day the distant sound of warfare had gradually moved closer. A couple of times German vehicles had come up the same tracks they had used, and on both occasions Guy had signalled to the watch, but each time they headed straight past the driveway and off up into the hills.

To Guy's mind they would have been better off leaving with their catch immediately, but for whatever reason they had been told to stay put and they had now spent an agonizing few days watching the Germans retreating into the distance.

The Jeeps and one of the large black cars had been put out of sight in an outbuilding, all the documents and paperwork had been gathered and stuffed in a disorganised fashion into any kind of bag that could be found, these they would be sitting on in the rear of the Jeeps on their return journey.

Dusk had started to fall, a cold grey mist slowly appeared from nowhere, drifting inexorably up from the valley below and into the hills, seemingly moving the massive concussions of the distant guns further away, as it crept in through the pine trees.

Each one of the team knew they were in for yet another long, cold, stiff night with very little sleep, the watch would be rotated with two men catching two hours sleep off guard. Hopefully in one of those perfectly made beds in the house, but more than likely in one of the out buildings.

Guy pulling his Commando helmet comforter down over his ears settles into a mossy indent in the side of a rock strewn slope, conscious not to make himself too comfortable and risk falling asleep. He uses the rifle-scope to scan around at each of the men on watch, worried that the mist might become too dense for sight contact to be maintained until nightfall. The sky is clear the stars twinkling into view as dusk slowly turns to night.

As DD scans back across the lawn at the edge of the tree line he can still just make out the movement of the rabbits, it always amazed him how their grey fur seemed to blend so well into the green of the background, making the outline seem to fade in perfect camouflage. He catches a small movement at the base of a tree trunk, the darkness and mist make it difficult to be certain of anything at this distance, was it a rabbit? It seemed darker, larger, he concentrates hard on the spot until his eye starts to water slightly, then again, the dark movement. Guy's heart rate increases, his muscles tensing, goose bumps make the hairs along his arms stand up as if in chill.

The curved back of a dark figure on the other side of large pine trunk can just be made out. Guy scans the outline, from the other side of the trunk a long rifle points out, slowly following the line and angle Guy moves the cross-hairs up and across to the viewing platform. The head and shoulders of Jock holding a Bren gun can just be seen against the broken background of the pines behind him, he is looking in the right direction but from his demeanour he's oblivious to the threat.

Light was fading rapidly. As Guy tries to relocate the figure he spots more dark movement, two, three, four men. Uncharacteristically he hesitates on the best course of action. Should he fire a loud burst to raise the alarm? If he brings the sniper down with one shot possibly no-one will hear it. Is it a German team or could it even be Americans? Locating the original, crouched figure his decision is made, even though he can only see the curve of his back and one of his boots underneath him, Guy senses the enemy sniper is about to make his shot. Aiming for the largest area he can make out, his boot, he has no time to compose himself, squeezing the trigger gently, again the whoosh of the virtually silent recoil, but now, at night, it seems so much louder. The bark at the back of the pine splinters outwards with a fizz of a spinning bullet. Rifle re-cocked, Guy watches the sniper sprawl himself low to the ground, inadvertently making himself a larger target, this time he won't miss. He watches with a start at the sound of the shot, the small paratroopers type helmet the enemy sniper is wearing kicks off to one side, Guy realises that the noise of the shot was not from his own gun as the tracer rounds light up in all directions. The peace of the night is shattered with the sound of machinegun fire and the explosions of grenades. Guy curses as he observes the sniper still moving, back and out of sight.

Scanning about, it is too dark, the movement too quick, for him to be effective from up here, he's up and running with no clear idea of what he's going to do, exchanging guns on the run down the ridge.

It comes to him, he'll try to flank their position, the sound of his stumbles and curses in the dark are completely lost in the melée of the fire-fight

As Guy rounds the fence towards the entrance and drive, bullets and tracer rounds thud into the ground and vegetation around him. He veers off into the pines, the thought that he might be shot at by his own team in the confusion hadn't really occurred to him. The noise fades very quickly upon entering the thick trees, he has to slow his pace to push through the branches, unable in the darkness to see anything in front of him, shouting in pain as both eyes are poked by the sharp needles of a pine branch, now he really is stumbling blindly forward. Pausing, trying to clear his tear filled eyes, the subdued sound of the fire-fight seems to pause at the same time with just the occasional crack of gunfire. The thought that his team is being overrun forces him forward again, he tumbles down a slope finding himself on his feet on a rough track he heads over in what he guesses is the right direction. The going is easier, slowing his pace, trying be more aware and to ease his breath, he creeps forward crouched, tree to tree, he can see the lighter shaded area of the compound ahead. He stops. Silence.

He slowly becomes aware of a quiet liquid gurgle close down to his right.

"Помогать , Помогать МЕНЯ нравиться!…"

Then, a shout from much further away to the right.

"Выкидывать , Выкидывать!"

He senses rather than sees movement backing away from the clearing, bracing himself against the pine trunk he squeezes the trigger, the noise is deafening, the muzzle flash makes the picture before him even darker, with all his strength and training he can't keep the barrel of the Tommy gun from climbing off the target area, he must have lost the Tommy guns compensator that clips to the muzzle. So he keeps the burst short and then immediately crouches and moves position over to the right. He finds himself virtually kneeling on the source of the gurgling as he ducks down away from the expected return fire, which never comes.

"nomowb…" *[Russian word for help]* the blood and gases escaping from the mans chest abruptly stop.

"JEEPS, JEEPS NOW!" It is the unmistakable sound of Jim's shout, quite close by. Guy knows he has to move quickly or risk being left behind. After a moment's hesitation and a pointless look over his shoulder to the right, at the blackness around him, he's up and moving as fast as he can through the forest. A large dark shape moving rapidly suddenly appears from behind a trunk on the left. Guy runs straight into it, guns clash, as both men are knocked violently off their feet, winded, dazed. Guy recovers to his knees groping for his gun. He finds it and tries to bring it to bare on the target, the man on the ground in front of him kicks out and up, the burst of gunfire shoots off harmlessly into the woods. The flash darkens the vision even more. The hefty kick deflects the gun to the side, then connects with his chest, knocking Guy backwards, his legs buckled awkwardly beneath him, he's stunned and scared at the speed at which the larger, heavier, man lands on top of him with both hands reaching for his throat. Guy knows he's only got seconds, his attacker's weight and strength feel immense, he uses his left hand to clasp at his attackers wrists while his right reaches down to the leather sheath holding the dagger on his right hip, his pistol is holstered behind him, he now realises that was a mistake as he can't get to it. His hours of practise had been time well spent, the dagger easily pops free of the sheath. Using all the strength he can muster he thrusts the heavy solid metal dagger up into the man's groin area. Instantly the murderous grip around his throat slackens and the crushing weight lifts from his chest. Guy coughs and gasps for air as he pushes the man off to his left, grabbing gun, stumbling up and forwards the ringing in his ears clears as the breath rasps though his constricted, swollen and bruised throat. Hearing the wheels spinning in the gravel and the whining engines of the Jeeps pushes him forward faster.

As he nears the drive outside the compound he watches as the first Jeep speeds by, he's shouting, "GUY, GUY" as loudly as he can manage, not only to try and make them wait but to make sure they don't shoot him on their way out. Bursting through the bushes and landing painfully and heavily down the bank and into the middle of the drive, Guy looks up into the front of the fast moving Jeep. It slides sideways under braking as it comes to rest a few inches from him. With a scream and a shout a smartly dressed body lands with a sickening crunch right next to where Guy is getting to his feet. Throwing his gun into the back of the Jeep Guy easily picks up the cursing captive and throws him back into the vehicle, climbing in on top of him.

Paddy, having lost his balance as the Jeep stopped, tries to resume his urgent wireless message.

"T one three WILDCAT, calling STAG, T one three WILDCAT, calling STAG, come back. WILDCAT contact, WILDCAT contact, possible BEAR, EAGLE or WOLF, come back..."

"They were Russian! The *stink of Russians I'm sure of it." Guy rasped out to anyone who was listening.

The Jeeps sped into the night, up into the dark forested hills, heading north.

*(Note:- Many of the 30AU men quickly noticed that each nations army had a very distinctive smell (stink!) unique only to them, the moment you entered a room or building you knew which side had previously occupied it. The only one they could never really notice was their own!)

Chapter Sixteen

December 2006. Liverpool, England.

"Hello Harry. Thanks for allowing me to come and see you." I shook his hand once Harry had balanced himself enough to let go of the Zimmer frame.

"We spoke on the phone, I'm the grandson of Ron Guy who served in 30AU with you, do you remember him?" I worried for a few seconds that the long drive up to Liverpool had been in vain, Harry's face remained blank.

"Guy, Guy, oh yes, yes, I certainly do, what was the first name again?"

"Ron, Ron Guy, sorry to say he passed away last January and it is only been since then that I discovered he was part of 30AU, one of Fleming's Red Indians, as you were."

"Ron Guy, yes, yes, I remember, he was a boy that liked to do things his own way, couldn't tell him anything! EastEnd hard nut. He used to call me Sergeant Scouser, yep, I remember him."

"How are you Harry, things well for you?"

"Well, not too good, not too good, I've been house bound here in Liverpool, three years now, three years on my Zimmer frame, but at ninety-one that's not too bad, not too bad."

"Sorry to hear that Harry, getting old is a bore, but you sound pretty good to me. I wanted to ask you about Guy, do you mind? Have you got time to talk?"

"Oh yes, plenty of time to talk." We walked though the small house hallway and sat themselves in the kitchen.

"Did you find Guy a handful then, were there problems?"

"Problems, no, no, no more than with any of our men, he was a good boy. Just a bit hard headed, liked to do things his own way." Harry smiled his mind slowly drifting back to those far off days. "Anyone of my boys could have been the troop sergeant, in my place, they were all great lads, without exception!"

"I can assure you that hard headedness never changed, my whole family knows only too well. Were you with B-troop in and around Vannes in Brittany in August 1944?

Ron met Margot there, mid August I think it was, she was a member of the Maquis, the French resistance. Margot was my grandmother, after the war she moved to England and married Ron."

"Well, wonderful, what a story, wonderful, you know what, I might have a photo of her, I think. Yes I was there. I had just rejoined the unit after my injury. I was wounded just after D-Day, when we were attacked by fighter planes."

"Ah yes, I read about that in Ron's memoirs and archive documents, right behind UTAH beach, seven fighter bombers dropped a series of anti-personnel bombs, none of you had dug in, you learnt to dig in the hard way. Five dead, about twenty wounded, it was said at that time they had homed in on an overlong radio signal. Although Ron always believed it was US planes, I'm sorry to say. I have some photos, Ganger Gates, Corporal Swann with Guy and Margot in an Orchard. Actually the story was that Corporal Swann was constantly putting Guy on duties to try and keep them apart, I think he was interested in Margot."

"Ha, Ha, yes, yes, wonderful, I was there. Did he ever tell you about the torpedo and the mine, when the truck blew up, he was there with us…"

"No he didn't, but he did write it down thankfully. In Ron's memoirs it mentions an incident on VE day. Do you remember putting Guy under close arrest on Job's orders, because of Commander Turner, on or around VE day, making him sleep on the fifteen CWT truck?"

"Ha, Ha, wonderful, oh yes, I remember…Guy's team had just re-joined us, from the Harz Mountains I believe, we were always easy to find, you only had to listen out for Job's bagpipes… oh yes, he was going to break his bloody neck…thank God I stopped him…but only just, mind you…just after that, a whole group of us used our training and acquired skills to go and liberate some food and drink, boy, did we get into trouble. What they never seemed to take into account was the fact that none of us Marines had eaten or hardly drunk anything for over three days, our only liquid came from sucking dew off the grass in the mornings! We either had to steal it or beg old Patton to give us supplies. If it wasn't for old 'Blood-n-Guts' we would have starved I'm sure of it. He used to give us some wonderful tinned chicken, on Thursdays I think it was... I remember Patton gave us a target one time... he used to call us his 'Limey Gangsters'... always cursing us he was, but he looked after us Royal Marines, some huge German forest, Riechwald... something like that, I think... he thought it was full of V2 launch sites, but it turned out to be a huge weapon making or testing facility concealed within the forest, beautiful it was, small kind of miniature railway engines, pulled long racks of bombs through the forest and we came across others as well, one at Volkenrode... We were constantly looking for fuel for the Jeeps, put anything in them we did. The Germans had taken a lot of trouble to hide any fuel tanks, a few times we put aviation fuel or what ever it was, more like rocket fuel, the Jeeps used to fly, well fly for a short while, before the engine blew up. Then we'd take it back to the Yanks and they would be perfectly happy just to point at a brand new Jeep and say take that one, no problem, no fuss, no paperwork, jump straight in it and back on our way... actually we took boxes and boxes from that bomb making forest, full of tinned fruit, peaches, kept us going for weeks it did. Lasted right up into Bremen and beyond..."

May 1945. Outside Bremerhaven. Germany.

...The approach to Bremerhaven was an unusual experience; it was the first time Guy, or any of 30AU, had seen steel helmet wearing German soldiers who were not prepared to shoot at them. Up until then he had known that if the Germans were wearing helmets they were going to put up a fight. There were modern relatively undamaged buildings throughout the outskirts of the town and everywhere the local people were coming out to greet them with cheers and smiles almost as if they were being liberated rather than defeated. As they neared the main part of the town the streets became more of a mess, the Allied bombing and artillery had decimated most of the fine architecture. The huge 51st Highlanders convoy, to which 30AU had attached themselves, entered the crumbled city at speed. Lieutenant Commander Job in the lead

30AU vehicle, pointed out his intentions to the rest of his team, he directed them away from the Black Watch and the Highlanders tanks and down into the docks and their target, specifically the SS Europa, which was the German mobile Naval Command Head Quarters and on NID30's 'Black List' and therefore in Job's 'Black Book'. Guy's small team, straight from their eventful jaunt down in the Harz Mountains, had handed over their precious cargo to the US agents hanging out of a C-47 at an empty and very basic airstrip, the plane barely stopped moving and then the small team quickly re-joined Commander Job's unit at Bremen. The city was devastated, full of the sickly sweet smell of death, a smell that Guy felt was permeating his very stomach, a smell that would stay with him until the very day of his own death.

Team Four, under Job took the surrender of Bremen, quickly followed by the capture of the huge Deschimag shipyards (by Job on a bicycle when the Staghound broke down) with a bag of some sixteen of the newest Type 21 and 25 German U-boats, most of which were still under-construction, and also two operational Destroyers, they had caught them all in the process of being rigged for demolition by the Germans. They had also managed to put even more Allied 'noses out of joint' by erecting a very professionally painted sign on the Bremen Dockyard gates saying, in effect, this place now belongs to 30AU. (In actual fact they had taken it and its contents for the US military who turned up very quickly to take possession).

Commander Job's Team eight 30AU now consisted of two Staghounds, two Jeeps, two fifteen CWT Trucks and about thirty-five or so men.

Job raised his arm from the Special Ops Jeep bringing the small convoy to an abrupt halt in front of the Dock security gates. "Right I want one Hound and one Truck to follow us. The next Jeep and Stag to follow in fifteen minutes, a few minutes later the last truck."

The lead Staghounds thirty-seven millimetre and the Jeeps twin Vickers machineguns shattered the relative silence of the misty early evening air drifting up from the dull green-grey seawater. The large dockyard security gates, flanked by some small grey painted wooden guard huts, slowly disintegrated in a satisfying noise of breaking glass and cracking wood.

The weakened gates exploded open into wooden splinters and twisted linking metal wire as they were hit hard by the lead Stag moving at considerable speed. Yet again they had managed to surprise their main target. No obvious defence seemed to be in effect. A few German sailors sprinted out of view as the vehicles slid over the cobbles and into the dockyard. The huge bulk of the SS Europa came quickly into view above the low-rise harbour buildings. She was an impressive sight, fifty thousand tons, and a Blue Ribband winner in her day. She looked even more imposing with her angular graphic camouflage. Some of the upper lifeboats had been removed to accommodate the high radio masts and gun emplacements that she needed for her new role in the North Atlantic, although as far as anyone knew the Allied Naval supremacy had kept her in dock for most of the war.

The first line of vehicles headed down into the dock area, they skidded to a simultaneous stop next to the ship's entrance ramps, the Marines dismounting at speed. All were keeping a wary eye on the upper decks of the ship towering some thirty or forty feet above them, while they set up defensive perimeters and rushed the gangways.

The few Kriegsmarines that were in view looked on in bewilderment, unsure as to what they might be expected to do, none of them seemed inclined to take up any kind of defence, as yet.

"Guy, Higgins, get that Nazi flag down, quick as you can." Commander Job instructed the two Marines nearest to him.

"Yes Sir." They headed off into the maze of the ships corridors and decks, always in the general direction of the stern, as the other Marines secured the ship. After a few dead ends and a couple of surprised and unintelligible encounters with amazed German sailors, that they either killed or managed to lock into any room they could find, they had procured a White Ensign from the flags held in the ships own stores and got it hoisted. Guy quickly folded and stuffed the lowered Nazi flag within his battledress. They returned to the gangplank at a more leisurely pace.

Commander Job and an interrogator had started to question the sailors of the Europa and had been informed, almost at once, of the 'Narvik-Class DD' Z29 Destroyer preparing to make a get away as the Allies advanced into the area, again 30AU had caught them unprepared and much earlier than the German commanders had expected.

As they approached Commander Job called urgently. " Sergeant Smith, grab some men on the double, there is a ship trying to make a get away, she's just off the Columbus Quay, over there, we've got to stop that Destroyer leaving the harbour!"

The Z29 had cast off from the dock, but was not yet ready to make steam, the three thousand ton ship slowly drifted out into the centre of the gently swaying water.

The Marines boots beat down the cobbles as they passed the Command Staghound on the quayside, Paddy on the wireless could clearly be heard.

"T eight OSPREY, calling STAG, T eight OSPREY calling STAG, over… OSPREY has the WHALE repeat OSPREY has the WHALE, over…KILLER in transit, repeat KILLER in transit, over…"

A small Tug was just in the process of casting off, near to the stern of the Europa. Guy, Higgins and Sergeant Smith quickly leapt off the dockside and on to its deck. It only took them the couple of minutes that the other five Marines needed to board and to relieve the crew of command.

Job and another few Marines came running along the quayside too late to board as Guy headed the Tug out into the harbour and straight at the dark looming hulk of the Destroyer.

The sun was low in the sky and shining from behind her silhouette, accentuating her size, it also meant that the Marines were temporarily unable to see if their approach was being monitored or maybe even about to be fired upon by any of the ship's numerous guns. It appeared luck was, as it always seemed to be, on their side or possibly it was just the sheer audacity and speed of the attack that just confirmed the old axiom 'luck favours the brave'.

The swell in the sheltered harbour was minimal as Guy guided the Tug up to the swaying hull of the freshly painted Destroyer. He used the controls to keep the boat firm against the ship until all the Marines had clambered up onto the deck a few feet above them. As Guy climbed up onto the railings, the Tug immediately drifted out of reach, he watched it drifting quickly away with a glance to the quayside, back the way they had come. He could see the rest of the unit watching from the dockside. It was only then that the thought occurred to him that all eight of them were now marooned on a fully operational German Destroyer probably manned by at least three hundred battle hardened Kriegsmarines. The sound of machinegun fire and loud shouts pulled him quickly up and over the railings, his Thompson sub-machine gun at the ready.

"Hands on Heads, Hände auf Köpfen! NOW!, JETZT!" Sergeant Smith and Marine Bonney were the only two of his team he could see. They had about six or seven hesitant looking German seamen in front of them; all were slowly looking about, almost in some kind of trance or daydream. Unusually they were all dressed in tropical whites, the ship had obviously been about to head for warmer seas. Eventually they all raised hands in surrender. The distinctive metallic thudding noise of Tommy gun fire sounded from both fore and aft of the four hundred feet or more of the ships decks.

"DD, Bonney, get yourselves up to that bridge, secure the radio room and the Captain, quick as you can. I'll get these boys below. Unten unten, durch diese Tür! COME ON, JETZT! JETZT!"

The wireless operator hadn't heard Guy and Bonney approach despite that fact that quite a lot of shouting had preceded them. The small door burst open from one swift but heavy boot. He virtually leapt to attention, up and out of his seat in shock and surprise, the coiled electrical wire ripping his headphones across his face as he stared intently at the end of each gun barrel. The large wireless set still crackled with life and the small electronic gurgles of unrecognisable messages.

As they dragged the radio operator forward to the bridge they could both make out the distinctive clicks of guns being prepared. They shoved the terrified German into the entrance door and followed him through.

"SCHIESSEN SIE NICHT!" The shaking wireless operator threw himself to the floor as the two Marines followed him onto the bridge. Three men flanked the German Captain. Two sailors and one Officer. All three held their guns at the ready. Everything stopped. A sudden silence broken only by the tiny distant shouts echoing about the ship.

"HALT! STOP! It is all right, es ist gut, I'm Commander von Mutius. Everyone remain calm, jeder bleiben ruhig."

The three Germans slowly lowered their guns.

"Get this ship back to the dockside. Now!" Guy turned and winked at Bonney. "I'll sort the flag." He left the bridge and once again located a White Ensign in the ships own supply of flags. He ran it up and stowed the Nazi flag within his webbing.

As the ships crew were disarmed and locked below decks some of the disgruntled Germans reacted in surprising ways to the capitulation of their Captain, whom they obviously respected enormously. Some broke down into sobbing fits while others became excessively aggressive. The mood improved somewhat when the Captain addressed his men via the ships speaker system, as the Destroyer slowly made its way back to dockside. Commander Job and Sub Lieutenant Grenfell and some more Marines were piped aboard by the ships own crewmen on Captain von Mutius's orders.

The docks had now become much busier with onlookers, mostly dirty, ravaged, half starved figures of Russians who had been released from a prison ship further along the quayside. The situation was getting difficult. Guy kept an eye from the ship's bridge, as he searched for cyphers and documents in the now open strong box. Some of the stronger Russian men seemed intent on boarding the Destroyer to take revenge on the Germans. It was only with great difficulty that Sub Lieutenant Grenfell, who was a bespectacled, fairly frail, studious looking man, but who was, thankfully, fluent in Russian and German, managed to get them under control and back to the prison ship, where Job promptly doubled the Germans own guard until a better solution could be found, but with only thirty-five 30AU men at his disposal at that time there was no other way.

Guy had the distinct impression the German Captain was more nervous about his situation than he should be. Some parts of the ship had been staunchly defended by the crew and Guy suspected they were harbouring some important Nazi's. Men who were probably trying to make their get away to warmer climates, which would have explained the Naval Whites and the freshly turned out ship, which looked immaculate.

The ships crew were mustered on the dockside and all but bare minimum were marched away to the naval barracks.

As darkness fell Commander Job accepted an invitation to dine with the Captain while the 30AU men liberated as much food as they could find in the circumstances and spent a long cold night making sure the Germans did not try to scuttle any of the captured ships. Certain areas remained off limits even to the 30AU men and Guy suspected the stowed Nazi's were going to remain hidden until the Americans arrived, which they did the following day.

The next few days were spent searching the whole dockyard and surrounding warehouses for technical information on weapons and mines. To Guy's immense frustration this meant he was, yet again, acting as no more than a 'skivvy' to the units mine expert, Lieutenant Commander Turner, who had made his position very clear with repeated complaints about the terrible reputation 30AU had already achieved for ill discipline and the general disregard for personal cleanliness in the field. He was an austere man of about forty with a hard bony face and a man that DD had taken an intense dislike to. While the Marines had to forage for themselves, they were supplied no food and drink at any time by their own supply teams, the Naval Officers, who they were there to protect and to keep alive at all costs, were mostly, to Guy's mind anyway, 'soft living' specialists and Guy found himself, after three days with virtually no food, having to serve fried breakfasts to Commander Turner, again.

DD grabbed the mess tin, into which he had scraped the breakfast that was making his stomach ache and his mouth sore with saliva. He stomped over to Commander Turner and 'plonked' it down in front of him and turned away instantly. He wanted to be away with his anger so that it may fester someplace else.

"Not like that boy! You WILL show me some respect boy! These damn bloody Marines, you can't trust a single bloody one of them. Come back and present it PROPERLY!" Commander Turner jumped to his feet raising himself to his full six foot two inch height.

The speed with which DD had reacted and was back at him, caught Turner entirely by surprise. Guy launched himself across the falling table, knocking the breakfast and everything else flying in all directions.

Turner found himself with his back facing his opponent and helpless, his arms, head and neck firmly held by the fantastic strength in Guy's arms.

"NO you don't boy!" In turn Guy found himself jumped on by Sergeant Smith, he'd been watching the scene unfold and was ready to intercept just in time, and at the crucial moment. Unknown to Turner, Guy had gone for his dagger, thankfully Smith had stayed his hand and the dagger remained sheathed. Smith heaved him backwards but Guy was not going to let go so easily.

"I've had enough of these fucking CAPTAIN BLIGH'S!" Guy shouted it into Turner's ear.

"Easy Boy, come on, calm down, this is not the way to end the war." Sergeant Smith liked Guy, he'd trained with him all through the many 30AU courses, and he was certainly one of 'his boy's'.

"What the hells' going on here?" Commander Job had heard the ruckus.

Everyone, except Guy, tried to pipe in at once.

"Alright, Alright, enough! Guy, let him go, NOW!" Shouted Job

DD had great respect for Job he would willingly have put his life on the line for Job at anytime and had done so many times. He relaxed his hold; Lieutenant Turner quickly straightened himself bristling with indignity.

Turner went to remonstrate.

"That's enough.." Job brought him to heel. "Sergeant Smith, place this man under close arrest, I've had enough of him disobeying orders, I can't spare him his duties, but he is to man the Bren on the back of the fifteen truck and he is also to sleep there forthwith. Get him out of my sight."

Guy, Smith and Job all knew this to be a completely arbitrary sanction in the circumstances, but thankfully it seemed to be enough to placate Turners obvious anger, for now, anyway. Guy was at least thankful that Job's tough and extremely diligent young sidekick was on the other side of Europe at that point in time otherwise he knew he would have really been in trouble.

That day's searching quickly led to the use of the very truck Guy had been assigned to. Interrogation of some captured personnel had led to the discovery of another depot for some advanced deep sea mine types, on the other side of town. A squad of 30AU headed through the town and quickly came upon the Fifty-first Highlanders tanks, held up by a pocket of German resistance ahead, medium mortar shells were landing nearby, they were being fired from a small copse over to the left of the road. The Germans spotters, if they even had any, were obviously not doing a very good job of trying to home the shells in on the tanks, and their aim was fairly random at that point in time.

Job arranged with the Highlander's tank commanders for a 'creeping barrage' which 30AU would use to advance behind to the target, which was just in view across some fields on the outskirts of town.

As Guy and his team moved behind the intense tank barrage the half-hearted German defence capitulated almost at once.

"WAFFEN UNTEN, HANDE AUF KOPFEN!, WEAPONS DOWN, HANDS ON HEADS!" Guy screamed above the noise of explosions, which did not cease for some considerable time.

The 30AU Stags and Jeeps were first up the road towards the slowly moving German prisoners. The Marines had disarmed them and lined them up on the side of the road in front of a freshly dug ditch. As the vehicles approached Guy and the other Marines were supposed to board the moving vehicles, but both Job, in the leading Jeep, and Guy, on the opposite side of the small road noticed a few of the prisoners looking extremely apprehensive, one or two even threw themselves to the ground as the Jeeps approached.

"STOP, STOP!" Guy and Job screamed the command together. Guy jumped in front of the lead Jeep, bringing the whole line to a swerving, screeching, halt. With at least one loud crunch as the two Stags collided. Curses and shouts could be heard along the line, even above the small arms fire and occasional mortar rounds still bursting out in the surrounding outskirts.

Job sprung from the Jeep and unbuckled one of the shovels, directing a couple of the Marines to fetch some more from the Stags and Trucks.

"Sie Manner, nehmen diese, anfangen, aus diesem Abzugsgraben zu graben!" He instructed some of the prisoners to start digging in the ditch, to which they stared, wild-eyed at him and around at their fellow countrymen.

"Bitte!, Der Abzugsgraben hat Explosivstoffe, Sir." The nearest prisoner started to plead at Job.

"Welches von Ilhnen kennt den Standort der Explosivstoffe?" Job instructed the prisoners who seemed to know the location of the mines to accompany

Lieutenant Commander Turner and help with the digging out and defusing of the mines lining the road. Meanwhile the Marines were instructed to make sure the surrounding terrain did not contain anything or anybody likely to try and take advantage of the sitting ducks their convoy had now become…

•   •   •

" …and that was how we saw out the days around VE day. I'm not even sure exactly which one was VE day; we were so busy running about, and so preoccupied trying to find food and not get killed. Around that time other 30AU teams were scattered all over Germany. Commander Postlethwaite captured the German Torpedo test facility at Eckenförde the whole Naval wing of 30AU was based there for weeks uncovering all their secrets. Commander Lambie and Team Four had followed some 'Special' clue to capture a top Nazi Professor, Professor Wagner, working on guided bombs somewhere in the Harz mountains, I think. I don't know who else was caught down that way but lots of rumours, lots of rumours. Apparently the Germans had tried to evacuate all their Naval people and intelligence down to some secret place in the Harz mountains."

"Any mention of von Braun? Could any of them have been the rocket scientists that ended up with the US military?" I desperately wanted to hear what these 'rumours' might be.

"I don't know, sorry, it was all so busy, so many secrets, no-one really knew what the hell was going on most of the time. Team fifty-five under old 'Sancho' Glanville had managed to secure the entire German Admiralty records and some very important Admirals and technical staff as well, at Schloss Tambach Castle, just south of Erfurt, mid Germany, and they had driven about all over the place, following tiny clues from each of the intelligence points they had captured. They ended up right inside the Russian sector and took them from under their very noses. Apparently they shipped out about fifty tons of stuff, all the way back to Blighty from that castle, and among others, one of the biggest problems they had was the large 'Fraulein Androde' who worked in the archives and was very determined to set fire to the whole lot! Sergeant Major Brereton and his small team had captured Admiral Karl Dönitz the new Führer, who had just taken command of Germany after Hitler's death. We were right there on the leading edge throughout the whole of Germany." Harry's voice still sounded strong, he seemed to have plenty of stamina left for conversation, even at his age. "After securing the mine depot at Bremerhaven and leaving Turner's team six to sort through the masses of mines and technical information, Guy and my team, twelve, I think it was, we got the call that we were required 'post haste' at the port city of Kiel, where Commander Curtis and team three, had captured Helmuth Walter one of the Nazi's top scientists and his whole facility and staff, they had prototypes of midget subs, torpedoes, guided missiles and even a rocket plane, without doubt one of the fastest aircraft in the world at that time…"

•   •   •

…The fast drive from the outskirts of Bremerhaven, through the ruined city of Hamburg was eventful, pockets of German resistance existed all around and it seemed the whole City was completely devastated, the roads were mostly impassable and the small convoy was constantly having to about turn, to find an alternative route. The sky was packed with Allied aircraft of all types. Jim's battered Jeep led the way, with two Stags and two trucks struggling to keep up. Guy didn't much like travelling in the trucks; he much preferred his usual place in the back of the lead Jeeps, where you could see what was around you and more importantly what was up ahead.

They had just managed to cross the river Elbe, when some small arms fire sounded up ahead, yet again the vehicles ground to a halt. This time the Marines were quickly out of the vehicles and taking up positions of cover. They found themselves with the men of the Seventh Armoured Division who had liberated Hamburg and were still trying to 'clear up'. Jim's Jeep reappeared from up ahead, travelling at speed, it slid to a stop along side the other vehicles.

"Guy, Flynn, get yourselves up to that point over there, snipe to keep their heads down. I'm going to call in some mortar fire on the ragtag bunch of Jerries that just fired on us." Jim sprinted off, over to the men of the Seventh who were a way further back down the road from which they had approached and gathered around one of the many Cromwell tanks and half tracks that were lined up and waiting to go.

Guy and Flynn quickly, but stealthily, moved into position. Guy shouldered his rifle and used the scope to scan the scene and to count the enemy numbers in obvious view. He eventually picked out the most likely candidate for an Officer, although it was far from easy as they all looked just about at 'deaths door', but before he had even had the chance to squeeze off one round, the mortar fire came in and everyone got their heads down, until, after a few intensive minutes, it had ceased.

As the smoke and dust from the mortar shells cleared the noise of the half-tracks came thundering up the road, and two low flying Spitfires that screamed overhead suddenly and completely drowned out all other sounds. Guy and Flynn were up and running at the bank along side the tracked vehicles. As they approached the Wehrmacht soldiers began to stand up from the bank with hands raised. Guy and Flynn were at first taken aback by their appearance. They were indeed a 'ragtag' bunch, gaunt pale faces with black sunken eyes, mostly boys and old men in baggy filthy ripped uniforms, barely recognisable as the enemy.

They started to disarm and line up the dazed Germans closest to them. The 30AU vehicles came forward along side a group of tanks.

"Guy, get yourself here!" Jim tried to scream above the din of diesel engines and tracks.

DD had just about caught the words, as he turned the filth covered Panzer-Grenadier next to him turned as well, his face was vacant as if in a state of shock.

"Guy? Votre nom est Guy?" He spoke slowly as if in a daze or on drugs.

"You're French? Votre Francais? Que le fuck vous font-elles dans cet uniforme?" DD had been working hard to improve his French ever since his time in Brittany. He couldn't understand why a Frenchman would be here, and dressed like that.

"Nous sommes de l'avant Russe, pour étre honnetes je n'avons aucune idée!" The mans head dipped, he looked as if he could barely manage to remain standing, let alone be able to fight.

"GUY, for fuck sake, MOVE!" Jim's voice sounded much nearer and he was obviously not in the mood to be kept waiting. DD turned and sprinted over to the Jeep and was promptly reminded by Sergeant Smith to get in the truck behind them. He grabbed the arm of Flynn who hung from the back and swung up into the trailer as the vehicles accelerated away, back on the road to Kiel and Commander Curtis and the eventual capture by Commander Postlethwaite of the Nazi submarine and torpedo testing facility at Ekenförde. Although in the event Guy's group ended up capturing the Neumünster Wireless Headquarters instead and spending a few warm sunny days relaxing on the lawns there...

•   •   •

...I was impressed with this ninety-one year old man, a man who still referred to my Grandad as one of 'his boys' but then again why shouldn't he, after all he never saw or heard of him again until now, over sixty years later. "Fantastic Harry, it's been an honour to speak with you, thank you so much for your time. If you don't mind I'd like to spend some more time chatting soon, I'd like to talk about the training and your time in Scotland? But I've got to get going, my sons have got competitions to go and take part in, fencing and tennis and we're going to be late at this rate."

"Oh yes, plenty of time to talk, anytime. One other thing, do you know how secret it all was at the time?"

"Well, I know that it was secret and a secret kept for fifty odd years after the war and everyone involved signed the Official Secrets Act, which does actually cover all memoirs, even up to seventy years after their deaths!"

"Oh Yes, that's right, lots of secrets still, but one chap, a Naval Petty Officer, I think it was, he was with us in Germany, when he went back to his unit in Blighty, they tried to charge him with desertion, never heard of 30AU or NID30, thought he'd done a runner for the whole bloody war. They nearly threw him in the clink when he turned up in his Khaki battledress at the Naval base, poor chap. He'd done a good job too. And another thing, no medals or awards, if they had tried to get medals for individuals they would have had to explain the circumstances under which they had been earned and as it was all secret they couldn't have any, not a single one I think!"

"Thanks Harry, what a story, that certainly demonstrates the secrecy at that time, right, I need to get going, bye-bye for now."

"Oh you might want this."

He handed me the group photo of B-troop, framed in grey cardboard, but this one actually had the men's names written on it unlike the one of Ron's.

"Thanks Harry, I've been trying to list the names but no-one even seems to have tried before."

"Bye, nice to meet Ron's Grandson, at last, see you again soon."

Chapter Seventeen

January 2007. Essex. England.

"Hello, hi, is it possible to speak to Jack please." I asked.

"Hello, well, yes, but he's not too well at the moment, in bed, bit of a chest." A lady had answered.

"Sorry to hear that, hopefully not too bad?"

"No not too bad, hang on, what is it you want?"

"I'm the Grandson of Ron Guy, one of 30AU, Jack's old wartime unit, I wondered if I could chat to him about it?"

"Oh yes, lovely, yes I'm sure he'd like to talk to you, hang on."

I listened intently to the noises on the other end of the line, as the kind sounding, but wheezing lady walked through the house and up some stairs.

"Jack, this man would like to talk to you about Thirty."

"Ah yes, okay. Hello."

"Hi Jack, I hope you're not feeling too unwell to talk?"

"No it is okay, you go ahead."

"Do you remember Ron Guy, one of 30AU?"

"Ron Guy, yes, yes, one of the new boys, I think. I was an original, one of the original men invited to make the unit. Not a part timer, HO whatever they were. These new boys were nothing but trouble. Looting, no discipline, most of them were RTU'd. There were about six or seven RTU'd around Paris time, we were blowing all these Safe Boxes, too much temptation I think, couldn't help themselves trying to keep some contents, if you ask me, although I don't know for sure what was involved, there was talk of payrolls, works of art, treasures… I know the names…"

"RTU'd, Returned to Unit? Was Ron trouble, do you remember if he had problems?"

"No, I'm not sure, I don't think so, I'll have to think about it, it will come back, the names are all familiar, but takes me some time to remember…"

"Of course, no rush, no pressure, I'm just keen to know all I can, that's all. You mentioned looting, I hear the Officers probably did quite well out of it all?" I had heard lots of rumours about some of the things 30AU had come across and possibly kept.

"WELL, bloody well. Some of them made a fortune, I'm sure of it." Jack had raised his voice, this subject had obviously got his hackles up.

"I'm thinking about doing a book, about Ron and my Grandmother, Margot, she was member of French Resistance, they met in Brittany while 30AU were down there." I wanted to try and slowly get round to the specific questions I wanted to ask.

"A book! We've got one, what's the point? No one knows the truth. What a load of Tripe! What's the point, it will not tell what really happened, no one will ever know. It is all secret, on the secret list. Why we went down to Cassis in South of France, certainly not to pick up a bloody Torpedo! We've had too many books, no one gets it right, one chap got published, made packet, then the book was banned, withdrawn, all wrong. Too many people trying to say what they don't and can't know about." Jack was beginning to sound distressed, upset, this wasn't going as well as I had hoped.

"Okay Jack, I'm sorry to hear that. I certainly do not want to upset anyone, as I said no pressure, I don't want anyone to say anything they don't want to tell me or do not feel comfortable telling me. I just really wanted to remember my Nan and Grandad and what they were involved in, certainly not to upset anyone else. Thank you very much for your time, if you do feel like talking about any of it please do get in touch, any and all information would be gratefully received. Maybe we can talk at one of the reunions? But thanks for now. Thanks Jack." I had decided it would not be wise to push this man who sounded as if he had a lot of pent up frustrations, probably festering for sixty odd years, just as they had in my own Grandad. It felt as though I had been listening to Ron rant again

"Okay, I'll think about it, we all took risks you know, risked being shot as spies if caught out of uniform and we were asked you know, asked to cover our uniforms, it was a constant battle just to do the right thing and we all knew that if caught we were on our own. Our own government would have denied our existence in an instant if we'd been caught photographing things we shouldn't have down on that coast. Maybe more will come back to me, it will come back to me. Bye for now."

"Bye." The phone clicked down, but did not cut off, I could still hear the conversation.

"Who was it dear?" Jack's wife, her voice was clearly audible.

"Guy, Guy yes all the names sound familiar. Thinks he's going to make a bloody bomb from his book, not with my help he's not, what a load of Tripe!" Jack was obviously still upset about something.

"Was this Guy older than you?" His wife was trying to calm him.

"No, new boy, trouble. Well they all were…"

*Click. I hung up, I desperately wanted to listen on, but it would not be right. He was upset. It had been just like listening to my grandparents. The same phrases, same tone of voice. Upsetting these people was certainly not my intention. It seemed some of them were still hung up, even after sixty years, hung up on who were the originals, who were the 'time serving' men, added for D-Day, and who were the 'part timers' (Hostilities Only) the replacements for the dead or wounded. Men who the original core of 30 Commando resented as having 'spoilt' 'their' special unit. It seemed to me they were all heroes and should be accepted as such. No one now could, or should, tell them apart. *(Or should they? I'm no longer sure. I have since learnt that at least one Royal Marine who had been RTU'd from France, in disgrace had entrenched himself in the Veterans Association to the chagrin of some!)* This was going to be a difficult road to take if I went ahead with the book as the only way of getting this important historical story out in the open, I was going to tread on toes no matter what I did, and still probably never really know the whole story of my Grandad or 30AU especially if the OSA got in the way.

As I read through Tom Bower's excellent book, I could not understand why the world seemed to have ignored it, when it seemed to prove conclusively that the US had lied and covered up their use of Nazi war criminals, who even went on to become world famous heroes of the American nation with institutions and colleges named in their honour. 'The Paperclip Conspiracy', also gave a very different perspective on British Intelligence and 30AU in particular, whose reputation was, according to his sources, more akin to Patton's view of them, an undisciplined private army running amok, complained and argued about for its entire existence, the 'Pirates and Gangsters' of his rants, far more interested in sexual conquests than scientific ones. Indeed maybe Fleming's famous character owed a lot more than had yet been credited to 30AU, who Fleming not only referred to as his 'Red Indians' but also, on occasion, as his 'Indecent Assault Unit'.

I had now to give more credence to the repeated reports I had come across that 30AU were controversial right from the start of their operations. A private army of the worst kind. Constant official complaints about behaviour in the field, drunkenness, direct orders being disobeyed, poor adherence to uniform rules and personal cleanliness. But maybe these were only caused by the very nature of the men chosen to undertake command of this type of unit, risk takers, adventurous explorers. Men like Riley a Polar explorer and 'Red' Ryder and Whiteley, Job, Glanville and others, these types of leader were essential to the success of a unit of this type and also meant they were only going to pick and select men of a similar nature to make up the bulk of the unit, fighters, rule breakers, risk takers, which was also only ever going to lead to one kind of reputation, unfortunately, not a good one. Especially if anyone who ever came to study them was never going to be able to uncover all the facts with which to make a considered opinion, facts and records which had probably been destroyed many years previously or even amended to suit their governments own ends.

Yet in the British governments own 'History of 30AU' it announced they had been 'Successful in the Extreme!' Which seemed to me to imply that not all of their successes were being eluded to within the pages of that very report.

* (I'm very pleased to say that I have since met this man in person and he was most gracious and welcoming and as helpful as possible.)

Chapter Eighteen

6th September 1946. Vannes, France.

Margot, her brother Guy and her Mother, Marguerite Wilthew walked up the precarious gangplank onto the ship that was to take them from St.Malo, Brittany to Britain for a visit to the estate in Shortlands Kent and then on to the larger estate in Scotland to Bridge of Allen, near Stirling. They were on the way to visit her uncle, Roy Wilthew, whom Margot only knew was something to do with the Knox Whisky Brewery. Her father's brother was now the guardian of the Wilthew Estate after the recent death of his mother, Harriet Wilthew (Margot's Grandmother on her father's side). This death meant that a visit had to be arranged to sort through the monies that were her family's due from the estate, as Guy Wilthew's (Snr) widow. It was not a situation Marguerite Wilthew was entirely happy with and she had a constant suspicion that some of the monies due were in fact going to go elsewhere, but without hard evidence she knew they could only take what was given and be as civil as was required to get it. Obviously the war had made communication somewhat difficult over the last few years and a visit had been arranged to try and bring everything up to date.

For the French people of Margot's home town of Vannes, life had improved rapidly after the liberation, with the Nazis no longer shipping everything back to the 'Fatherland' the food supplies had quickly begun to improve, although it would obviously take a lot longer for things to really start to approach the way they were before the Nazi occupation.

The family had been overwhelmed with joy the day that Guy Wilthew (Jnr) had arrived back at the house. Unannounced he had just appeared as if from thin air, he arrived on a Wehrmacht motorbike, in a German helmet and with a German machine gun slung on his back. His FFI armbands were clearly visible. Physically he looked much as he always had, slightly thinner maybe, his smart suit hung loosely from the shoulders and obviously a few years older but other than that, he looked just the way he had when he had left in his pristine uniform to fight in the French Army, all those years before. But Margot could see there something else within his eyes. She knew they were all different people, but the depth of his gaze had changed, probably forever, more than it had in the rest of the family.

Margot initially tried to spend as many hours with Guy as she was able. They often rode out together on his motorcycle into the Bretagne countryside, which he loved to photograph and she loved to paint. But no matter how she approached the subject and tried to draw out of him some emotion, or small story, something with which to begin to rebuild and repair the damage so obviously and deeply done, nothing was forthcoming. Although he was alive, something else inside him had clearly passed away, she prayed that whatever it was it was not completely dead and it would, in time, return.

She had received Ron's first letter at Christmas 1944, she had at that time been upset that he had not written earlier and constantly found herself wondering if he had survived the Liberation of Paris and the rest of Northern France. The memory of that one and only kiss in the Cathedral Vault had remained as perfectly fresh in her mind as the day that it had happened and she felt it would always remain so, even if she lived to be one hundred.

The letters exchanged between them had slowly increased in intensity and passion and culminated in Ron's reaffirmed proposal of marriage to which she had eagerly accepted. She had begun to sign her return letters with 'your future wife'.

Her mother, whom Margot found herself unable to discuss Ron with, remained mainly ignorant of the growing feelings between the two and was determined that Margot should marry one of the men she had picked out of the well-to-do families they mixed with socially. A constant stream of wealthy sons would come calling to try and make some kind of impression on a woman whose mind was entirely focused on a 'working class' English soldier, nine years her junior, on the other side of the globe and who seemed likely to remain so for the foreseeable future.

A plan had slowly begun to form in Margot's mind. She knew that her father's will had made provision for her, even though she had only been about three when he had died, a provision had been set aside that would become due when or if she married. She found herself constantly wondering if money was the true reason her mother was so keen on her daughters finding husbands. But the idea had slowly begun to make itself larger in her mind, a plan for her escape that seemed to her the only way forward.

•　　　　•　　　　•

Margot had found the journey to Dagenham by train and then through central London all a bit overwhelming on her own after the large row that had preceded her departure, which still felt as though it was ringing in her ears. Unbeknownst to her the white five pound note she had intended to use had just been withdrawn as legal tender, so she had found herself short of money and fairly lost. On top of that she was still very upset at the parting words that had been used by her mother.

The row had erupted in the Scottish Wilthew household, accusations had flown that her mother had been caught trying to go through private papers. When Margot had then also suddenly announced she was not going to return to Bretagne but to use her joint English/French nationality to stay in Britain, Marguerite Wilthew had lost her temper almost instantly. Then Neville and Roy had started to argue with each other until the whole family household had been in turmoil, from which, apparently, it has never recovered, even to this day!

Her mother still referred to the man Margot had unexpectedly and proudly informed them she was leaving to marry as *'Beau Bête'* and she had made it very clear she only considered him a young peasant, brought up from the depths of the London slums and who would never amount to anymore than just that. Certainly far too far down the class scale to ever be considered worthy of her daughter's hand in marriage. But Margot had refused to give way.

Roy and Neville Wilthew, her uncles had listened intently to Margot's plan and expressed their support for what she intended to do and had also informed her that once she was married, her father's provision, as set in his Will, would indeed become hers by right.

Margot, still in a thoughtful daze, walked through one of the entrances to the District line Underground Station, she stared up at the arrivals and departures board, trying to make some kind of sense of it, feeling a sense of rising confusion and a slight panic.

"Excusez-moi Monsieur... Sir, excuse me ...veuillez me dire la manière... ermm Dagenham station please, Foxlands Cresent, could you tell me how to get there, please?" Margot spotted a uniformed man walking purposefully through the waiting passengers, one of the underground workers, who looked friendly and strangely familiar to her, like a long lost friend.

"Hello Luv, of course I can help, that's what I'm here for! Now let's have a look shall we. You're in luck, that's the very road I live on, Foxlands Cresent, so I should know the way, shouldn't I..." He smiled warmly and Margot instantly felt very much better.

He looked at the address on the small piece of paper she was holding. "Well now, would you look at that, number eight..." he seemed surprised.

"Yes, number eight, Ron Guy, I'm going to meet Ron Guy." Margot smiled hesitantly, unsure as to the uniformed man's reaction and huge beaming smile.

"Well I'm pleased to meet you young lady, my name is Frank, Frank Guy, I'm Ron's Dad... his father... you understand?"

The next few weeks were difficult for Margot while she stayed in Ron's small room not really knowing when he might return or what to expect when he did. There was also a very awkward moment when one of the girls Ron had met while stationed on the south coast of England had turned up at the door asking for him.

Frank, she felt, had a genuine affection for her, but his wife, Dorothy, Ron's mother, seemed cold and austere. Frank tried to reassure Margot that 'Doll' as he had always called her, had become that way because of the war, he was of the opinion that she was even suffering some kind of 'shell shock', numerous bombs had landed nearby and one or two virtually right on top of her and she never really recovered from the effects. *(These effects lasted her entire life, I even remember her repeatedly throwing me, as a very young child, out of Bluebells and into the street when she had reacted badly to my constant childhood wargames.)* It had certainly left in her an uneasy dislike for all things foreign. Unfortunately that seemed to include Margot. She constantly found herself wondering if she'd made the right decision as she waited in this tiny house in Dagenham, London.

Dorothy and Frank had received the telegram from Hong Kong informing them of their son's illness and the fact that he was on his way to the military asylum at Fareham, but they had kept the main details to themselves. There was an obvious stigma attached to mental illness. But Margot had picked up that something was seriously wrong and the fact that she did not actually know what it was only made her that much more concerned and upset. She naturally feared the worst.

The day she knew Ron was on his way home she spent sitting in the front living room in her coat, watching out of the window. All attempts to remove or distract her were futile.

When she eventually saw him round the far corner of the Street she ran out to meet him. He looked tired, thin, but very smart in his dress uniform and just as handsome. She embraced him right there in the middle of the street with a passionate kiss.

Chapter Nineteen

6th September 1946. South China Sea.

Ron Guy laid in the filthy hammock rocking wildly from side to side, the noise of retching and the stench of vomit and faeces was overpowering, the typhoon was to rage for three long days. The sound of the waves hammered and boomed against the sides of the ship, the stresses being put through the hull structure were audible. He'd had no choice but to take the lower hammock as the stupefied madmen, of whom he was now officially one, had been forcibly loaded onto the hospital ship and locked away in the already stinking lower decks.

As soon as the war in Europe had come to an end he found himself initially in Wrexham and then moved about all over England, transferring from 30 to 44 and then shipped out with 42 Commando, B-troop, to guard Japanese prisoners of war in Kowloon. He missed the men of 30AU desperately, but so much more than that, his mind and heart had been overpowered by a need, by love, by Margot.

Unbeknownst to either of them, on the very same day Ron's hospital ship had sailed from the Hong Kong port bound for England, Margot had left Brittany with her mother and brother and her unannounced intention of staying in Britain to be with Ron.

His mind drifted as randomly as the massive seas about him as Ron recalled the chain of events that had led him to this hellish pit...

•   •   •

Angus and Guy had become close friends in 46 Commando during its time in Wrexham, England immediately after cessation of hostilities in Europe and now were together again in 42 Commando and after the Bay of Biscay storm had tried to sink their converted aircraft carrier cum troopship, where Ron had again found himself in the unfortunate position of being in a very low hammock, they now found themselves in south-east Asia. After a tour of 'Pirate Patrol' trying to protect the mail boats and other trading vessels that were being harassed by communist backed Pirates, they were now guarding death row prisoners.

Three men sweated profusely holding the difficult, powerful martial art stance that their prisoner, Jalea was instructing. Clark, Angus and Guy, already well trained in hand-to-hand combat had been mightily impressed by the discipline and training of their Japanese prisoners-of-war, who had taken it upon themselves to instruct their guards, not only in their language, but also in their martial art skills. Jalea had formed a close relationship with Guy, who had even begun, slowly, to divulge 30AU stories to him and been given, in return, a hand drawn Marines emblem entitled 'Woolies Looters', a reference to Guy's original D-Day landing team of Woolforce under Colonel Woolley and their haul of loot found within the German safe boxes throughout Europe.

Angus dramatically and totally unexpectedly, burst into twisted spasms of pain, convulsing back and forth across the floor. Guy had been worried about his friend for a while. A few days before he had started to act strangely when he'd begun to tell him of the bloodbath that had been the liberation of Walcheren Island.

His Commando Brigade had sustained the highest percentage of casualties in the war. Guy had listened intently to the story, although his mind could not help wandering to his own tales, but he was so very wary of re-telling his own stories to the other Marines of his troop. The threats and need for secrecy had been so firmly drilled into the ex-30AU men, they just dare not speak about any of it. But the need to express his feelings and thoughts about his experiences had begun to almost involuntarily leak out to one of the Japanese prisoners he guarded.

As Angus had told his story, he had slowly descended into a jabbering wreck, unable to control his own actions, sweating, twitching and finally passing out and now this.

"You two, get him to the military hospital in Hong Kong." Major Gardener-

Brown shouted at them, in obvious anger. "Corporal Guy, get to my office quick as you can when you've finished with him at the infirmary."

"Yes, Sir." Guy and Clark picked up Angus and carried him off on a stretcher, they eventually found their way to the ferry to take them across to the island hospital.

"Do you think this must be what delayed shell-shock looks like?" Clark was a virtually silent man and very rarely expressed any opinions. "You know this is how you're going to end up if you don't stop behaving like a 'Little Devil'."

Guy smiled, he knew Clark was referring to an incident when he'd been chased, while naked, around the kitchens of a large restaurant by the cleaver wielding father of one of the waitresses he'd been caught with.

"His Commando Brigade were decimated by German crossfire on the flooded land of Walcheren Island, Angus only just made it through, he lost a lot of good friends." Guy then informed him of the story as he'd heard it previously from Angus.

The nurse was a huge man, an ex-professional wrestler. Guy liked him instantly, he reminded him of his grandfather, Sonny, who had been a bare-knuckle fist fighter of some renown in the Docks of London. They helped him to change and administer Angus. The nurse tried to re-assure them both about Angus's care as they reluctantly left.

Upon his return to the barracks Guy headed straight to the Major's office. The Major had been good to him, even quickly approving his promotion to Corporal upon his troop Captains recommendation and Guy respected him for it. He entered on request. "You wanted to see me Sir?"

"Yes Guy. At ease. How was Angus?" The Major finished with his paperwork.

"Not too bad Sir, he seemed to settle once we got him away from here, Sir."

"Good, good. Now look here, it has come to my attention you're spending far too much intimate time with these prisoners. They are death row war criminals you know. Not your own personal tutors. It's got to stop and stop now." The Major gave Guy an intense look.

"Yes Sir." Guy knew only too well the mental torment and anguish being with these prisoners over the last few months had brought him. He had learned enough of their language to enjoy the company of some of the men, only to discover, as he stood guard next to them in the military courts, that they were accused of the most heinous crimes imaginable. The evidence was enough to make anyone sick. There seemed to be no correlation to the crimes and the punishments either. Some of the worst mass murderers and torturers were not being punished, while men who seemed to be guilty of so much less, Guy had had to stand guard over and watch executed. The men who had been in charge also seemed to be receiving more lenient punishments than the men who were probably just obeying their orders. Everything had begun to feel twisted and distorted, nothing was fair, NOTHING. Ron now knew there was no such thing as justice in this world. It was all taking its toll and he had found his constant nightmares were getting worse, much worse, he was being awoken every night by the screams of dying people. He had to get out.

Two days later Guy headed straight back to the island hospital to see Angus, when he arrived he was shocked. Angus was still in the same bed, but tightly strapped into a dirty straightjacket and belted down to the white metal bed frame. His eyes were black and sunken, the pupils dilated, they darted back and forth unable to focus, his face bruised and cut, his front teeth had been knocked out and his lips were a bloodied and swollen mess. Coherent conversation was virtually impossible.

"What the hell happened to him?" Guy angrily confronted the huge nurse.

"Whoa, whoa, slow down boy. He exploded in a fit of violence. When you two blokes left and we tried to examine him he attacked anyone who approached. We had to restrain him." The nurse looked as if he was ready for another fight.

Guy was upset and angry, he continued to visit Angus as often as he could, until one day the bed was empty. He was gone.

"Back to England mate. On his way home." The nurse explained that Angus had been loaded onto an Asylum ship, which had already left port for England.

Ron and Margot's acquaintance had continued by mail and memory alone, since that fateful day in August 1944. Ron sent his first letter in the Christmas of that same year and since then they had started to correspond regularly. At first the letters had been slow and formal but gradually the letters increased in intensity and frequency, a passion had slowly entered their writings and continued to grow and develop until it had evolved into a desperate longing, both now expressed the urgent need to be together as soon as possible. Their lives now revolving entirely around the arrival of the postman. Finally it had culminated in Ron's reaffirmed proposal of marriage and Margot's eager acceptance. Both needed to be together, but together without any obligation to a military force.

He had had enough of killing and death, he felt the very stench of death had somehow entered him, infected his soul and stomach, the pale watery blue eyes of the pleading SS guard at Ohrdruf were beginning to haunt his dreams, a dying man that he had ignored. How and why could he ever have been turned by his country and its war from an innocent young man into a killer, a killer cold bloodied enough to have ignored a dying man to have denied him even one last sip of water? It was something he would never understand as long as he lived. Was he really capable of that? How had the '*powers that be*' turned him into a monster?

The nightmares only continued to get worse, they echoed with ever loudening screams of trapped and dying people. Dreams which somehow managed to carry that sickly sweet smell of death, a smell that would never quite leave him. He found himself constantly wondering if maybe by escaping the military he could relieve his tortured mind of the nightmares and his past? He even found himself wondering if one of these 'Samurai Warriors' some of whom he had found himself respecting and liking had cursed him as they looked him in the eye at the very moment their necks were snapped at the end of a rope.

The thought of the other 30AU Marine colleagues that had only signed for 'Hostilities Only' and were therefore free of service already, just added to the feeling of desperation. He now couldn't understand why he'd ever signed a twelve-year contract, he had to get out, it had started to become an obsession.

It was June 1946, just six weeks after Angus's departure when a letter arrived from him, explaining what he'd been through since leaving the Far East and ending with the revelation that in fourteen days time he would be discharged, back to the 'Sanity of Civvy Street'. Guy was pleased for him.

That night, again awaking with a start in the early hours, dripping with sweat and expecting to find himself surrounding by mangled, stinking bodies, it

255

came to him, his plan for escape.

He began first thing in the morning, bombarding the poor Major with 'chits', requests for courses that no longer existed. A few days later he made constant requests to see the Major.

Eventually the duty Sergeant at arms marched him into the Major's office, Gardener-Brown's stony look confirmed that Guy was no longer flavour of the month.

"What do you want this time?" Snapped the Major.

"Sir, it is my conclusion that you have taken a dislike to me for some unknown reason. I therefore request a transfer. Sir." Guy had, for once, rendered the Major speechless.

The Major reflected for a few moments, "Dismissed. And Guy, do not darken my door again." The anger clearly etched into his already stern face.

When Guy returned to the lads of the troop he immediately began to speak gibberish, just as Angus had done previously. After a few days he requested an appointment with the Psychiatrist and a week later he sat in front of an Indian Sikh Doctor in the Hong Kong hospital spouting garbled stories about his grown sister. In reality his sister had died in a cot death as a baby and he only had two brothers, Frank and Ted.

Still he found himself as Corporal of the guard on sentry duty, when his chance finally came.

A fire had started in the petrol depot opposite the guardroom gate.

Guy quickly organised his men into key control points to keep back the rapidly enlarging crowd who were eager to watch the spectacle. The Chinese firemen had arrived quickly enough but seemed to be unable to extinguish the raging inferno.

Acting on impulse, Guy realised this was the moment. Looking about all seemed as under control as it could be at that stage. No one was obviously in danger of losing his or her life. Deciding that if sanity was doing what was expected, insanity must be the opposite.

He ran at the engrossed firemen intent on their task. He knocked the leading fire-fighter off his hose and started to drag the other two with him into the tornado of exploding fireballs engulfing the structures of the surrounding buildings. Every drag forward threatened to start blistering his skin with the heat.

Major Gardener-Brown had arrived with a team of A-troop men just in time to witness the events unfolding before an ever-enlarging crowd of onlookers.

"Get that man under control, now!" The Major was horrified at the confusion being caused as a direct result of Guy's irrational actions, he sent in two men to restore some law and order.

The intense heat of the inferno he was approaching certainly had his attention, but Guy was aware enough of the goings on behind him to realise the men were coming for him. He relinquished the hose to the competent firemen.

"Sorry mates." He flattened the first two Commandos' to reach him. The Major moved forward with more men. From behind the lead Chinese fire fighter, whom he'd knocked off the hose approached unheard in the roar of the blaze, a pickaxe handle raised to strike.

"No." Major Gardener-Brown darted at Guy as he tried to turn, but too late. Thankfully the Major deflected the main force of the blow with his outstretched arms, but it still connected with Guy's head and shoulder stunning him down onto one knee. Three more men were felled in the ensuing struggle until Guy found himself spread-eagled and upside-down held by many hands. He stopped his futile struggles and relaxed.

"OK men, put him down." The Colonel had arrived to the sound of the crowd cheering and applauding the entertainment. Guy struggled to his feet and stood to attention before the Colonel and the Major who was nursing his badly bruised arms.

"Give me a thousand men with an appetite for a fight like him and I'll march on Red China tomorrow!" The Colonel smiled, unconcerned about the scene before him.

"Get him to the sick-bay." Guy was marched off into the comparatively cold and quiet solitude of the barracks.

The next day he found himself being escorted to the hospital. The only thought on his mind was how to accomplish the next stage of his plan.

"Strip." The guard handed him the obligatory striped pyjamas, which he changed into in the middle of the ward. The doctor appeared with the biggest needle Guy had ever seen. Bent over the metal-framed bed a sample of spinal fluid was extracted. He was then handed over to his friend the ex-wrestler nurse and given the very same bed that had been Angus's all those weeks before.

Two weeks later on the 6th of September 1946 he boarded the H.M. Hospital ship, the Empire Clyde, that was to take him back to his love. He was desperately worried, having been unable to communicate his intentions, how would Margot feel about marrying an official madman? How would he provide? He had been trained solely in the art of killing, camouflage and intelligence gathering from the enemies of his nation, a powerful, alert and formidable enemy, how could he be returned to an unsuspecting normal English community? How was he going to fit back into civilian life? Could he ever fit back in? What work was he suited to do? How in the hell was anything ever going to compare to the bond that he had had with his fellow 30AU Marines and the tension and excitement of overcoming impossible odds during their secret missions to conquer the Nazi nation? Was he now passed his best at 21? Was he now a spent force? Was his nation and its people finished with him?

After the relentless pounding of the typhoon, Guy had spent the next few days shunning the advances of the ships Captain who had taken a fancy to him. The Captain was constantly requesting Guy to be brought to his quarters and Guy had an uneasy feeling this man had done this many times before with others in his charge and was also very concerned that if he knocked him out, as was his first impulse, he would find himself trying to swim back to Hong Kong. Thankfully the Captain seemed to take the rejection fairly calmly. The same skipper had arranged for a rope cargo net cage to be constructed by the ship's crew, which allowed the demented below decks, access to the outside world. The sailors of the ship watched the freak show from any vantage point they could find. Guy only took the lift up to the cage once, he preferred the company of the chaos below decks. Amongst them morphine addicts, a vicar's son who had contracted syphilis and men like himself, men who only wanted to escape their own nightmares. All were drugged up to the eyeballs.

After weeks of travel they eventually arrived at the Royal Naval hospital in Fareham. His mail awaited him and also his friend Angus, still unable to leave the Asylum.

The months of stress had taken their toll. From a fighting weight of twelve stone Guy now barely topped nine, the news that Margot awaited him at his parent's home in Dagenham just added to the stress. Had he done the right thing? How could she ever love a skeletal madman like him? How in the hell was he going to make a living? All these thoughts and more made themselves very real as he boarded the Gravesend - Tilbury ferry on the final journey home.

He needn't have worried; as he walked, in full Royal Marines dress uniform, down the partially bombed out east London estate and to Foxlands Cresent towards number eight, his parents house, the vision of his 'Angel' approached him.

He knew she was the 'Angel' to his 'Little Devil'. He knew with all of his heart and soul that his one and only chance of redemption from the things he had done in the name of his country lay within this 'Angel'. Jet black hair, stylish French coat and perfect blue shoes. Completely oblivious to the disapproving looks of the local gossips, right there in the middle of the street they embraced in a passionate kiss.*

(They married on 17th January 1947).

Beau Bête

Chapter Twenty

1947 Vannes, France.

Margot and Ron stared up at the huge Cathedral as they walked hand in hand up the sloping cobbled street, through the Prison arch of the City Wall in Vannes, Brittany. For Ron the last time he had seen this street had been during the liberation in August 1944, three years previously, as he had strolled with his friend 'Ganger' Gates to call on Margot. For Margot she was returning as a married woman, on her way to try and repair the damage done to her mother's emotions from losing her daughter to a man she considered unworthy. Ron and Margot had talked long and hard and both came to the conclusion maybe a life in France might be preferable to the East End of London or England, which was still suffering the after effects of war and the endless rebuilding required to repair damage done by the bombing raids.

They had walked slowly from the railway station down towards Cathêdrale Saint-Pierre-et-Saint-Patern on this beautiful warm mid summer's day. Ron was concerned that the visit was going to be a mistake, but Margot had been insistent, she wanted to try and patch up her broken relationship with her family and she considered now the right time to do that.

Armelle, her sister, had just given birth to her first child. Margot had found herself to be unhappily lost in an unfamiliar country, with a man she loved deeply but who was suffering terribly from the after effects of war. He was racked with guilt for some of the things he had seen or done, could barely function at times, unable to sleep or escape the constant nightmares filled with screaming dying people and the pleading watery blue eyes of a dying man he had ignored. He wondered if he would ever sleep soundly again, he'd even awoken to find himself physically attacking Margot in the early hours of the morning, which had obviously only made his mental state that much more fragile.

In his early twenties the war had all but destroyed him physically and mentally, he was very, very nearly at the end of his tether, he felt almost unable to even look for work, any work and at times he couldn't even mentally lift himself from the armchair it was all just too much. *(It was over two years before he finally felt ready to face his first job after leaving the Marines, a milkman).* Up until then they had been existing on the money that Margot had, but both knew that could certainly not last forever and both had begun to worry about what would happen when that income had finally dried up. This trip to France was maybe one way forward for them both.

They found themselves at the front door of the terraced house in Rue des Chanoines, knocking loudly, but with no answer. After a time they walked slowly in the mid day heat round to the back gate and let themselves in with the key that was still hidden in the same spot, and had been for as many years as Margot could remember. She instantly felt so much better at the sight of her beloved bird tables still teeming with her birds. She was convinced they were happy to see her come back into the garden.

The house was cool, dark and silent. She called for her mother and was surprised to find still no answer. They walked together through the house taking in the atmosphere of the beautifully decorated rooms. Her family's works of art returned to their rightful places.

They made their way up the stairs conscious of the silence in front of them.

The nursery, freshly decorated, her heart rejoiced at this obvious display of expectant new life. Entering the room she made towards the large crib that had been in the family for decades and which took pride of place in the room by the window, as she approached it Ron grabbed at her arm.

"No, stop!" a faint smell had caught his attention, a smell that he could never escape, it filled his nightmares and he found himself constantly wondering if he would ever again truly escape its memory. The smell of Death.

A tiny baby beautifully dressed and wrapped in a crocheted blanket lay in the traditional lace covered crib. It looked like a perfect porcelain doll, pure white and just as cold.

As they walked down the main isle of the Cathedral, still in a shocked empty daze, on their way to pray, they spotted the small group of her family. They were kneeling in prayer in the St. Ann Chapel in front of the statue of

St. Anne d'Auray the patron saint of Bretagne (Brittany). The reunion was tearful and awkward.

Armelle's baby had died an unexplained cot death in the early hours of the previous morning and all were quite understandably inconsolable.

Margot was in emotional turmoil, the thoughts of beginning her own family were so near that her sister's loss was that much more real to her. The difficult task of bringing her family round to accept her new husband had become impossible. Everyone was trying to deal with their own individual grief and everyone had to do that in their own way and in their own time.

The visit was made short.

•   •   •

1950 Vannes France.

On this visit Margot was determined to bridge the family rift. Ron and Margot had their first child, just a toddler, Gwen, and Margot was heavily pregnant again. Ron's fragile mental state had improved rapidly as soon as he had immersed himself in work, any work, and he found himself in various states of employment, Milkman, Bus Conductor, Mailman but none managed to hold his attention for long. Armelle had her first child, Richard, and Margot deeply longed for the family to be properly reunited...

Ron sat on the bare floorboards in the dusty attic room surrounded by piles of photographs and negatives; the last few days had been difficult, the job of turning her mother's mind on Ron was going to be a long one.

Margot had started to sort through some of her stored possessions and had been distracted by these photographs that now surrounded both her and Ron.

Her brother Guy Wilthew had returned from the war a changed man, introverted, quiet, distracted, he had not and would not discuss his war. He had poured his energies into photography; postcards and books published under the name of Gaby or Gabriel, his wartime wireless codename. It was something that he had always shown a keen interest in even before the war had interrupted all their lives.

Most of these photographs were taken by him of the Wilthew family and friends, if they had not been taken by him they were taken on one of his cameras in his absence.

"Who's this?" Ron had started to become irritated by the many photographs of Margot with, to him, unknown men. His fierce jealous streak was starting to get the better of him. "and this, who is he?"

It was a jealous streak brought about the constant awareness of their class difference and the fact that Margot's money was at present providing for the pair of them, he felt, and very strongly, that it should be his job to be the provider. But how? He just did not know. The worry and the nightmares were already starting to force his mind into a cycle of highs and lows. *(A cycle which would continue for the rest of his life and eventually lead to his early death).*

"Oh Ron, they are suitors, men who my mother thought suitable for me. There was never anything between myself and those men. They just called in and tried in vain to gain my attention." Margot ignored his growing agitation.

"Well you won't be needing them anymore then will you." He knew these were rich men. He picked a few of the offending pictures and moved over to a tiny fireplace within the attic, where he set alight to them.

"Ron, please, that fireplace has not been used in years. It is not safe to use it, please put them out. I'd like to keep them anyway." Margot pleaded in genuine concern for safety and also dismay at the loss of treasured memories, that and the fact that the air in the attic was already far too hot.

Ron ignored her and continued to throw the odd picture into the fire, which certainly made him feel better.

Then a *photo caught his eye that made his heart miss a beat. Nazi SS uniforms. A group of men standing in what looked like a dark factory. The group of men were top ranking German Nazi leaders, he instantly recognised some of the faces and uniforms from his training for 30AU and also from the press and newspapers articles of the war crime trials that had taken place in Germany over the past years.

Top ranking German Nazi's, he recognised faces, some of these men 30AU had captured. He picked up the pile of pictures that it had come from. A strange knotted ball made itself felt at the base of his stomach as he looked through these photographs. He recognised V2 rockets or at least small parts of them. These prints were detailed, close-up pictures of the working parts of Nazi rockets. Mainly the fin and rudder parts.

"Who's this?" Ron held a picture of three suited men in front of Margot. She tried to ignore him, thinking it was only going to add to his fire. "Who's this?" He insisted.

"Oh… that one is my brother, Guy, you met him yesterday, I've no idea who the other two men are. Why?" She looked at him, puzzled as to his sudden change in demeanour.

"Only what you already know, he spied for the French Communists, he won't talk about it. He was never actually of the mind of the communists. It was not his political ideology, but it was at that time the only way to fight the Nazi's, when he first arrived in Vichy, France they were backing the new occupation. The communists were his only opportunity to fight back against the country that killed Alphonse and invaded his home." Margot was distracted by the small fireplace.

A slow rumble had begun to accompany the sounds of the flames that were consuming the pictures of her ex-suitors.

Ron was completely distracted by his thoughts as he watched Margot stand and move over to the tiny fireplace. He slowly became aware her face was one of concern, she was listening to the slow roar of flames, which had increased,

(It is never fully explained what these photo's were actually of, other than photo's of V weapons and Nazi's, but whatever it was, it seems to have left Ron in no doubt that Guy Wilthew was somehow connected to 30AU missions and that he eventually was murdered because of it. It was something Ron never fully discussed with anyone, although he had been heard by many members of the family to mumble that his opinion of Guy's death was murder. Whether he ever actually discussed these things previously with Guy I guess we will never know, but I do know that they did meet on occasions.) In my own opinion it seems so incredibly unlikely that possibly it was all just in Ron's own head, some kind of connection that came to him in later life as his mental state deteriorated.

rapidly. It was now fast becoming a vibration, the floor and walls of the attic had begun to shake. Ron knew instantly, the chimney was ablaze. The knot in his stomach had just doubled in size as he realised he had now managed to set fire to his new 'French-in-Laws' house.

"Ron, RON! Do something! I told you not to burn those stupid pictures! They meant nothing, and now look! MERDE! DO SOMETHING! FAITES QUELQUE CHOSE RAPIDEMENT!" Margot stood looking back at him, as she used her hands to support her large round belly.

He grabbed a plain solid metal fireguard and tried to wedge it in front of the fireplace, in order to try and restrict the airflow up into the chimney. But it would not fit.

His only thought now was to get her out, as quickly as possible and everyone else in the house who were downstairs with the children, Richard and Gwen. The bricks in front of his face had begun to smoke with smouldering dust, as had the wooden beams on the inside of the roof. He swung Margot into his arms and carried her down the stairs, screaming "FIRE, POMPIERS!" at the top of his voice.

As the family left the house into the narrow cobbled street they joined a crowd that had already started to gather. All faces were raised skywards watching the flames that were shooting out of the large chimney stack. These flames were accompanied by ever increasing clouds of black smoke, which had already started to billow from the open windows of the attic rooms.

Thankfully the Brigade des Pompiers were quickly on the scene and the damage was relatively minor considering the amount of smoke that had preceded it and was restricted mainly to the attic and a small part of the roof at the back of the building.

In the next few days both Ron and Margot quickly came to the conclusion they would have to leave. If there had been any chance of changing Marguerite Wilthew's mind about Ron's eventual acceptance into the Wilthew family, the events of the last two visits understandably seemed to have dispelled them, completely.

They returned to England as quickly as possible to their new house at twenty-six, Leigh Park Road, Leigh-on-Sea in Essex, which they had fallen in love with during their honeymoon; and bought upon the return from their first trip to France. They had both thought France might just be the better option, obviously they both now knew that was not going to be the case.

They were in time for the birth of their second daughter of the eventual six children. Gwen, Mag, Kath, Ronny, Margot and Rosie, that they would happily and eventfully raise in and around the south east of England.

BEAU BÊTE

Epilogue

I spent days and days going over and over the documents, notes and information I had collected from the 30AU Veterans, the National Archives, Libraries and Websites and the Royal Marines service record of Ron's. There did not appear to be any record of the incident over the breakfast table, no reprimands recorded up until he was discharged for being 'below the standard expected of a Royal Marine' while out in the Far East.

The documents together did form a substantial list of Intelligence gathered by 30AU, which was an amazingly eclectic and extremely long list, all gathered by about six field teams according to the Official Documents. There were at least a dozen Admirals listed, one of which was actually the Führer (just promoted) as well as their entourages. The entire German Naval records. Lord Haw-Haw's premises. Any amount of technical weapons installations and the hardware associated therein. Certainly it would appear on the face value of these lists, that to collect that much information and material would have needed far greater logistical input, many more teams and back-up than were listed in these documents anyway.

I started to look into what happened to these captured men and their innovations. Professor Herbert Wagner, caught near Blankenberg, within the Russian sector by 30AU team four, led by a US Naval Officer, as recorded in the National Archives. Wagner was a brilliant scientist working on highly advanced guided missiles and bombs that had already been used against Allied shipping to devastating effect. He too had been handed straight to American Secret Agents by 30AU along with all his plans and prototypes, ending up working and living with the US Navy and according to Tom Bower's 'The Paperclip Conspiracy' and his source of 'ALSOS' (American Intelligence) mission reports the Professor had apparently 'surrendered' at the same time as the von Braun and Dornberger in Bavaria. This was the first official documentary evidence, albeit separated by the Atlantic, that the official military version of the US capture of these scientists was fabricated, just made up. A Professor Martin, a chemist working on fuels for V weapons, again captured in the Harz Mountains and handed over to US agents. The Z29 Destroyer, captured at Bremerhaven, within the British sector, apparently packed with technical plans and top Nazis (who were they?) trying to escape to southern seas, that too was handed straight to the US military. All the brand new Type 21& 25 German U-boats captured (by Job on a bicycle) while still partially built and rigged for demolition by the retreating Nazi's at the Bremen dockyards (British Sector), then controversially signposted on the dockyard gates as belonging to 30AU, all handed over to the US military. Helmut Walter captured at Kiel by Curtis and team two, with SAS support, in the British sector, was kept, at least for the short term by the British Secret Service at Barrow-in-Furness, but again, as with Wagner and the Von Brauns, his inventions were certainly verging on the genius, years ahead of anything else going on at that time.

It was also recorded that Wernher von Braun was handed back to the British Secret Service in Wimbledon London, (the recent target of some of his very own V2 missiles), for their two week long interrogation, before his transportation to the USA. Why? Were all the Nazi scientists given over to Britain to be questioned? Or just the ones the British had captured for the US?

In fact it appeared that the entire modern US military owed the beginnings of a vast majority of it advanced weaponry to Nazi Germany and a great deal of it was originally captured by 30AU, were they working for the Allies or just the USA?

It was also recorded that a small detachment of US officers had been 'attached' to 30AU, one of whom was Angus MacLean Thuermer, who later went on to a high position in the CIA, were they using Fleming's 'Black List' as well or following their own target list or just keeping an eye on what we British were capturing?

Ballistic missiles, Cruise missiles, torpedoes of all types (guided, jet propelled, homing), guided missiles and bombs. Submarines (Midget and other), Type 21 & 25 U-Boats, probably the fastest submarines in the world at that time. Rocket planes, Jet fighters some in production others as plans, radar installations of a type that only other scientists would recognise, early warning systems, acoustic scanning systems, harbour defences, endless lists of mine types, (deep sea, undetectable, anti-personnel, anti-tank, anti-life!) and many more technical innovations, the lists just kept getting bigger and who knows what else they found and decided never to reveal to anyone. Chemical? Biological? Weapons of mass destruction!? Plasma fire-balls?

Was all this information collected by 30AU and just handed straight to the US?

Was it now possible the CIA, like most of their hi-tech weaponry, were just an extension of the Nazi SS, without such fantastically striking black *Hugo Boss* uniforms (although maybe they were also wearing *Hugo Boss*, quite probably in fact!) prepared to lie, murder and to hide the facts in order to serve their own ends?

Had 30AU captured either Wernher or Magnus von Braun or even both and handed them straight to the US military? They had certainly captured more scientists than were officially recorded, snatched in their family homes in front of their own families as recorded in these scribbles?

Or was it all dreamt up by a madman in an Essex mental institution while under a combination of electric shock treatment and heavy sedation?

•   •   •

I had written to the French side of the family, who amazingly still lived in the same house that Grandad had called upon, sixty years previously during the liberation of France. I had asked for all or any information regarding Nan's brother, who had died on his motorbike in 1968. But I did not hold out much hope of receiving anything back. Nan's one lifetime wish had been to retrieve some of her father's paintings that should rightfully have been hers according to her brother's Will, but the French relatives had refused all efforts at communication about the subject and when one of my aunts had finally taken up the cause late in Nan's life the resulting stress had probably brought on Margot's first stroke much to her extremely distressed daughters upset.

To my delight I received an unexpected letter back from France, but what it told of Guy Wilthew's wartime, to my disappointment, seemed mainly shrouded in mystery, even to his closest relatives. They referred to his training in the army to operate a wireless, but from what I had heard from Nan, Guy would not have even needed much training for that, she had often remarked on Guy's electronic wizardry. Telling me the story of how he had built his own quadraphonic music system throughout the living rooms of the house while still in his teens. They also referred to his unit being one of the very few who tried to resist the initial Nazi invasion of Northern France, with catastrophic consequences, virtually the whole unit was wiped out. Guy had somehow managed to escape and had made his way south into Vichy, France, eventually joining a communist resistance movement which was involved in various operations against the Nazi occupation, but what they were no one seemed to know. Although whatever they had been had left Guy Wilthew as a lifelong and vehement anti-fascist campaigner.

I had been only a baby when Guy had died. Nan had often spoken very fondly of her brother and told me that on one of his visits to her in England just before his death he had been very taken with me as a baby and only relinquished holding me with a great deal of reluctance, having never had any children of his own. Margot had also been desperately worried about his well being on that visit, he and therefore she, had been convinced it was to be their last contact. For some unknown reason he had been worried for his life, Nan had been entirely sure of that.

I had begun to wonder if having these historic revelations in the public domain would keep me and my family safe? Or would that just mean being swamped with crackpot conspiracy theorists? Or Americans, with guns, defending the heritage of their country? Was I thinking as my Grandad would have done? Or was I going as mad as he had ended up? None of these were very comforting thoughts.

April 2007. Channel Tunnel. England, France.

My mother, Gwen and I sat together in my car, talking earnestly as the train hurtled through the channel tunnel.

I had been working hard putting together the love letters and memoirs into some kind of order, when I wasn't forced to try and earn some money and keep my clients happy. I had at first worried about the fact that Grandad would have signed the 'Official Secrets Act' which would make his memoirs, however manic they appeared, legally subject to a Government censorship, but any OSA intervention would of course only prove beyond doubt the story was true and increase peoples' awareness and help get the important 'facts' out in the public domain. If I was eventually thwarted by publishers or the OSA I had decided I was going to publish the story on the 30AU website which was already attracting a lot of attention even without this part of its history. I had begun to realize that no one was interested in trying to discover the truth, the world at large was just happy to sit back and absorb what they were fed by the authorities, just so long as they had money in their pocket, gutter press with topless girls and satellite television channels with which to occupy their time, their nation was content. I had also begun to wonder if those were the very same basic human traits that would allow a strong passionate leader, during a time of harsh countrywide difficulties, to brainwash and control an entire nation, even if that leader did turn out to be as insane as Hitler.

I took the half an hour sitting in the car going through the channel tunnel to try and explain my discoveries and motives to Gwen, my mother.

"This may come as a bit of a shock, but all Ron's writing and these letters, seem prove that the Allied military has lied to world for the last sixty years, lied about how Nazi scientists were captured and exploited, some of them even ended up as national heroes, rich and world famous, when they might even have been complicit in war crimes or at the very least turning a blind eye to Nazi atrocities. I've even found documents that seem to confirm that they hid the truth. But there may be even more to it than that. I showed her a leaflet, it was in French, and some photographs of paintings.

"Kathy, your sister (Ron and Margot's third daughter of six children) and her family, they recently went to visit Brittany. Margot's birthplace, where her family still lives. They went to see if they could contact any of the French family and to see some of the paintings that Nan had wanted to retrieve all of her life, but had never found a way of doing so without the use of the law courts. The French relatives refused to see Kathy at that time, in fact they have so far refused all contact, but I've been in touch, they have agreed to meet us.

I think they are still concerned about what should have been Margot's according to her brother Guy's Will, anyway they still own the same house, the same house where Ron met Margot, the same house where he says he found photographs of Nazi's that were taken by Guy (Wilthew). Kathy brought these things back with them on her visit, this leaflet 'Musée du Faouët' and these photographs. They are photos of the paintings, paintings by my Great Great Grandfather, Louis Le Luexhe, he was the French Imperial court painter over a hundred years ago, although he quickly refused to work for them because he felt they were living too decadently. And these, the paintings of his son, Alphonse, they were religious painters and Louis's son-in-law, Guy Wilthew, my Great Grandfather, your Grandfather, he was an Aristocratic English artist who owned properties in Kent and Scotland, he travelled the world painting portraits of the rich and famous from all the countries he visited. He fell in love with twelve year old Marguerite Le Luexhe when he rented a vacant studio in Le Faouët, then he returned there every year until she was eighteen so he could ask for her hand in marriage. This painting on the front cover of the museum brochure, it was by him, the father of Guy Wilthew, they both had the same name, father and son. The son was your uncle, my Great Uncle. No one in the family ever knew what he had been up to during the war, only that he had been a wireless operator, spying for the French Communists, even though his political ideology was not that of a Communist, it was at that time the only way to fight back at the Germans.

I tracked down and contacted a second cousin in France. Armelle's son, Gildas, I sent him some photos of his mother that I found at 'Bluebells', he'd never seen them before and was very grateful, despite all the problems between the families he has agreed to see us. I asked about his Uncle Guy's time fighting the Nazi's, he eventually wrote back explaining that he didn't know anything more than us, but he sent me these photographs of Guy, taken shortly before his death that he got from his twin sister, Guénhaële and his older brother Richard. In Ron's writing he talks about Guy's photography and photos he found of Nazi's in the Attic at Vannes and incredibly they own the same house in the medieval town of Vannes, which is where we're going now.

Guénhaële still has photographs and writing that were Guy's maybe his memoirs, still there in the house at Vannes, possibly even with the photographs that Ron wrote about. Nan told me many times she suspected her brother Guy had been fearing for his life, had even come to visit her in England she felt as a goodbye, a last farewell, just before his death. Ron's scribbling, that I'm still trying to make sense of, in amongst all those crazy coloured drawings and rants that speak about Guy's murder, at least he had believed it was murder and not an accident. He seems to have become obsessed with coincidences, there is all sorts of diagrams and equations, none of which seem to make any sense at all, but they seem to refer to the coincidences. Like Guy's accident, one year to the day before the 'Eagle' landing craft touched down on the moon and the day both Ron and Margot left for England the 6th September, neither one aware of the other as well as other dates and the names, just about everyone is called Guy! He was convinced Guy Wilthew was some kind of connection between 30AU and the Nazi scientists they captured, that's what drove him to depression throughout the later years, a fact that he could reveal to no one or risk bringing the attentions of… I don't know, deadly attentions, from whoever *they* are. He thought he was protecting his family. Maybe he was never sure if that threat was real himself, but how could he take the risk? If he believed that Guy's ex-ladyfriend, Barbara was only visiting him and his family to keep an eye on them, to try and find out if they knew anything or if Guy had passed on his knowledge. Gildas thinks she is now dead and no one else knows anything about her, no family, no numbers, no addresses, no photographs, her face is obscured in every one. Maybe she was actively looking for that very manuscript, Guy's memoirs or the photographs Ron says he found, maybe she even found them or more probably they all went up in flames when Ron set fire to the house by accident. Maybe Ron had to just sit there and live with it, his entire life worrying that he and his family may be in danger, we know he was never politically active, although he actively criticized all politicians.

The men of 30AU were trained to keep secrets, not to discuss their activities, it was all operated on a strictly 'need to know' basis, so he probably never even knew the names of the people they were capturing or why or what they had done, he was just a grunt, the muscle, there to do as he was told at just nineteen or twenty years of age. So it's quite possible he was guessing about who they captured or just paying heed to the rumours and gossip that must have been passing about at that time.

Margot's mother, your grandmother, in this painting, kneeling in prayer in the same Church. She had dinner with Patrick Dalzel-Job, during the Liberation of France, he was Commander in the field of 30AU, maybe that was the connection between Guy? All 30AU would have needed was the radio code the Communists were using for their wireless broadcasts and maybe she knew how to get that, or at least who they needed to contact to get it. Then they could have pinpointed targets, just from monitoring their wireless broadcasts?" It felt as if there was some real connection there however unlikely it seemed. "And that's the reason Ron never told anyone he was 30AU, never made contact with any of his old wartime buddies, never attended a reunion. Spent the last years of his life afraid that his family still might be in danger, for something he and his brother-in-law were involved in sixty years earlier?" Had I come to that same mistaken conclusion as Ron? I still did not know. It all seemed to make sense, to fit into place. It was possible but surely fantastically unlikely.

Look at this, I was looking into the history of it for most of last night." I opened up the laptop and clicked open a few files. "I found documents online that there was a factory in northern France manufacturing fin and rudder parts for V2 rockets and the Nazi SS packed the whole lot, including the people and moved everything into Nordhausen, the secret underground facility, to protect them from the Allied bombings. It also said there was a Communist spy infiltration discovered by the Nazi's and they were hanged with thin wire from a crane, up to fifty of them, tied and gagged with wire and slowly throttled, while the slave workers were forced to watch right in the middle of the factory. Over 20,000 slave workers died at Nordhausen while building V2 rockets for the Nazi's, 20,000! That's even more people than the rockets themselves ever killed... In among all those mad scribbles and that manic writing there's clues, I think that Ron Guy believed Guy Wilthew was part of that infiltration and that 30AU used him to capture important Nazi scientists, before the Russians communists got hold of them. Could that have been possible do you think?" I tried to stay quiet for a few seconds, trying to let these thoughts have enough time to be absorbed by my blanked faced mother.

"Bloody hell, I don't know, I can't take it all in so quickly, this sounds like some kind of *James Bond* movie, incredible... but true?" Gwen opened the sunroof on the car trying to get some fresher air.

"*James Bond*, very apt, but I'll tell you all about that bit later...Ian Fleming was actually the units commander, behind a desk...and in the field it was commanded by the very Naval officer he supposedly used as his inspiration for his books..."

"You're kidding me!" Gwen looked gobsmacked.

"Anyway...look, I've mapped it out. Von Braun left the Peenemünde Rocket facility right up there on the north German coast, he left in February 1945; he headed for the Harz Mountain range, which is there, dead centre of Germany. Look, the green arrows are the recorded movements of 30AU, the red, the Nazi scientists movements according to the history books. For two months, March and April, they actually could have been anywhere, anywhere in Germany. Apparently von Braun took with him somewhere between two hundred and five hundred scientists with him! Right across the entire length of an invaded Germany while nursing a badly broken arm, which some accounts say happened near Peenemünde in a truck crash and others say happened near Bleichrode in a car crash and while four lots of very intent secret Military were actively searching for them! The Americans whittled that down to one hundred and twenty-eight scientists, which they eventually took to the US. But if von Braun didn't take all those men to Bavaria as it says in the history books, how the fuck did they all get there? Obviously they are all going to stick to any story they are told to, or they would be out in the cold, just another Nazi, or dead. "Take a look at these websites I've cached." I opened up the laptop and put it on Gwen's lap. "Kammler was von Braun's boss, well indirectly, but he was the main Nazi responsible for all these scientists. Kammler disappeared off the face of the earth, never stood trial at Nuremburg with the rest of the war criminals. No one has ever been able to trace what happened to him. If the Americans were that keen on keeping these scientists for themselves, they had to make sure it was not possible to link them to any Nazi atrocities. It was the Americans who could have been involved in the disappearance of Kammler, after all they were the ones with most to gain if he didn't stand trial for war crimes. Maybe they did that because that severed the link between these scientists and atrocities? Toftoy was the American military man responsible for tracking these scientists and getting them to America to work for their military. Maybe Kammler did a deal with Toftoy to gather these men together? He would have been trying to trade what he had to save his skin and do a deal for himself, which ultimately led to his own disappearance. Either fed to the pigs or a nice pad in Rio, whichever the Americans thought was the safer bet. Obviously I'm sure that's a massive oversimplification, they probably never even met but that doesn't make it any less accurate. Maybe the Americans had thought that had worked and then twenty years later another link popped up, this time in France. Another link that had to be disappeared?" A shiver went down my spine. Could the US military be capable of such a thing? I felt very small suddenly, sitting here in the Mini, under the Channel. My mind snapped to a vision of all the young Allied soldiers on D-Day, on the very sea above our heads, thousands upon thousands of innocent young male lives, most of them American, most of them virgins, but all were about to be thrown at a Nazi wall by their countries and the men in charge of them. I looked at Gwen, she looked just as pale and shaken as I felt. The links made too much sense, fitted together too nicely. It had the simple ring of truth.

"What the hell should I do, should I try to get this story out?" I looked to Gwen for some way forward. "Maybe we should just go back home, forget this quest, wipe the website. Just go back to our lives? Are we going to be murdered in our beds? Killed in a road traffic pile up, with no-one ever being the wiser?" I looked through the car windows as the train emerged from the tunnel back into daylight the journey had seemed to take only minutes.

"I honestly think we need to see it through, get the story out. For my parents, your grandparents and our family, they all fought for what they believed to be right, put their very lives on the line to fight for the truth and against tyranny.

We can't do anything but the same, no matter how it ends." Gwen took my hand.

I knew she was right. Turning around could and would never be the right option.

"I came across some "heavy" websites last night. All the conspiracy stuff got to me. There are stories of an American man, something to do with the shipping of V2's and the gyroscopes and guidance systems of the rockets straight after the war, how his family is totally convinced he was murdered by the CIA, their website is huge, they have been trying for years to get justice and others, many others, hundreds of conspiracy websites all trying to accuse American Secret agencies of one thing or another, it all got to me. But what if Grandad was right? Maybe the CIA are the new Nazi's, murderers of innocent people, maybe if we go ahead with this quest to find out more we are going to disappear, believe me if you look through these conspiracy websites you'd be as scared as I was last night." I stopped myself. Was I now 'going mad', becoming paranoid? Why was I trying to convince Gwen to be scared? This was all wrong, (it could still be nothing more than a crazy fantasy dreamt up by my Grandfather while high on a cocktail of medicinal drugs). The same drugs he had raved and protested about in his scribbles for his last years. "Let's just go and see what we can find, then we'll make a considered choice eh!?"

I also wanted to visit the subjects of the religious paintings and the scene of Ron and Margot's first kiss, in the Cathedral at Vannes and that was where we were heading.

On the brochure of the museum in Le Faouët, was featured Guy Wilthew's (Snr) painting entitled 'Bénitier de l'église Saint-Fiacre' and a quick web search informed us that Saint Fiacre was a fifth century Irish Monk and there was one town named after him, just North East of Paris and many Chapels, even a Paris Hotel. A quick study of the museum brochure listed many other paintings of a lot of Chapelles in and around Le Faouët, it seemed at the turn of the century a whole group of renowned artists had gathered there to work in the area and some stayed for good. One painting subject was a La Chapelle Saint-Fiacre two kilometres south of the small town that I knew to be the birth place of Margot, Nan, where she had lived with her family in the town square right opposite the huge covered market until she was ten. It was the town where Guy Wilthew her father, the English aristocrat and painter had rented the recently deceased Louis-Marie's vacant studio from his widow, and then eventually taken their daughter's hand in marriage, Marguerite Le Leuxhe/Wilthew. The couple had also kept on his house, which was on the corner of the market square, opposite the covered market where Louis-Marie had died suddenly while adjusting the town clock in 1896. That was where the font would be.

The old part of Vannes was beautiful, still surrounded by the massive Ramparts of the old city wall. I found it very difficult to imagine Ron and Corporal 'Ganger' Gates, in the August of 1944, passing through the Prison arch of the city wall which led into Rue des Chanoines, as we were now doing. The house looked just as it had done in the pictures I had seen of it, exactly the same, even after sixty years, right opposite the huge Cathedral that was talked about so much in their writing and letters. I instantly decided that if I should ever win the lottery or come into money I would try to find a way to make this house into a museum and art gallery dedicated to the art of the Le Leuxhe/Wilthew family and the contribution they had made during the war - 30 Assault Unit, the Maquis and the 'Rote Kappelle' (Red Orchestra, the Germans term for the Communist Resistance).

Richard, Guénhaële and Gildas and their families seemed very pleased to greet us, which was unexpected to Gwen and I considering the problems that had occurred upon Guy Wilthew's (the son) death and the bitter words that had flowed with regards to the terms of his Will, but that had been between Armelle, their mother and Margot her sister, hopefully now we could all finally put those unfortunate problems behind us.

Although they had politely refused all previous attempts at reconciliation, not only did they seemed pleased to meet us they even took us in and put us up for the next few days with gracious and unexpected warmth. It was a wonderful experience. Gwen and I found the whole thing somewhat surreal, like some kind of time warp. Although Gwen did not know it at that stage she had visited this house before as a child with Ron and Margot, she had also met with these relatives thirty odd years previously when the family had still been closer, before Guy had died. The cousins travelled to England and stayed at 'Bluebells'. All three even remembered me as a small child and specifically the fact that a small child of the family was speaking English rather than French, when I had been frightened by a spider.

The food the family cooked was all prepared in the traditional Breton way, just as Margot had always prepared it in England as the family were growing up. We sat in among the many works of art painted by Guy Wilthew (Snr), that were at the same time familiar, in style and content, and yet completely different from the few paintings of his that used to hang in 'Bluebells', it was an odd and emotional experience.

Margot's childhood bedroom was unchanged in over seventy years, in it hung stunning works of art, masterpieces, completely covering all the walls. I held the photo's of the American airmen she had helped escape and the photo's of Ron and Margot in the garden, everything was the same, it was purely timeless, these pictures could have been taken yesterday, it was stunning, breathtaking. The paintings of Margot's mother, Marguerite Wilthew, one praying in a chapel was ten feet high and heart stopping, there was also a painting of her sitting on a chapel pew in contemplation looking at a crucifix, all were painted by her future husband Guy Wilthew, it depicted her trying to make the decision between a life dedicated to religion as a nun, as was her original intention, or a life married to Guy, *(Thankfully she had chosen the latter!)*. It was painted immediately after his proposal of marriage, after he had waited six years to ask her father Louis Marie Le Luexhe for her hand.

The Le Leuxhe paintings were just as stunning, by the father Louis and also one of his sons, Alphonse, one of the fifteen children all brought up in Le Faouët square. Unfortunately Alphonse's obvious talents were cut very short by his death at the hands of the Germans at the beginning of World War One.

At times I found it hard to push the thought from my mind that some of these oil painted wonders could, by rights, have one day belonged to me. But I had made a promise to my hosts that that was not reason for the visit, we were here to find out about Guy Wilthew's(Jnr) war and that as far as I was concerned if Margot, Nan, had not wished to pursue the matter by whatever means at that time, then I would respect her decision. But it was something that would now always haunt me (unless I could somehow find a way to get them on display to the world).

Richard, Armelle's oldest son was an amazing man. A professor of philosophy who had travelled the world extensively and spent time living in Afghanistan as a young man, he could speak Greek, Persian and English, and read Latin, a collector of ancient weapons and many other things beside, which filled the large house. I thought that maybe one day they could all form part of a display at a museum. One item in particular caught my eye the moment we stepped into the room. It hung above another dark but mesmerizing painting of the inside of Saint-Fiacre Chapelle, it was a perfect Red Indian Eagle feather headdress, along with some of their ancient weaponry, I wondered if it had been there when Ron called in and if he had paid it any attention when he entered the house with Margot sixty years earlier.

Richard was also a champion musket marksman who still competed all over France. He informed me that Guy Wilthew, Richard's uncle, was also an expert marksman and as far as he was aware had spent the entire war chopping wood in various forests in France and Germany and had then become embroiled in a battle alongside the FFI, to clear up pockets of Nazi occupation that had still persisted, even after the majority of Germany had been overrun. He had returned home to Bretagne on a Wehrmacht motorbike in a Nazi Helmet and with a Mauser slung across his back. I could not help but imagine him escaping Nazi Germany on the motorbike as a 'French Steve McQueen', but this time succeeding in making the impossible second jump! Richard had been as close to Guy as anyone, if he did not know of his precise activities during the war, then no one was going to, unless we could find clues within his writing, memoirs or photographs.

But upon inspection there was nothing within the collected works of Guy that shed any light on Ron's belief that he had been involved with the capture of Nazi scientists and they were not aware of the existence of any other photographs, or information that may cast light on his lady friend Barbara. Maybe she had been successful in finding and destroying any evidence that had existed, or maybe she and he were not involved in any way shape or form and it had been a mistaken belief from the start, maybe she was just unlucky enough to have been witness to three male friends killed in two separate vehicle accidents on roads in which she was travelling as well, even though, on each occasion, she had managed to remain entirely unharmed; which was the more unlikely?

Could those photo's have got into Guy's possession by another means? (Or could so many of these happenings just have been born of Ron's drug induced imagination?) Or could Guy have been murdered for another reason, entirely unrelated, he had been a politically active anti-fascist, could that have led to his murder? Why would he have spent the five years of the war with no apparent contact with his family, at least as far as his sister Margot was concerned, maybe Marguerite, her mother, did know where he was and what he was doing? Or did he leave them without word of his well being for five whole years and if so, why? After all, Vichy France was backing the Nazi's at the time of their invasion, could Guy have found himself forced into the Wehrmacht or at least to do their biding, then connecting to the communists at a later date? Marshal Pétain received the death penalty for backing the Germans in his trial after the war, although the sentence was commuted because of his age. Ron had even mentioned in his writing taking the surrender of a Frenchman in a German uniform at the end of the war, could Guy have found himself in a similar position? Or could he have just hidden himself away for five years, while the female side of his family were actively resisting the Nazi's on their own? How in the hell was I ever going to know when I would never truly believe another official document or statement again?

The Basilica Cathédrale Saint-Pierre-et-Saint-Patern was stunning, a huge dark gothic building, even on a sunny day it was darker and even more overbearing on the inside and the obvious entrances to any vaults were blocked with huge stone blocks with large iron rings attached, there was also no sign within the house cellar that a tunnel had ever existed between the two buildings.

After a wonderful few days staying in Vannes we headed on to Le Fäouet, booking into the Hotel Le Croix D'or which turned out to be the very same hotel that my Great Grandfather Guy Wilthew had checked into when he had originally come to Le Faouët to paint over one hundred years ago. A visit to the Museum where some of Guy Wilthew's works of art, owned by our cousin Richard but on loan to the Museum for display, were alongside other pieces painted by ancestors, Louis and Alphonse Le Leuxhe which were all fantastic.

I have never been a religious person, although I do consider the whole family deeply spiritual, without being religious, if that is possible. In fact I was, up until now, of the firm opinion that most of the devoutly religious people only became that way because they were fighting their own demons within their heads and felt that the church might be able help them with that losing battle. Every other child molestation case I ever heard of seemed to involve some devoutly religious person, that and most of the wars and acts of terrorism of course! But the events of this last year had really given me something to think about. Certainly I felt some external force was at work within, leading me inexorably to some point in the future. All the coincidences had just piled one on top of the other, I felt somehow detached from it all, just a spectator. I had begun to feel I was just a passenger and now walking into these chapels I was moved, emotions welled up inside. Especially at Saint Barbe which was stunning, perched overlooking a deep valley where the loud gurgle of the swollen river could be heard through the trees, it was an immensely tranquil spot and I also realised that the photo of Nan, Margot, taken by her brother Guy, with her on a plinth as a statue was taken at the main entrance to the Chapelle.

When we stepped through that very entrance on a hot sunny spring day, the temperature plummeted, I could clearly see my own breath as if it was a sub zero winters day, it was a very spiritual moment as it was also at the Fountaine of St. Barbe the apparent site of some miraculous spiritual healing and the subject of some of Alphonse's paintings.

The Chapelle Saint Fiacre was magnificent, very unusual with three small offset spires, it reminded me of an ancient fairy tale, gothic with just a hint of evil lurking somewhere within all that detailed architecture and stonework, but not a particular aspect you could actually point out. It was the site of the painting depicting the stained glass window that had so captivated me at the house in Vannes, I had hardly been able to keep my eyes away from it, as we walked into the Chapelle it was like actually walking into the painting, were all these feelings and emotions déjà vu? Was it a revelation? Some kind of confirmation of God, it certainly felt like it! For the only time in my life I felt I was actually in the presence of God, a real God. It was all very real and it filled me now, I was overwhelmed with a passion, an unexplained passion… for God? for life? for the truth? I could not be sure, but I now believed my whole life had been leading to this one point and the quest to get this story into a book.

I had the pictures of the paintings with me and the Museum had actually erected permanent easels in the very spot that my Great Grandfather had sat at, nearly one hundred years previously. There it was, the stone font. I held up the photo of the painting by Guy Wilthew, completed in 1914. It could have been painted only yesterday if we had dressed two Breton people in their traditional garb with the wooden clogs. Nothing had changed; it was timeless. My mind's eye caught a brief glimpse of the traditional Breton wooden clogs that had always hung in Margot and Ron's kitchen, next to the back door at 'Bluebells'. I felt my grandparent's powerful spirit was with us, in fact I was entirely sure of that.

"So, what do we do now? Where do we look for this connection, if it even existed at all?" Gwen looked quizzically at me.

"Fuck knows." I walked over to a dark wooden pew of the church and slid along until the beam of sunlight from the high stained glass window illuminated us as we sat.

"Jesus Christ! …" I exclaimed after a few minutes.

"Don't blaspheme, you're in a bloody church" Gwen tried to smile.

"So are you. You don't blaspheme… I guess we'll never know what Guy did during the war, other than the fact he spied on the Nazi's and worked with the Communists even though he didn't agree with them, but it seems obvious to me that the Americans were the ones who were involved in the disappearance of Kammler and then lied to the world about how all these scientists ended up in their hands, working and living in their country, treated like heroes instead of war criminals. If they did make people and documents disappear, it would have been to hide the evidence that linked the scientists they had kept to Nazi war crimes, seemingly one of the von Brauns, which if discovered would have made it impossible for them to have any chance of a green card! Or whatever it was they needed to work for NASA. So the Americans had to hide it, they had no choice if they wanted to keep all those brilliant minds working for them and just maybe 30AU and possibly members of our family were the ones who set that whole chain of events in motion. Hopefully that same family line can now bring that chain of events to a close. For good."

I stared up at the window and the sun glinting through the beautiful stained glass, the very window of the painting that had transfixed me so much in the house at Vannes, I was filled with... I didn't know...

...just filled.

FURTHER READING:-

Attain by Surprise *edited by David Nutting*

Artic Snow to Dust of Normandy *by Patrick Dalzel-Job*

The Paperclip Conspiracy *by Tom Bower*

From Pole to Pole *by J.P. Riley*

The Hazard Mesh *by J.A. Hugill*

**Honours and awards made to 30AU men.
Taken from 'Official History':-**

Colonel Quill	- D.S.O.
Lt.Col. de Courcy-Ireland and Captain Pike	- D.S.C.
Lt. Commander Glanville and Lt. Lambie	- D.S.C.
C.S.M. Day, Colour Sgt. Lund and Sgt. Brereton	- D.S.M.
Cmdr. Curtis, Lt. Cmdrs Hugill and Postlethwaite	- Mentioned in despatches
Captain Ward and Captain Cunningham	- Mentioned in despatches
Sergeants Whyman and Wilkins	- Mentioned in despatches